THOMAS KENT MILLER'S
Holmes Behind the Veil Series

Book 1
SHERLOCK HOLMES
ON THE ROOF OF THE WORLD;
Or, The Adventure of the Wayfaring God

Book 2
THE GREAT DETECTIVE
AT THE CRUCIBLE OF LIFE;
Or, The Adventure of the Rose of Fire

Book 3
THE SUSSEX BEEKEEPER
AT THE DAWN OF TIME
Or, The Adventure of the Star of Wonder

"[*The Sussex Beekeeper*] has James Clerk Maxwell in it, and Pope Pius IX, and a beautiful Roman maiden cast out by her imperial father. And quite a bit more. It's very readable."

—Chris Redmond, www.sherlockian.net

"[*The Sussex Beekeeper*] is an incredible book. I can't believe how much material and research has been put into it; truly stunning; a massive undertaking. The Holmes/Mycroft comments were fun. I think it is a special book, very well done. Holmes/Quatermain and all readers who like anything in that area will simply adore the book. I was astonished by all the info and facts that were woven together so well."

—Gary Lovisi, Sherlock Holmes authority

"Any lover of Rider Haggard's works will be intrigued to see the innovative use of his main hero in what is a most unusual and original book. Throwing all traditional story-telling formats firmly out of the window the author has woven a book of many possibilities. if you want a real challenge and an intriguing thought-provoking read then this is worth a try."

— Roger Allen, Rider Haggard Society

ATTENTION! WARNING!

You are holding a haunted book.
You may set it down right now and no possible causal
effect can beset you; *however,* **if you read farther, I cannot**
be held accountable for whatever may affect you—
for good or ill.

This volume was fashioned from several manuscripts set down long ago at various times by people in the throes of huge events and huge emotions, who could not help but to infuse, that is, print upon, these assorted writings strong impressions, exactly in the manner that some houses and other locales have been imprinted with intense personalities or incidents long passed. Such impressions, or recordings, as it were, are sometimes observed to repeat themselves over and again—phenomena often interpreted as "ghosts." In other words, this volume contains the haunted descriptions of several incidents. The different documents that make up this book have been, in turn, lost and forgotten for ages, only to be found for a time, mulled over, then passed on, only to be lost again from both view and memory. They have passed through diverse hands, always affecting the lives of whoever touches them or has been touched by them. Furthermore, each individual to whom Fate has dealt these awesome and sublime manuscripts has felt obliged to add a marginal word or attach a note, sometimes of explanation, sometimes of warning, before Providence set to work burying again each in turn, only to later have them surface and move on to the next person by whatever happenstance or means. And it is I—and I alone—who has been fated to act as the focus or locus wherein all these several texts have been brought together. While the actual disparate manuscripts from which this book has been derived are without a doubt haunted in their own right in the manner described—except perhaps my own jottings—I have reason to believe that the essence of the haunted thoughts and accounts contained therein have been transferred to this entirely new work by virtue that the ideas and histories are in themselves haunted, regardless of the medium in which they are presented.

All things considered, then, it is only natural that the book you are holding consists of myriad layers. Please read it attentively, especially without preconceptions as to what a pastiche should be; follow its diverse channels and rivulets from the start: see them join up at the end. T.K.M

"[*The Sussex Beekeeper at the Dawn of Time*] is a highly postmodern creation, conveying its narrative through many different sources, each inflected with different shades of irony or doubt. The author has structured the work as in one sense an 'epistolary novel' (perhaps 'documentary novel' might be a better term). One outer document leads to another, and these to further, inner documents, so that the reader experiences the book as if going through a series of doors in a labyrinth of secret passages. This approach is complex—the reader must keep their wits about them—and allusive. It asks for an alertness and constant curiosity. An impatient reader might be daunted by the layers of what appear to be preamble at the outset, but these are in fact essential to the way the book works. This experimental approach is accompanied, however, by a thorough understanding of the enthralling themes found in the mysteries and romances of the Haggardian tradition: ancient secrets, hidden adepts, enigmatic heroes, strange sects, resonant spiritual symbols, a quest across time and space. They are all there, even if not always laid out plainly in a linear plot. Instead, we must regard the book as like a curious crystal, which reveals some new dimension as each facet is caught in the light of our understanding."

—Mark Valentine, *fin de siècle* authority, in *Wormwoodiana*

THE SUSSEX BEEKEEPER
AT THE DAWN OF TIME
Or, The Adventure of the Star of Wonder

At the Heart of Which is a Ghost Story

Experienced in 1873 By

Hans the Hottentot

Aide-de-Camp to Allan Quatermain and His Father Before Him

As Immediately Related to, Then Recounted Nine Years Later

In 1882 By,

Allan Quatermain

Author of "King Solomon's Mines," "She and Allan," ETC.

To His Friend and Companion of Harrowing Adventures,

Who Set Down the Tale as It Was Told to Her, Later Bequeathing

It to Her Mysterious Cousin "M"

Lady Luna Holmes Ragnall

Heroine of "The Ivory Child" and "The Ancient Allan"

1905 Annotation and Apicultural Commentary By

M* Ably Assisted By **SS†**

Including a Letter By, and Extracts From the Journals of,

Maria Mitchell

America's First Woman Astronomer

Entire Monograph Assembled, Edited, Supplemented,

And Annotated By

Thomas Kent Miller

Editor of "The Great Detective at the Crucible of Life," ETC.

* Some authorities have argued from internal evidence that "M" is the initial of a pseudonymous name used by a certain Great Detective during his retirement in Sussex.

† The same authorities sometimes suggest that "SS" are the initials of a neighbor, fellow honey fancier, and occasional assistant of M during this late interlude.

Paperback ISBN 978-1-78705-163-8
ePub ISBN 978-1-78705-164-5
PDF ISBN 978-1-78705-165-2

Published in the UK by MX Publishing
335 Princess Park Manor, Royal Drive,
London, N11 3GX
www.mxpublishing.co.uk

Cover design by Brian Belanger
Interior drawings by Elizabeth Davies

For my mother, father, and
and two brothers

Astronomers used the James Clerk Maxwell Telescope to detect cosmic ashes from the dawn of time. It comes from stars that died more than 10 billion years ago. It is the first time stellar dust has been detected at such an early stage in the evolution of the Universe, say British scientists.

—BBC News

Oh, Star of wonder, Star of night/
Star with royal beauty bright/
Westward leading, still proceeding/
Guide us to the Perfect Light.
—John H. Hopkins, Jr.

Suddenly, in the air before them, not farther up than a low hill-top, flared a lambent flame; as they looked at it, the apparition contracted into a focus of dazzling lustre. Their hearts beat fast; their souls thrilled; and they shouted with one voice, "The Star! The Star! God is with us!"
—Lew Wallace in *Ben-Hur: A Tale of the Christ,*
Book I Chapter V

Contents

List of Illustrations

Dedication

To the Alexander F. Morrison Planetarium of Yesteryear,
California Academy of Sciences, Golden Gate Park,
San Francisco, California, Circa 1960

From the late 1950s through the early 1960s, during which time my mean age was 15, I lived on the San Francisco Bay Peninsula in California and would often ride a Greyhound Bus the twenty miles or so north to San Francisco and take in an epic road-show "event" movie, such as *Ben-Hur*, *Exodus*, *King of Kings*, or *The Wonderful World of the Brothers Grimm*, which in those days were presented in huge movie palaces and were treated with the sort of reverence that we expected for Broadway theatrical productions. One could not merely buy a ticket and enter the theater. It was necessary for me to purchase tickets long in advance at the sole bookstore in my hometown. These moments were really big events in my young life.

Around this same time, a star suddenly burst onto my life. It was joy and tranquility and peace and awe and amazement and wonderment all wrapped up in one. It was the Alexander F. Morrison Planetarium in San Francisco's Golden Gate Park. The planetarium was part of the vast

6

California Academy of Sciences complex that included the Steinhart Aquarium, and was just across from the De Young Museum.

At the Morrison in those far-off days, after you paid admission, you entered a domed theater big enough to hold perhaps one hundred lounge chairs. The dome was lit in such a way as to simulate a gold- and orange-tinged dusk, and classical music played softly through invisible speakers. On a platform in the middle of the dome was the most fantastic single object I had ever seen up until then, and its fantastic quality never lessened, no matter how many times I saw it. This was the planetarium projector, and it looked rather like a giant insect. It was this elaborate mech anism (built from scratch soon after World War II by Academy optical technicians) that projected thousands of stars of varying brightness onto the inside of the dome.

Once the round theater filled, the doors closed, the light of dusk faded as night arrived, and then, miraculously, before my eyes, the stars slowly came out (and I had to remind myself that we were indoors and that outside it was broad daylight) while the classical music continued softly. When it was completely dark, and the heavens sparkled with myriad crystal points as though seen from the top of the

Rocky Mountains, the presenter, who was at a discreetly placed podium near the edge of the dome and not noticed by most of the audience, began to speak in quiet tones and presented a family-friendly astronomy lesson that utilized all sorts of multimedia tools—film, slides, models, animation— all pointed out with a magical red arrow of light wielded by the speaker.

The star projector at the Morrison Planetarium circa 1960. (Courtesy of and © The California Academy of Sciences, photo catalog number N3612.tif.)

But this calm ambiance simply went away in the early 1970s as commercialism crept into this bastion of science and learning, and, in lieu of the carefully crafted air of relaxation and peace, advertisements were projected onto the dome. Away went the tranquility that I had always prized. Away went the deliciously orchestrated merging of dusk into night accompanied by serene classical music.

More recently, the entire California Academy of Sciences has been renovated, and the 2008 version of the planetarium entered the 21st century by going entirely digital—with the result that the projector I so loved and admired was boxed up and put into storage more than a decade ago, as I've lately learned while trying to establish its location. Attempts by Academy staff to interest outside collectors or other museums have been, sadly, for naught. Can it be that the magnificent star projector that so touched my life will simply be forgotten?

I mourn this loss to this day, more than 40 years later.

It is to the memory of that institution, the Alexander F. Morrison Planetarium, at that moment in time, that I dedicate this book.

Thomas Kent Miller
December 2013

There is in life an element of elfin coincidence which people reckoning on the prosaic may perpetually miss.

—G.K. Chesterton

Preface

By Thomas Kent Miller

i

Thrice in the last five decades, recognition of the name Allan Quatermain has experienced a revival.

A century ago there were bestselling authors much as there are today, but human nature being what it is, before very long something like 95 percent of those popular authors had been utterly forgotten or, at best, relegated to the domain of the cognoscenti. For example, do the names Mrs. Henry Wood, Bertram Mitford, Elizabeth Stuart Phelps, Allen Upward, and Marjorie Bowen sound familiar? I suppose not, yet, in various studies, we are told that Wood (1814-1887) attained sales of 5 million copies; that Mitford (1855-1914) wrote more than 40 novels, many of which sold briskly and were well reviewed; that Phelps (1844-1911) was an extremely popular writer in her day who had achieved phenomenal success; that Upward (1863-1926) was a prolific best-selling author of mysteries and novels; and that Bowen (1885-1952) had more than 180 novels and collections to her credit. In other cases, once-successful authors may not be utterly forgotten—just *almost* utterly forgotten. One such almost utterly forgotten bestseller was Allan Quatermain, who was the author of the African memoir published in 1885, *King Solomon's Mines,* which became an international best-seller overnight—the most popular book of its day (sort of *The Da Vinci Code* of 1885).

Quatermain himself, however, never enjoyed the benefits of this popularity, as he, with some stalwart friends, even before the book was published, had already returned to Africa seeking adventure and had lost all communication with the civilized world. It was while on this journey that Quatermain received a wound that proved fatal . . . but he died slowly enough that he had time to pen his final memoir titled simply *Allan Quatermain.*

Following the publication of *King Solomon's Mines* Quatermain's close friend Henry Rider Haggard came into possession of that final memoir and various other manuscripts and autobiographies, most of which Quatermain had dashed onto paper to wile away his time (and left behind) during his three years of retirement in England. Rider Haggard, who became in effect Quatermain's literary executor, arranged for these memoirs to be published, piecemeal, as they had a habit of popping up unexpectedly, the last in 1927.

Thus, from the mid-1880s to the mid-1920s, that is to say, for a forty year period roughly a century ago, the name Allan Quatermain was common currency. During that bygone era, most literate persons in England recognized the name and attached to it certain striking images of African adventure, as did readers throughout the world once the translators began their work.

However, even before the last of his books had been published, cultures and time had moved forward and changed, and, as is natural, the name Allan Quatermain faded from the consciousness of the public at large, though he was one of those lucky few who wasn't totally forgotten because, on one hand, most public libraries usually kept a copy of *King Solomon's Mines* lying about, and, on the other, there have been at least five movies based on that memoir; however, it is the exceedingly and extraordinarily rare movie-goer who would be able to identify the author of the original book!

And thus it stood for about 50 years until in the mid-1970s, when the Newcastle Publishing Company of North Hollywood, California, reprinted a few of Quatermain's out-of-print books, which stimulated a minor revival that lasted a decade.

Thirty years after that, and more than seventy years after the last of Quatermain's books had appeared, around the turn of the twentieth century into the twenty-first century, writer Alan Moore and illustrator Kevin O'Neill resurrected the name when they made Quatermain the primary character amongst many resurrected Victorian characters in their series of extraordinarily popular and clever graphic novels, *The League of Extraordinary Gentlemen*. And before long, Sean Connery was playing Quatermain in a popular movie based on the series.

Meanwhile, however, a decade before the *League* came into existence, in the early 1990s, a long lost Quatermain memoir had come to light, and it was my good fortune, in 1994, to be offered the opportunity to edit and shepherd that memoir into publication. The provenance of that manuscript is most interesting. Beginning as Quatermain's oral account of an 1872 adventure told before a roaring fire in a sitting room in upstate New York, it was put into writing by Dr. John H. Watson *(a full month before he'd even met the great detective!)*; and then bestowed onto Frederick Church, the great landscape painter of the mid-19th century. Following

Church's death in 1900, the memoir remained in the possession of his heirs, though stored in a wine cellar for 25 years. By chance, H.P. Lovecraft was presented by the heirs with the opportunity to prepare the manuscript for publication, and he enthusiastically accepted. However, it seems he lost interest in it, and it basically fell off the earth for 65 years. After Lovecraft's death, the box of papers that contained the manuscript was misplaced and the manuscript's very existence remained unknown until it came to light in the early 1990s. At that point, Lovecraft's original (posthumous) book publisher, Arkham House, took on the responsibility of deciding how best to deal with it. However, its then editor had a full plate, and based on his awareness of my prior editing of *Sherlock Holmes on the Roof of the World*, he asked me if I would be interested in taking up the challenge.

Of course I grabbed at the chance and eventually, after its own thoroughly bumpy and exceedingly convoluted publication road (that included, believe it or not, an abortive and embarrassing $75 million movie titled *The Rose of Fire* with Michael Caine, Gene Hackman, and Sigourney Weaver that I had absolutely no responsibility for), the scholarly book that I had originally envisioned and had labored to prepare finally appeared as *The Great Detective at the Crucible of*

Life; or, The Adventure of the Rose of Fire—an adventure involving both Quatermain and the Great Detective. Thereupon, Quatermain's memoirs of his 1872 travails gained the notice of anthropologists and conservationists around the world—the end result being that Quatermain's words helped to literally change the face of Africa and revolutionize public awareness of human origins, all of which is detailed in the prefaces of that book.

Thus, you can imagine what a staggering shock it was, after all this time, to learn that all the while that I was editing both *Sherlock Holmes on the Roof of the World* and *The Great Detective at the Crucible of Life*, with absolutely no awareness of it, by some miracle of chance, I had had in my possession still another unknown Quatermain memoir.

That new memoir is now the book you are holding, *The Sussex Beekeeper at the Dawn of Time; or, The Adventure of the Star of Wonder*.

ii

I am a pack rat.

Without this defining aspect of my life, I wouldn't be writing these words, I wouldn't be beginning this book.

In the early 1980s, my wife and I bought our first house in the Emerald Lake district of Redwood City, California. Emerald Lake is a forested, rustic pocket of turn-of-the-century log houses in an otherwise normal suburb of San Francisco. As it happened, by pure chance, down the road apiece, around a few bends, lived E. Hoffmann Price— making him my neighbor. Price was a popular and successful contributor to pulp magazines from the 1920s to the 1950s. His first sales were to *Weird Tales* magazine, whereupon he became a friend of many popular writers of the day through correspondence. Before long, he was selling stories to a long string of magazines with titles like *Spicy Detective, Adventure,* and *Magic Carpet*. In time, he developed a wanderlust that he sated by automobile "touring," then a new pastime, and he drove around the country meeting his colleagues and friends, writers and editors, such as Henry Kuttner, Seabury Quinn, Clark Ashton Smith, Otis Adelbert Kline, Robert E. Howard, and H.P. Lovecraft. In the 1950s, however, the pulp magazines faded, and Price gave up writing as no longer lucrative and began work as a microfilm technician with his local government. He'd lived in his house for about sixty years, for nearly all the time he had been writing for the pulps.

17

Thomas Kent Miller and E. Hoffmann Price approximately 1985.
(Photo: Jayne Miller)

I had first met Price in his home in 1977 where he regaled myself and two friends for hours with tales of his myriad adventures the world over and plied us with various liquors. One of those friends and I wrote a profile of Price that ran in a local magazine, and eventually an expanded version was printed in the fanzine *The Weird Tales Collector* # 6. This was thirty-five years ago.

Later, after we became neighbors, Price and his wife and my family visited one another often in the course of the next four years.

Then, on April 25, 1986, a life-altering event happened in my family's life, and we unexpectedly and

18

literally moved overnight from northern California to southern California, a distance of 450 miles.

During the few hours (literally) when this was happening and while I was away from the house, Price came to visit, and my wife, who was in the midst of chaos, received him, apologizing that I wasn't around. Price gave Jayne a thick manila envelope and asked that she give it to me. Within moments of his leaving, she threw the envelope in a box and promptly forgot totally about it, never mentioning this incident to me, as she had far more important things on her mind. During the next year, we sold our house and I moved my family and our belongings nine times (again literally). In the end, my wife and I settled in a small southern California community, where we have been living since. As things quieted down, I finished up the last editorial tasks on *Sherlock Holmes on the Roof of the World* and shepherded that slim book through publication in 1987, the centenary of the Great Detective's first appearance in *Beeton's Christmas Annual.*

Of course, many wonderful books and other treasured possessions vanished from my cognizance during all that 1986 shell game of packing and moving, and moving and packing; much of it was stored and languished in unopened boxes (eventually tattered boxes) in various places. That was more than a quarter century ago as I type, and treasures are still resurfacing to this very day.

It was in 2008, then, 21 years after *Roof of the World* was published and 14 years after Quatermain's Ethiopian memoir (*Crucible of Life*) had come to my attention, that I was rummaging in our rent-a-storage unit in a nearby town looking for some *Weird Tales* magazines that I knew I had somewhere. I opened a box . . . and there on top was a fat, faded-manila envelope that I didn't recall ever having seen before. In a broad, bold hand, my name was written in capital letters in the middle of the envelope in faded blue ball-point pen. When I opened the envelope, I found the following extraordinary note to me from E. Hoffmann Price clipped to a somewhat smaller envelope with a seriously rusty paperclip. Within this second envelope was a succession of five other envelopes, each smaller than the previous, a circumstance exactly analogous to a set of Russian nesting dolls.

The typed note read thusly:

Dear Tom,

I was puttering under the house recently and came across the enclosed, which has been tucked away in my basement since 1936, surviving floods and mud and other disasters where other possessions, such as cartons of Weird Tales and Adventure, didn't. Bob Howard's dad, Isaac, sent it to me within a few days of Bob's suicide and of the simultaneous passing of Isaac's wife. Those many years ago I perused it, and could not for the life of me determine why Bob had thought to send it to me. During my correspondence with Isaac over the years before his own passing in 1944, he told me how Bob had spent upwards of a week organizing his files and even made funeral arrangements, so it seems logical that at that transitional moment, shipping me the enclosed was something he felt was important. Nevertheless, frankly, I could not decide what to do with it, and as is common in this kind of instance, I eventually did nothing at all and soon forgot about it. You know that Dr. Howard sent me a trunk of Bob's papers that I eventually sent to more capable hands, and it never occurred to me to add this packet to that collection. Now that it has surfaced again, I thought of you. My assessment is pretty much the same as Bob's. It is hard to think of it in any other manner than as a hoax. I am letting you have it as you are interested in our doings during those days and maybe you'll be able to do something practical with it.

 Geoffrey a. Price

April 25, 1986

Inside the second envelope and clipped to the third was this short typed note from Robert E. Howard's father to Price:

Cross Plains, Texas

July 3, 1936

Mr. E. Hoffmann Price

Redwood City, Calif.

Dear Mr. Price:

I am so sorry to write you again so soon after my letter of the 27th. However, Robert, I think, wanted you to have this package. At the least he had it all wrapped and sealed and addressed to you. I am enclosing his sealed envelope herewith.

Yours truly,

Dr. I.M. Howard

Box 313

In that third envelope was this note from Robert E. Howard to Price, the first of seven missives clipped to the fourth envelope:

Cross Plains, Texas
June 9, 1936

Dear Ed:

The contents of this package are quite extraordinary, so much so that I can only assume it is an elaborate turn-of-the-century hoax. I received it via an antiquarian bookstore located in Ireland. I doubt the bookseller was the architect of the joke. Anyway, it is too out-of-the-ordinary to merely toss away. Therefore I bequeath it to you.

I've included the pertinent correspondence that resulted in my possession of the envelope and its contents

Very truly yours
Bob

Then there came this series of six linked formal letters. Those written by Howard are all carbon copies:

[carbon copy]   Box 313
                                     Cross Plains, Texas
W.H. Smith & Sons Ltd.   April 2, 1930
24 High Street
Newtown, Powys, Wales

To whom it may concern:

I was recently intrigued by your advertisement that I happened to see in a travel magazine. I am writing to enquire if you have the following book that I would be able to purchase, The Romance of Early British Life; From the Earliest Times to the Coming of the Danes, by G.F. Scott Elliot, and published by Seeley and Co. (1909) which is not readily available in the states, though I have seen a copy in a library. In lieu of that particular title I am also interested in anything touching upon Celtic history and folklore.

Yours Sincerely,
R.E. Howard

5 May 1930

W.H. Smith & Sons Ltd.
24 High Street
Newtown, Powys
Wales

Dear Mr. R.E. Howard
Box 313
Cross Plains, Texas
USA

Dear Mr. Howard:

Thank you for your correspondence dated 2 April.
However, W.H. Smith & Sons stocks only books of
contemporary interest. I suggest that you try the
following bookstore that may be able to help you:
Hodges & Figgis Books, 56-58 Dawson Street,
Dublin.

All best regards,
E. Fitzgerald

Box 313

                                           Cross Plains, Texas

                                              July 6, 1930

Hodges & Figgis Books

56-58 Dawson Street

Dublin, Ireland

To whom it may concern:

Mr. Fitzgerald of W.H. Smith suggested I contact

your shop to enquire about the availability of The

Romance of Early British Life; From the Earliest

Times to the Coming of the Danes, by G.F. Scott

Elliot, and published by Seeley and Co. (1909). I am

also interested to know about Celtic histories and

folklore in general.

Yours Sincerely,

R.E. Howard

7 August 1930

Hodges & Figgis Books
56-58 Dawson Street
Mr. Robert E. Howard   Dublin, Ireland
Box 313
Cross Plains, Texas, USA

Dear Mr. Howard:

At this present time, we do not have in stock the
title you asked about on 6 July, though I will make a
point of communicating with other stores to check
its availability. In the meantime, I can recommend
the following ($3.00 each after conversion):

The Witch Cult in Western Europe by Murray
Fairy Faith in Celtic Countries by W.Y. Evans-Wentz
The Welsh Fairy Book by W. Jenkyn Thomas
Celtic Folklore: Welsh and Manx by John Rhys

I look forward to hearing from you,
Yours sincerely,
Edward Nicholson, Manager

[carbon copy]   Cross Plains, Texas
                                  Sept. 6, 1930

Hodges & Figgis Books
56-58 Dawson Street
Dublin, Ireland

Dear Mr. Nicholson:

Thank you for your response to my enquiry. I am in
fact most interested in two of the books that you
list. I enclose my United States Postal Office money
order for $8.00, which should be sufficient funds to
cover also postage and handling,

The Welsh Fairy Book by W. Jenkyn Thomas
Celtic Folklore: Welsh and Manx by John Rhys

I look forward to receiving these unique titles.

Yours truly,
Robert E. Howard

24 October 1930

Hodges & Figgis Books
56-58 Dawson Street
Dublin, Ireland

Dear Mr. Howard:

Many thanks for your order.

Also, though I am taking a chance, I
nonetheless feel certain that you must be THE
Robert E. Howard, the author of "Skull-Face," etc. I
frankly feel honoured that you should do business
with my store. As a small gesture of appreciation, I
am enclosing along with your books an odd item
that, in point of fact, was already part of the
inventory of the store when the current owners
purchased it from Mr. Webster more than 25 years
ago. That this item is old goes without saying, but its
authenticity is highly suspect. I have shown it to
some experts and they all have spent a few minutes
examining it and then smiled and told me it is a
rather sophisticated hoax and worthless. Because it
doesn't appear that I can sell it to anyone with a
clear conscience, and because it has been in the

store for so long, I am, rather impulsively I admit, including the item in question along with the books I am sending you. As a well-known author of fantasy and the like, perhaps you will have better use for it than I. It is a sort of diary, or purports to be.

In any event, it is now yours.

All the best,
Edward Nicholson, Manager

The fourth envelope, to which these last seven letters were clipped, bore the Dublin address of the Hodges & Figgis bookstore in the top left corner. I opened this envelope, mindful of its age and brittleness, and I found yet another envelope, this time with no accompanying message. In the center of the envelope was scribbled "To JW" and nothing else. Opening this envelope I found still another with a single defaced formal typewritten letter attached. A hand-written note was scrawled at the bottom of the letter. This is that letter along with the note (in bold italics) at the bottom:

31

Mellis & Mellis
Solicitors
50 Broad Street
London

21 Dec. 1905

[HERE IS A HOLE CUT WITH A SHARP BLADE WHERE THE RECIPIENT'S NAME AND ADDRESS WOULD HAVE BEEN.]

Dear Mr. [ANOTHER HOLE]

Our late client, the Lady Luna Holmes Ragnall's, final request was that we hand-deliver this envelope to you following her death in 1884, but not before we could determine, by whatever means, and as soon as possible following such determination, that you had conclusively retired from your career as a [ANOTHER HOLE].

Respectfully yours.

Anderson Mellis

am:lbn

What a hoot cousin Luna sent me this ms.—via her solicitors 21 years after the fact. Thus after more than 3 decades, I'm again crossing paths with dear old Quatermain!

When I opened the next envelope, I found a small diary of indeterminate color because it had long faded into a sort of grey. Placed between the cover and the first page of the book was a fat bulging envelope that we would call legal-sized today. The words "To My Cousin—Please Read BEFORE Negotiating the Contents of This Old Diary" had been written on the envelope in the pleasant script that I would soon come to know so well. However, I set that smaller envelope aside and gave the diary a careful examination page by page.

As I had already worked with two similar documents professionally, I saw quickly that this was neither a joke nor a hoax. Rather, I saw that it was authentic and priceless. It was, quite amazingly, another new Allan Quatermain memoir, this time telling of an experience in west Africa. Examination showed that it comprised an oral account by Quatermain told to Luna Holmes in her bedroom in Ragnall Castle and written down by Luna herself. This document, as you have just seen, was eventually delivered to Luna's presumed cousin via her solicitors, Mellis & Mellis, but that cousin's name had been carefully expurgated—no doubt at the direction of the person we will come to know as "M"—from the various documents that had come into my possession. The cuttings, that is to say the holes, had edges that were either yellowed or browned depending on the paper type, affirming for me that the mutilation had happened long ago. He, that is the cousin (we presume the male gender), is known to us only as, as just mentioned, "M". The only conclusive or apparent information we learn about M is that he was somehow affiliated with beekeeping, and that he rather rudely ordered about an individual identified only as "SS".

The vast almost incalculable irony is that I had actually possessed this memoir for two years, stuffed in an envelope addressed to me and packed in a box gathering dust in a garage, even as I was finishing up my first book, *Sherlock Holmes on the Roof of the World*, in 1987—and there it remained for another 26 years, unknown to me and packed away in that moldering cardboard box until I finally stumbled upon it in our storage unit 17 years after I'd received that momentous call from James Turner that resulted in the publication of my second book *The Great Detective at the Crucible of Life* and all the earth-shattering events that fell from that!

After examining the contents of the diary that first time, I picked up the bulging legal-sized envelope that I had found in the diary and which I had set aside. It contained a letter to M from Lady Luna Holmes Ragnall consisting of nineteen sheets of feminine notepaper topped with the Ragnall crest, which still retained a faint aroma of roses. Following that were letters from Professor Maria *[Editor's note: Pronounced Ma-RYE-ah]* Mitchell to Luna and another from Quatermain to Maria. In the mid-1800s, Maria Mitchell had risen to fame as America's first woman astronomer and subsequently taught at Vassar College. She also figured prominently in *The Great Detective at the Crucible of Life*.

Here follows the contents of those letters followed by Quatermain's memoir as set down by Luna Holmes. *The reader will note that in these documents as I am presenting them there are a number of separate, often terse, bold italic notes printed alongside Luna's entries.* These are an attempt to represent the numerous handwritten marginal notes that appear throughout the letters and diary. These notes are all dictated by a person identified only as "M" to another identified as "SS". It appears, thus, that SS must have read aloud Luna's documents to M (SS apparently being conversant in the same singular shorthand that M had taught Luna), while M regularly interrupted to give terse instructions or make some comment or another that SS was obliged to copy into the margins. You will observe that many of these notes appear to focus on the minutia of beekeeping and have nothing to do with either Luna's record or Quatermain's tale, though these notes grow in prolixity, profundity, and relevance as Quatermain's story draws out.

The first of these boxes is a request to SS to send the diary and associated materials to a "W". Of course, while we don't know who either SS or W was (aside from whatever one chooses to deduce from the scribbled "To JW" on the corresponding envelope), we can certainly make educated guesses. However, the fact that the diary languished in a Dublin bookstore for 25 years indicates that something went wrong. Anything is possible; maybe SS did not ship it, or maybe W mislaid it, or maybe some mischief occurred while the package was en route, that is, between points SS and W. All we can say for sure is that M requested it be sent to W, and not much afterward, it found its way to Mr. Webster's antiquarian bookshop.

Thus, Luna Holmes' diary traveled as follows: She wrote it in 1884 and soon thereafter put it in an envelope labeled to go to her cousin. She may have hand delivered that envelope to the offices of Mellis & Mellis with instructions that it be delivered to her cousin only when certain conditions had been met. The envelope, therefore, was tucked in the solicitors' safe for more than 20 years, whereupon they delivered it to M in 1905. M did not keep it long and requested that it be sent to W. It apparently did not get to its destination, but instead it further languished in a Dublin bookstore for another 25 years. Then it was sent to Robert E. Howard, who kept it for six years before he made sure it was sent to E. Hoffmann Price, who, for lack of any other reason

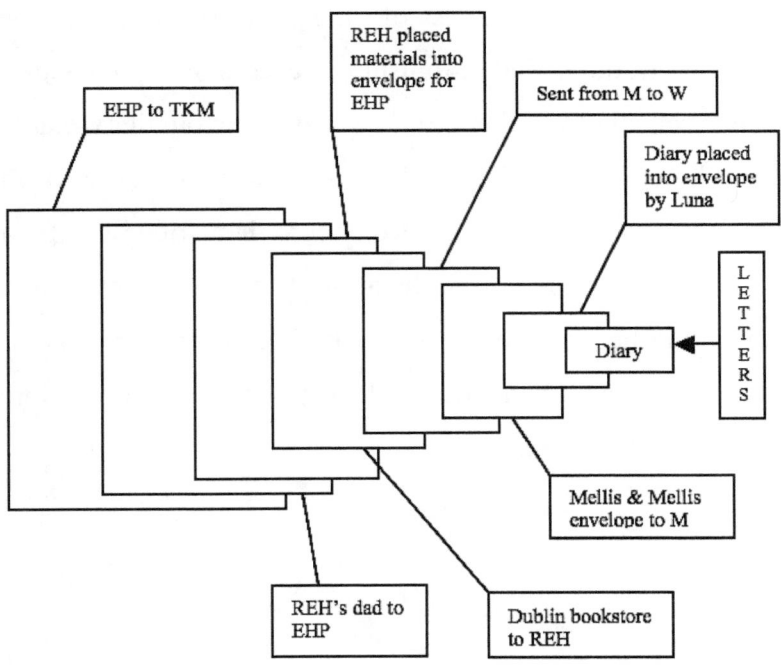

The succession of envelopes shown schematically.

to treat it any differently, kept it under his house for about 50 more years and then delivered it to me, who unknowingly possessed it for another 22 years or so in a succession of garages and storage units. Therefore, from the time the diary was written to the time it arrived at my front door was slightly more than a century, and two more decades passed until I stumbled upon it! In round numbers, that's a journey of 125 years.

Thus, in the fullness of time, so to speak, I burrowed my way through that astonishing succession of envelopes, shown schematically here, finding at last the old diary that the Lady Luna Holmes Ragnall had grabbed in her haste to find writing materials on which to record her friend's African adventure and which diary she arranged to be delivered to her cousin via her attorneys, along with her scented explanatory letter and some others, all of which follow here as forewords to Quatermain's tale.

First Foreword: A Typed Letter
FROM LADY LUNA HOLMES RAGNALL
TO HER UNNAMED COUSIN

SS—

Send to W all this material from my

18 August, 1884   *dear departed cousin. It's astronom-*

ically interesting, of course. I'm quite

My dear cousin: *positive that he will want to add it to*

his files for eventual embellishment.

Boo!!   *—M*

I'm haunting you now perhaps long after my passing because I wish you to have something of mine. I am requesting my solicitors to deliver it to you only after all principal parties are gone . . . and after they have deemed (through whatever sources) that you are no longer active in the [A HOLE] business, per se, for I have no wish to distract you from your proper affairs.

The gentlemen who have delivered this packet to you have no idea of our blood relationship—per your request.

At best, from your viewpoint, the enclosed diary will be a curiosity, I suppose.

I doubt I have mentioned him to you since your and my paths cross so infrequently, but I have a friend by the name of Allan Quatermain. He recently came into a fortune having to do with—I speak the truth!— King Solomon's Mines. He tells me that he has written the whole thing down and that he expects it to be published as a book next year (that is, next year from my point of view— heaven only knows when from yours). With that fortune he bought an estate in Yorkshire.

Allan's and my association has been long and multifarious to say the least! In fact, now I do recall that he and you were both at a garden party held here at the castle in the summer of 1870, though you were but a lad, and Allan is rather shy in social situations, so it is doubtful that you will remember him.

You know of course that I left nothing whatsoever to you as was your request, and, further, I've never mentioned my relationship to you since you made it clear that time years ago how utterly inconvenient my dropping your name could prove to you. Even disastrous!

Though I have bequeathed my monies and possessions to Allan from my heart, I strongly suspect that he will decline—for much the same reason as yourself—namely the inconvenience of riches would impinge on his quiet life. Besides, he is rich already from having cashed in those diamonds that he and his friends brought back from King Solomon's Mines.

However, getting to the point, the thing that I want to give you, and which I believe you will find rather interesting, is the attached ms. written in my hand in the shorthand that you taught me, as Allan relayed the astonishing events of his experience in west Africa.

You will be interested in learning how I happened to hear Allan's adventure!

As you know, as a woman and a noble one by marriage, I can be fickle. And during the evening in question, I had suffered through indignities unimaginable from those horrible Atterby-Smith relatives of Lord Ragnall, who have been harassing me about what they believe is their rightful inheritance—namely all of it! The fact is that I would have embarrassed myself if I hadn't in a fury stomped up those stairs before I could lose my temper, leaving poor Allan to suffer the load and no doubt ponder the peculiar ways of my sex [Editor's note: See *The Ancient Allan*].

Be that as it may, in only a little time I felt lonely in my rooms and asked Alfred [Luna's footman] to fetch Allan. Arriving a little while later, he seemed confused but as docile as a puppy dog. I just needed company, you see, after having to endure those awful people, and I had no intention beyond merely chatting about whatever came to mind—anything but a certain adventure he and I shared some time ago for quite a duration. Now of course, you don't know, or at least I shouldn't think that you would know, that due to various factors having to do with my being kidnapped and being forced to take on the role of priestess of the Kandah tribe in Central Africa, my senses are now ever heightened and it was easy enough to see that poor Allan—who had fought in infinitely more terrible mêlées than I can ever imagine—felt distinctly uncomfortable being alone with me in my chambers behind closed doors. Thus with the intent of distracting him from his immediate plight, I poured him a drink and asked him some leading questions hoping he would tell me in some detail of one or more of his other expeditions that did not involve me, particularly of the curious ones—(by that I mean expeditions over and beyond those ordinary hunting and trading ones by which he plied his trade of hunter and guide, usually with the end being some poor young elephant was left orphaned, though, once when I admonished him on the subject, he admitted that such wanton killing was beginning to give him pause)—for I knew of course that some of his adventures were especially unique.

Picking a subject at random, I asked him to elaborate on some points he had mentioned earlier in the day regarding K.S.M. and the safari leading up to the mines. (Oh, I'm putting the cart before the horse! He had earlier told me that he'd only just finished writing a manuscript that detailed that journey in all its particulars and that he would bring it over for me to read if I was interested.) But, just then he told me how he was tired of that subject and preferred not to discuss it then.

Perhaps, I suggested, over the years he had encountered other lost treasures—wonders to stir the soul. Then I was amazed to see dear Allan become wistful. He was quiet, using his fingertips to make tracks through the condensation on his glass. In time, I saw that the pattern he was making was that of stars, or rather, a star repeated over and over. Finally I had to interrupt his reverie and ask what was he thinking, whereupon he said, "Well Luna, there was a time in west Africa that had more than its fair share of the out of the ordinary about it."

"And the stars?" I asked, for I am nothing if not bold, but you already know that, dear cousin.

"Stars?" he responded confused, and when I pointed to his glass, he frankly blushed. "Oh, I gave myself away! Your questions following so close on one another brought to mind the other time I had a fortune in diamonds in my hands—or, I mean, one fabulous diamond. I didn't have it long enough for it to be christened any particular name, but I thought of it then and still do as my "Star of Wonder." It was mine to do with as I wished . . . but as you can easily conclude, the one thing I didn't do with it was bring it home and cash it in."

"Heavens! Why on earth not?"

"You know what they say, my dear, 'And therein lies a tale!' and to tell it properly would require most of the night."

"Well." I said, "do you see me doing anything else of importance?"

A simple enough argument that won the day, and for several hours I was treated to the joy of beholding a new Allan Quatermain, one that I was not acquainted with—a loquacious Allan Quatermain!

He refilled his glass, stretched his legs toward the blazing fire in my bedroom hearth and quietly began his story. After a few minutes I realized that I was missing the chance of a lifetime and that this was an opportunity to capture all the spirit of the man, so I interrupted him to ask if he wouldn't mind if I took down his words, to which he assented.

When I had grabbed an old unused diary from my corner press and with some pencils in hand, I spent a few minutes hastily summarizing what he had already narrated. All the time I was catching up, he sat silently, apparently in thought. When I was done, rather than continue his story, he communicated the following, as I recall it from memory:

"You know, Luna, here is a queer thing. There are three people who are no longer in this world who touched me to such a degree that mentioning their names or the circumstances that I shared with them in common conversation feels like irreverence. Thus, to remember their loss, or, rather, the loss of them which is my loss, brings down on me a torrent of emotions that I would prefer to avoid."

"Allan," I say, "please tell me."

"Well, there are my two wives, Marie and Stella, and the third is Hans. With regard to Marie and Stella, I want you to know that during my leisure time here in England at the Grange, which is about all I have these days, I have jotted down some memories of them and there are two volumes that are devoted to their lives as I knew them—but that is all I wish to say on that subject—Luna, are you crying?" [Editor's note: See *Marie* and *Allan's Wife*.]

"No, Allan. Well, yes. Yes, I was, as I can only imagine the strength and devotion of such women must assuredly be beyond my ken!"

Allan smiled reflectively, or at least as I imagined it to be, and said passionately, "No more!" Then after pausing to reflect for a minute or two, he asked, "You remember Hans?"

"Clearly and with much fondness, I have wonderful memories of Hans," I replied, as that old Hottentot was more like Allan's shadow than his servant, and we had shared some little time together before his passing, through the agency of an enraged terrible and giant elephant [Editor's note: See *The Ivory Child*], though admittedly I was not on my best form, having been recently kidnapped, drugged for months on end, and suffered indignities numerous and unmentionable.

But Allan continued, "I was about to say that with people who never knew Hans, there is no point

47

at all in mentioning him, because one really needed to know him and experience him and have a clear picture of him in mind, or else the exercise of discussing him in conversation is pointless . . . ."

Again, Allan seemed lost in thought for a while.

"But you were saying about Hans."

"Well, here is that queer thing that I meant to say—and, Luna, since you did in fact know him for some time, I can speak comfortably about him to you. Well you remember how exceedingly bright and astute he was, despite never having any formal schooling in the European sense, at least none beyond the lessons my father furnished to all the staff of our Cape Colony station where he performed his duties as a Church of England clergyman. What I'm trying to say is that I can never remember Hans saying, that is speaking out loud, anything to any European either in his own language or about his language, which is called Khoi. It's that distinct clicking language that the Hottentot people use along with Bushmen and a few other native groups. Of course, as you know first hand, he and I could speak fluently to one another in English, Dutch, Arabic, and Zulu, and he, as I, could communicate in a whole spectrum of languages as one must be able to in order to survive in the distant reaches of Africa where we trekked. I bring this up now because the story I have to tell depends greatly on the nature of his own native language, the language of his birth, which is extremely difficult for Europeans to reproduce . . . . I'm sorry to be wandering, Luna, but there is a point, or rather a story, or perhaps anecdote is a better term to which all the preceding is preface. There was the time in 1873 . . . ."

The tale that he told that night of an adventure with his manservant Hans astonished even I, who have known and seen so terribly much: I who am not easily astonished due to the peculiarities of my own life and certain adventures I endured against my will.

But I have finished my little introduction to what follows. Knowing you, I expect it has some points of interest, and as I dispose my will, there is nothing else I can imagine doing with Allan's record of Hans' encounter with—what?

SS—

Your eternally loving cousin,
Luna

The honey is crystal-lising again in the far-ther hives. √ *temps.*

P.S. I must be growing feeble because there is another item

—*M*

that is for all intents and purposes a prequel of sorts to Allan's long story and which I have been meaning to also give you. I am tiring, so I will say this in as few words as I can. Within a few days of Allan sharing his story with me, I impulsively wrote to Professor Maria Mitchell, the noted astronomy professor at Vassar College in New York, who you will learn when you read the diary, was a major participant in the events Allan described. I don't know what I expected, but . . . lo! she responded. I attach her epistle here. Her letter, which is actually several, is an admirable introduction to Allan's tale. And, now that I have already said farewell, I hasten to do so again, as I don't wish to appear flighty.

L.

Second Foreword: A Typed Letter
FROM PROFESSOR MARIA MITCHELL
TO LADY LUNA HOLMES RAGNALL

8 January, 1884

Dear Lady Ragnall:

Thank you for your extended
message of this last November.

Oh, I wish I could say how delighted I was that you
wrote and that I have heard much about you from
our mutual friend, and that aside from that, I am
honored beyond human word's ability to convey the
extremity of my pleasure—but, alas!, none of that
would be true because (1) my social circles are
limited at best, (2) my knowledge of the intricacies
of the British hierarchy, of peers and knights and so
forth is abominable, and (3) I can't recall that Allan
ever mentioned you—and as a result, I have never
heard of you, though I don't doubt for one second
that you are in fact who you say you are, and that as

SS—

Let's repurpose the wax.
Put on calendar to discuss.
REMEMBER!
—M

51

a natural consequence of that status, you must be richer than Croesus.

Please forgive my clumsy manner of introducing this letter, for I am in fact so happy you wrote and I often wonder about dear Allan, and heaven knows that correspondence was never his forte and I wish to respect his privacy at all costs.

It seems that we have in common that we have both experienced intimate and long adventures with Allan and his man Hans. Mine were twofold, first in east Africa on the Horn and close beside the Red Sea and the second was in west Africa, just a stone's throw from the Atlantic Ocean on the border region between Sierra Leone and Liberia. However . . . however interesting my experiences were, I cannot imagine the degree of yours. Being kidnapped as you have described and suffering the lot of being drugged and violated body and soul—I cannot fathom it! And to think that you have been able to retain some semblance of sanity and normalcy, for which I much admire you. It seems that it was the courage and persistence of both Allan and your husband, Lord Ragnall, by which you survived. God protect them both—the one in life and the other in Heaven.

In my own case, Allan's and my first meeting was pure happenstance, unwittingly arranged by the highest powers of both government and church, and as full as it was with incident, it lasted only a few days. In the second instance, Allan and Hans, again unwittingly, stumbled onto a scientific encampment of which I was part. Of course, upon their unexpected appearance at the gates of the place, my scientific colleagues would have turned them away if it had not been for my insistence that they remain. But once having entered, due to the situation, Q and H were obliged to be our guests for some weeks, but of course, he has already explained or confided to you this much or else you would never have gone to the trouble of contacting me! Never-theless, of course, he, or they, he and Hans, were not privy to anything much more than the surface details of daily life in the encampment, or laboratory, and despite my high regard for Allan, neither could I then, nor now, say too much as I am ever bound by oath.

Yet, as you are so close to him, it is incumbent on me to share something with you. There is so much I want to share with you, but all that must wait because I have something particular to say, and Heaven only knows how, if I get sidetracked and if exhaustion sets in due to the digression, it may be a whole day until I can circuitously get back to my point. What I wish to share needs to be done now and not put off. It is namely this:

Twelve years ago in the summer of 1872, after Allan and the rest of our little group parted at the edge of the Red Sea and once I was home and had begun my life again—though, as it turned out, this would not be for long—I received a most unusual letter from Allan. Indeed, it wasn't really from Allan at all, because he was mainly the agent by whom another wanted to speak to me, but I will not put the cart before the horse. I wish now to include here that letter of a dozen years ago. The reason is that I believe that the message so revealed (despite its flattering reflection on my own person, which modesty would have me exclude, but which act would render the message meaningless) must be shared, that is to say, must become known to another beyond my poor humble self. I think there is something here (despite its strangeness) that ought to be better known and so here is the letter. It is odd because, there is a letter within a letter within a letter but you will see for yourself.

Now, I must wind down this note, as I am very excited that Mr. Matthew Arnold will be presenting in just a few hours his views on Emerson to an expected group of 600 students and townspeople! I've been looking forward to this lecture for some time, and must now get ready.

Yours,
M. M.

Third Foreword: A Letter
FROM ALLAN QUATERMAIN
TO PROFESSOR MARIA MITCHELL

July 1872

My dear Maria:

I am sorry to impose on your normal life in America so soon. I am doing so, however, at the request of a mutual friend. But before that—as I have this unexpected opportunity to communicate with you—something I would not have ordinarily thought to do—not because of avoidance nor rudeness, but because I do not like myself to be imposed on, therefore I tend to assume that any outreach from me to anybody would be construed as an imposition—I wish now to state how pleasant I found your company during our odd little safari three or four months ago. I need not remind you that you were the only woman in our group of a dozen opinionated and some disingenuous men, which might have been an intimidating circumstance for many a woman, but never seemed to faze you in the least. From first to last I must admit you had inspired in me the greatest respect and admiration not only for the heights to which you have risen in academia, as well as your scientific attainments, but for your honest ability to participate in our group without resorting to the feminine tricks that your gender, regardless of race, can do so well, much to the bafflement and embarrassment of us poor men. As I said, I am taking this opportunity now to sing your praises because this correspondence has been pressed on me, on one hand, and because it is only right to speak the truth in a world so absorbed with self-advancement and appearances and so much other nonsense that it is often difficult merely to live and let live and be content within our own skins, and I must say that Hans *[Editor's note: See "Appendix: H. Rider Haggard's Character Hans the Hottentot" in the second book of this series* The Great Detective at the Crucible of Life, *for vital information about Hans.]*, in his own way, feels much the same as I and seldom does a day go by that he doesn't mention you with his own brand of fondness and admiration. ("Baas, remember that crazy lady who risked her life, first, seeking that pile of rocks they called the Heaven's Dead, and, then, by thrusting herself into a man's battle and thereby winning the day, much to the chagrin of many men, including many of those tall, skinny desert folk, especially of the one whose head she lopped off; well, if ever you chance to talk to her in a letter, tell her that I believe she did the right thing, and that my only regret is that I didn't think just then to kick that fool's head around just for fun until my foot ached!") But the true reason I am writing now is that another member of our troop is requesting that I do so (though, please note that his message includes an addendum addressed to me from Zikali, that awful Zulu wizard Shaka once named "The Thing That Should Never Have Been Born").

It is Bayushtiak *[Editor's note: See* The Great Detective at the Crucible of Life*]* who asks that I communicate with you. Here following are the impressions he wished me to convey to you, and that I will leave you with. I tried to keep true to his intentions, neither taking away nor adding any thought or statement of consequence of my own or by extrapolating any more than I ought, though I was sorely tempted to soften the edges of his remarks, which I believe sprang forth during moments wherein he forgot himself, and during which his words were colored by some dreadful experience or experiences perhaps having to do with betrayal, I would imagine, or else some other onerous happening, of which I don't presume to comment one way or another.

Still, his positive remarks are kind and reflect some of my own feelings *vis à vis* both you and Mariam *[Editor's note: Again, see* The Great Detective at the Crucible of Life*]*

I have nothing more to add here and now, but I do hope our paths cross again.

Your friend and fellow adventurer,
Allan Quatermain

A Tribute to Professor Maria Mitchell
From Bayustiak the Zulu Warrior

Macumazana—

It has been my experience that women as a rule, by and large, are evil creatures, prevaricators who are not loath to be false time and again with regard to the men in their lives in order to get their own way, but mostly to hurt men for the joy of doing so and merely to raise themselves up. I have loved many times and have deeply regretted each time, for all there is at the end of that black cave is boundless sorrow. With a woman the pain is all the more searing because each time it is always the one you least suspect, because she can wield magic and blind you and cause you to forget and she will laugh all the while. O, Macumazana, the great spirits did ill by creating these creatures, for some shine like the sun and lift the soul and make a man feel he is one with heaven; others are ugly or malformed or overtly evil or vindictive, and no-one would ever think differently about these last, but, O, Macumazana, all of them, every last one is nothing more or less the seed of death and pain and suffering.

Were that the spirits had thought better of their plan!

[Here I broke in and said, "O, Leopard (for you remember he was so called, that is to say his honorific title was, "The Steaming Hot Breath of the Crouching Black Leopard"), why are you making a speech to me, of all people, who knows well of what you speak, for, with only—five exceptions (here I confess I counted on my fingers), I would manifestly agree with much of what you say. From women often comes confusion and despair. But why are you, without warning, thundering so in my ear?]

Because, Macumazana, for months now, ever since we returned from that land of more wonders than can be remembered, I have been aware of my mind slowly changing in some measure with regard to these opinions of women which I have just stated and that I have held so true for so long, because not long ago, I—indeed you as well—met two women who broke the mold, who are unlike other women, neither of whom I believe could ever harm a single hair on any man's head. Of course, one is not a true woman but the girl who speaks in tongues and who has so much wisdom, and the other is the sky talker. I have never encountered such two stalwart, apparently honest women who seem not to have some ulterior motive and whose existence almost balances the unbalance caused by all the others. I say "almost" because, on balance, even these two pure souls cannot save the race from the folly that women cause! The beauty of some women is like the sweet sap of fragrant flowers that betrays some poor little insect to feel intoxicated and be off guard so that they let themselves be fooled and in the end must inevitably be not so much destroyed, but eaten alive. O, only suffering and doom is the fruit for any man who is attracted to any woman. It is the wise man who imprisons his women in a *kraal* and does not suffer them to leave. What good is a woman except to make babies and what is the good of that when half the babies grow to become girls, then women. O, evil begets evil! It is an old story!

Still, I want you to tell sky talker that I am quite fond of her and that I am sure that I need not ever fear any evil originating from her, and that she is truly different and I am honored to have known her, and I wish you to convey that to her with those magic markings that you white people often use in the manner that we Zulus employ runners and messengers and, too, as we use the fathers of fathers and the mothers of mothers [that is, elderly repositories of tribal lore]. Tell her I hope to see her again in the Land of Fires where we are all bound.

And now, Macumazana, I also have a message for you from the Opener of Roads [that is, Zikali].

[Here, my Zulu friend was quiet for a time, his head and face lowered, clearly trying to focus. And when I saw his face again, his eyes showed only white, and he spoke, the timbre of his voice having changed, and thus his wizard master, the dwarf Zikali, chose to send me a few chosen words or remarks that I place here on paper, as they have points of interest.]

A Message to Allan Quatermain
From the Zulu Wizard Zikali, "Opener of Roads"
Through the Medium of Bayushtiak the Zulu Warrior

Ho, Ho, Macumazana:

"The Steaming Breath of the Crouching Black Leopard" ho, ho, tells me he plans to seek you and speak to you. Well, as I am never one to let slip an opportunity, I am giving him a message to repeat to you. I don't know if he will remember it or not, and even if he doesn't, there will be no harm. For their own mysterious purposes, the spirits that continually enshroud me have caused me to see a little into the future, and then they showed me the end of the world, or maybe it was the beginning, I don't know, for they are all the same to me (and O, I fought it, as there are some things I would rather not see nor know about). What I saw was that little yellow monkey of a fellow who is as close to you as your own skin—the one called "Light in Darkness"— earnestly listening to matters that were, or rather will be, far beyond his ken. But, you know I must know all things knowable so I eavesdropped, or rather, again, will do so, over your man's shoulder and heard what he heard, and more, I

63

saw something he couldn't see! O, ow! And what I looked at turned around and looked at me and I knew the uttermost fear that a being could know. It knew I was there and stared at me and I could not have closed my eyes if I had tried. Moreover, we stared at one another for what seemed an eternity and I feared, O, I feared. By now you are wanting to know why I am telling you all this business through the agency of my servant. It is because I have little choice. As I have slaves, so there are things to which I am a slave (yes, I confess this, though you will think I am making up only another wizard's trick). That Spirit, who is the Spirit to which the other great spirits bow, took pains to lay hands on my heart and commanded just this: that I bear witness from afar to that which Light in Darkness will someday tell you after a certain incident, and confirm to you that such matters were not the drunken dream of your servant, but rather accurate reporting. Thus I do not yet know the secret but must needs to wait as you must also do now that I have told this to you. Well, be that as it may, I am bored speaking to you through my servant. Farewell, Macumazana, Watcher by Night!

[At this point Bayushtiak's eyes rolled back into place and he shook his head and drew in a sharp breath and looked

64

bewildered, or as much so as such a man can appear, but only for a moment, and I asked him if he remembered what he had just spoken, and he replied, "O, no, Macumazana, those who are the vessels of the words of the Opener of Roads do not live long if they remember, and, thus, being a man of some sense, I cannot remember anything at all." Which was just as well because I believe that Zikali was playing me the fool yet again and was in the midst of some elaborate joke and I could see him making that horrible sound that was his laughter and rocking back and forth on his haunches, making merry at my expense!]

Editor's Note

Here follows Lady Luna Holmes Ragnall's diary, which she bequeathed to her mysterious cousin, an individual we know only by the initial M. The diary was written in the personal shorthand that M seems to have taught her, and with time and effort, money and expertise, I was able to have it rendered readable. Here are the contents of the actual diary in which Lady Luna Holmes Ragnall recorded Allan Quatermain's adventure as he told it to her.

The epigraphs, division into chapters, chapter titles, illustrations, and captions are all my additions, because they offer a perspective and dimensions that would otherwise be missing.

Please see the adjacent note calling out separately, or explaining, a most important aspect of the book's structure that some may notice and deem curious.

A Further Note About the Organization That
The Editor Has Superimposed onto
Quatermain's Memoir

The section of this Quatermain memoir that I've titled "Hans' Story" is, I believe—and which belief ought to be abundantly clear from the title page—the very core of this book and everything before it is treated as introduction, or prologue, once again in my view.

Prologue

By Allan Quatermain

After this Lady Ragnall [retired], having instructed Moxley to show us the smoking room . . . . Over the rest of the night I draw a veil . . . . [W]hile pretending to help myself to whiskey and soda, slipped through the door and fled upstairs. I arrived late to breakfast.

—Allan Quatermain in the *The Ancient Allan*

Here I will stop this tale, for to describe all my adventures and experiences on my way to the West Coast would take another book, which I have neither the time nor the inclination to write.

Allan Quatermain in *The Treasure of the Lake*

First Prologue Chapter

The Whale

There was the time in 1873, deciding to follow the advice of John Arkle, a man who was central to a story *[Editor's note: See* The Treasure of the Lake*]* irrelevant to the one I'm about to tell, as to the direction of travel when leaving the country of the Dabanda and the Holy Lake of Mone in Central Africa, I, with Hans* turned west with the intention of reaching the coast around Sierra Leone and locating an expedient ship or some such with which to return to South Africa and Durban, our home.

That journey took more months than I care to recall and can be divided into two distinct chapters. There was the actual trek between the country of the Holy Lake and the southeastern region of Sierra Leone contiguous with Liberia, a journey full of incident both good and bad, but totally separate

---

* Editor's note: See "Appendix: H. Rider Haggard's Character Hans the Hottentot" in the second book of this series, *The Great Detective at the Crucible of Life*, for vital information about Hans.—T.K.M.

from the subject of this tale. And then there were our experiences on the coast.

As we headed out of that amorphous and still largely unexplored region that we call for convenience Central Africa or Darkest Africa, despite my own journeys which *in toto* covered very little ground when considered geographically, we began to hear rumors from the various villages and occasional safari of a tribe of great white witch doctors and of the peculiar magic they wielded that required the building of a railroad for transport. When I asked what it was that was being transported, I received no clear answer but eventually concluded that it consisted of some sort of heavy equipment.

And since it was our encounter with those so-called white witch doctors, which description, by the way, could not be further from the truth, I will skip the fairly routine matters of signing papers, greasing palms, and stating intentions to officials, and get to the root of the episode.

With our retinue of wagons, oxen, and bearers, Hans and I entered the port community of Freetown, which was then in 1873 a growing hub of trading, with the aim of booking passage on the first vessel heading south. At this point we sold the wagons and oxen and dismissed the bearers

70

and sold the various goods we'd accumulated on our trek from the various peoples we'd encountered.

That left only Hans and myself in this foreign land, as certainly neither of us had ever been this far west, and so the sights were new and different, and, of course, we were always comfortable around each other, having shared so much over the years.

In due course, I had us booked onto the commercial trading vessel *Carlson*, which was expected to arrive in some weeks, and was thence bound to various ports along the west African coast, making stops at Cape Town and Port Elizabeth and then on to our home Durban, of which I saw little enough due to my livelihood. Thus Hans and I had time on our hands, and then I remembered those white witch doctors of which we had heard rumors. I mentioned to Hans that I had half a mind to scout about and see if there was any substance to these rumors.

"Baas! You can go wherever you want! But I intend to stay comfortable at that rooming house you fixed up, for it reminds me of the missionary station of the Predikant, your Reverend father, where I met you years ago when you lost your way in the spirit world and arrived in this land, which is really the very last place a sane spirit would venture, but who am I to judge such things, as I am only the drunken yellow dog that the Zulu cannot be bothered with."

"Or perhaps," I said, "you've noticed that the saloon is only a couple of doors down, and one way or another you will become drunk on square-face [Luna, you remember that by square-face, he meant gin], since my moderating influence would be gone."

Hans looked struck and said, "Baas! You think so little of me, your servant!"

"It's not a matter of what I think, Hans. It is what I *know*."

"Well, Baas, since you put it that way, and since I promised your Reverend father, the Predikant, that I would watch over you and protect you for as long as the spirits allow—and let me tell you a secret, Baas, even after I am swept into the Place of Fires, I will bargain and cajole with whomever it is necessary to do so, so that I will still be with you, which is something you can depend on."

Thus we argued for a day or so, with Hans ever trying to change my mind about my little side expedition, and which he came close to succeeding and winning me over to his side, but then my sense returned. I said, "Be my guest if you wish to get drunk when I'm not here to get you out of your scrapes! Do as you please!"

And in the end, days later, he and I were marching south without bearers through the forested region that there served as a buffer between the town and the black jungle. My internal navigation system is usually pretty good and I seldom get lost, even in places I've never seen or ever known, but this time as forest transitioned from jungle and the sky was a great stage where various brands of air collided and rolled and changed the color of land and hills, I confess that I lost my bearings, though my plan had been simple enough, namely to keep as much as possible within sight of the majestic ocean on our right.

***

"Baas, smell it! The sea of the west! Smell the salt!" Hans' wrinkled little face was turned upward and his nostrils quivered, and a glow spread across his face.

He was quite correct. After suffering through a maze of steamy jungle on one hand, followed by arid desert on the other, we finally found ourselves exiting a dank forest within view of a hilltop. Hans ran ahead, as he does when he is excited, and in a few moments I heard him cry out, "Baas! Come quickly."

I remember that the sound of his voice was muffled by the sea breeze that refreshed my face. I ran to the top of the hill only to find that it was not a hill at all, but a rise that fronted on and ended in a sheer cliff overlooking a small crescent-shaped bay with mighty waves crashing on the rocks far below. I then fixed my attention in the direction Hans was pointing.

"See, Baas, a great whale coming up to breathe!"

Greatly disappointed, for though I knew not what I expected, it was certainly more than a mere whale, of which I had seen many over the years. Nevertheless, I acknowledged that there certainly was a large vortex of water below.

"Hans, is that all? Have you not seen as many whales as I?"

"Yes, Baas, perhaps even more, but never have I seen such a whale as the big black brother yonder. He is a mountain, this whale, but wait, you have not seen anything but his splash. You have not seen him with your own eyes. He should rise to the surface again any moment."

Impatiently I watched the swirling waters. Then suddenly the waters parted with a mighty frothing and a titanic blue-black-maroon mottled monster fully two hundred feet in length exploded into sight, leaping straight into the air and spouting a prodigious tower of spray and foam nearly half its length across the sky.

"Great God!" I exclaimed, "Such a fish!" Just then the great whale hurled itself back into water and submerged again causing a grand swelling of the waves, and all at once its mighty double-bladed tail heaved into the air, then smoothly slipped under the churning waters.

Hans and I were mesmerized by the sight, so much so that he was speechless, which is rare enough to be sure. Even as we watched, the waves roared and parted once more and the great blunt nose of the blue-black hide poked up from the madly swirling blue-green waters, snorted a blast of spray arcing through the air, then submerged again.

Such a proud spectacle to see! Frolicking there in nature's bosom, skipping about the waters joyfully, was the earth's largest creature, the hugest fish which God ever made. The greatest of the great whales. Fully three times larger than the greatest I had ever seen. Then Hans and I found ourselves being showered with a watery mist and bits of foam as the wind carried the beast's spout up the cliff face. When it settled on the surrounding rocks, it vanished in wisps of steam. Over and again we watched that cavorting monster cross and recross that crescent bay.

But one could only be so mesmerized for so long before more practical matters intruded, and we continued on the path that would lead us to our quarry, at least as suggested by some local natives we had met.

Half a day after this, we heard faintly at the edge of our hearing, or more accurately, Hans' hearing—for his ears were more attuned than mine, and have been as long as I knew him which was long indeed, since my childhood—the distinct chug-chug of a locomotive and then a piercing whistle. Within a day we encountered the wide tracks. Hans ventured up and down the tracks for some distance but saw nothing worth reporting except more track. Insofar as it was late, I decided to throw up some prickly sage and set down our packs and rolls and make a fire, in other words to set up camp, right there near the tracks so that we would be able to learn about the train, and maybe even get a ride. Sure enough, the next morning we heard the whistle again and eventually saw a locomotive appear in the distance with one passenger car and several flat trucks loaded with equipment, all of which was covered with canvas, or oil cloth, as we could not at that distance identify its nature.

I'm sure the engineer saw our camp, but the train's momentum did not waver as it grew closer, so I said, "Hans, stand in the middle of the track and wave your arms to stop this fool train. Don't you agree that it would be at least polite for it to slow down?"

He looked at me and said, "Baas, I don't mean any disrespect for your Reverend Predikant father—who I served for years, or to you for that matter—but you can stand in front of your own damn train!"

In the end we both watched, helplessly, close alongside the track and made futile gestures. However, I don't believe that engineer would have hesitated running us down, if it came to that, for though it slowed a little in a perfect riot of squealing, sparks, steam, and the acrid stink of burnt metal, and so forth, it showed no intention of stopping, and Hans and I had to jump for our lives. As it raced past us, I noticed the name of the railroad company emblazoned on the side of the engine—Kingdom–Elias R.R.—in elaborate ornate and scrolled lettering. The mustached engineer was shaking his fist at us and had thunder in his face. As it roared by, we saw its one passenger coach along with two or three indistinct faces staring at us from within. To their credit, they seemed confused, and I gave them the benefit of the doubt.

Thereafter, assuming that the track must end somewhere, or, at the very least go through somewhere, Hans and I chose to follow the track in the direction that the train had raced off. The country all around was a patchwork of all kinds of terrain both high and low and of foliage both tropical and temperate type, but I couldn't help but be impressed that in every case, if there was a hill or other formidable obstacle in the path of the track, the train builders had drilled right through solid rock with tunnels rather than move the track around the obstacle, even in instances when the terrain included more than enough land to facilitate that approach.

For three or four days—I don't remember now, as these things do tend to blend together after a while—we continued down this deserted metal path, but a path that showed every indication of being recently created and used often enough.

Then all at once the wind shifted and Hans' little body reacted as though it was touched with a hot prod.

"Baas! I smell roasting meat—and beer! May the Predikant, your Reverend father's heaven, that he loved to talk about so long and so often, be praised for I am tired of biltong and warm water."

"Perhaps we are finally approaching the origin or destination of the railroad," I ventured. "Or perhaps that tribe of white witches is around the bend!"

But Hans had already run ahead and he didn't stop until he was out of sight due to the undulating nature of that landscape. "Hans, you monkey, come back!" I cried, but heard no response. Rather irritated at my servant for his impetuous behavior, especially as I valued his gun in this unknown territory and it was certain that two guns were better than one in the event they were needed at all. The end of it was, still following the wide track and stepping around a stand of trees, I finally found Hans, sitting on an outcrop of rock and twirling his filthy hat and grinning.

"Well, Baas, it is nice of you to finally join me, for as you can see, we have company, which can only be to the good as I am hungry and it seems that my nose did not fool me," and he gestured in the direction of the sea which was again visible from this vantage point. But that is not all I saw! Down below and in the distance a mile or so ahead and built at the bottom of a kind of valley that ended at the Atlantic Ocean, was what appeared to be a town of sorts, or village, at any rate a thriving community, or at least that was our first impression of the place as we viewed it from on high from the top of one of the cascading natural walls that formed the north face of the valley. My gaze lingered and then I spotted in the distance half hidden in the ocean mist the oddest sight.

At the far end of the community, I thought I could see through the mist a small Greek temple. But then the vision disappeared, leaving me to rub my eyes and wonder.

Such a proud spectacle to see! Frolicking there in nature's bosom, skipping about the waters joyfully.

Second Prologue Chapter

The City Where There
Shouldn't Be One

I said I thought there was a village or town down below us, but in a few moments I realized that the distance and the mist, or what I at first thought was mist, had deceived me. In a moment I began to understand what in fact it was that hovered below in the valley that opened to the sea! What I had interpreted as mist and dark clouds was in fact smoke billowing from heaven knows how many chimneys from numerous large buildings, which at first I took for factories. I rubbed my eyes, and looked at Hans, who was likewise studying the sight, his eyes moving rapidly, calculatingly. It is interesting how one often sees what one expects to see, rather than what actually is. Though any kind of village was unexpected, still when we saw first a cluster of

SS—

We need a new smoker, as repairing ours won't do at all, as it would be only a temporary solution. We should have a spare in any case. Put it on the list.

—M

buildings away in the mist, we naturally assumed on some level that the cluster was relatively contained, that is, smaller rather than larger. But when our eyes took in the sight, and expectations vanished, the vast operation below became evident. Our path fell steeply into the valley and ran straight into the middle of a veritable small city throughout which huge construction projects were underway. By far most of the activity was somewhat north-west of the city. It took me a moment to grasp the scale of the scene, but when I finally understood just what I was seeing, I counted nineteen towering steam shovels at work grabbing claw loads of rock and earth and dumping it all into a hundred or more waiting train cars that were attached to a dozen waiting steaming and smoking black locomotives, most waiting their turn. This screeching and clanging equipment was at work excavating an enormous hole in the ground, a vast bowl-shaped pit that somehow reminded me of active volcano craters or titanic meteorite craters, of which I have seen my fair share! The roar and piercing whistles of the locomotives and the cry of the earth being rent and disemboweled were horrible.

Then I saw that the clouds were made of just as much dirt and dust from the excavation as black smoke from the chimneys—and it hung over everything and severely blocked

Excavating an enormous hole in the ground, a vast bowl-shaped pit.

the waning late-afternoon sunlight—already turning crimson—slanting in from over the sea, casting long red shadows upon the whole scene, magnifying my impression of vulcanism. And once my brain was able to assemble all the pieces, what I saw was this: The buildings with the chimneys surrounded the pit and were arranged equidistant from one another. Massive pipes with enormous valves extended from each building and were intended, it seemed likely upon first observation, to pour some material or another into the pits, but the pipes were not active at that point.

The tracks for the trains I have mentioned were mainly laid so that they began between the "factories" and ran to the edge of the pits and were situated so that the excavators could

83

dump their claw loads into the railcars. They mostly jutted out at first rather like the spokes of a wheel for a distance and then they all veered gently to the southeast and disappeared into the nearly opaque, poisonous, roiling red air towards wherever they dumped the debris, I suppose.

It was an uncanny sight to find this immense hub of activity where there was supposed to be nothing at all. "A tribe of white witch doctors, indeed!" I muttered to myself, which act stimulated Hans to make his first utterance since this sight had come into view.

But then, as my senses became acquainted with the waves of sensory imagery that assailed me, I blinked and stared and realized that in the distance was a second giant pit being excavated with just as much activity as the one below where Hans and I stood.

"Baas!" Hans was saying, "I am not as well-traveled as some, and Durban is as big a town as I have known, but I remember your father, the Predikant, telling stories to his poor staff about white men's kraals many times bigger than Shaka's, many times bigger than Durban, and I have never ventured out of the land of my fathers, but I do have ears and I have heard from many white men of big towns, and I suppose I am seeing such a place being born down below even now!"

"I suppose so, Hans, for such a sight is as new to me as it is to you. But be quiet now, as I need to think."

And, as it was now growing dark, Hans and I retreated and found a sheltered spot in a hollow to sleep, and at dawn we were trekking down the hill following the easiest path, as now that we saw our destination, we no longer needed to confine ourselves to following the train tracks. In so doing we traveled into some ravines and such so that we lost sight of the town for most of the distance. But toward midday, we came to the crest of a hill, and there, right before us, so close you could almost touch it, was the vital and bustling community, doing its best to live and work despite the huge disturbance and the construction going on all around it. Up close, it seemed still larger than it had from a distance. What passed for the passenger train station was off to the right, and the locomotive we had seen—it was the same because I recognized the number on its side—steaming and huffing and puffing, presumably nearly ready to move out and run down whatever poor innocent pedestrians happened to get in its way!

From our vantage point, we could look straight over the main street, which was pressed earth, with sixty or so spartan buildings with shops. At the end of the street a second

In the distance was a second giant pit being excavated with just as much activity as the one below.

street crossed and formed a T. At that crossroads and facing down the main street was the tallest building that was within our view. Perhaps two hundred men and women were on the streets, none strolling, each with a mission and walking with purpose in various directions. None seemed to be taking in the sights. There was no loitering in this place. Despite the crowd, the ebb and flow of its movements were remarkably organized, and I felt that the architects of this mysterious metropolis knew what they were doing and had planned well.

In addition, I was amazed to see that a dwarf-sized railroad system crisscrossed the town. You heard me right, Luna: a miniature railroad system with tiny engines and cars. This turned out to be a transportation system, a handy way to move people and equipment around within the limits of the town. The locomotives were perhaps ten feet in length, yet looking for all the world like their big brothers that hauled rubble from the pits. These were driven by men and women who rode the engines much as they would ride horses, their legs hugging and pressing hard into either side of the black metal engines. All in all, it proved to be a very efficient tram system.

In a moment, Hans was pulling at my sleeve, and he said reflectively, "Baas, do you see someplace where they sell square-face, for I am thirsty, and what is the use of a town like this unless it has a saloon?"

I inspected what I could see and had to admit that there didn't appear to be a saloon, at least within our view.

Instead of horse-drawn hansoms and carriages
or omnibuses, the laboratory used small trains
powered by tiny locomotives on which sat the drivers.

But I ventured a guess. "Maybe that tall building has something of the sort."

Well there was nothing for it but to continue ahead, but before we started, I peered into the distance, hoping to see the temple that I'd noticed the day before, but I couldn't see anything of the sort. In a couple of hours, we emerged from the undergrowth through which we had traversed onto a road paved with stone. This led into the town, which was just ahead. But now I noticed a queer fact that was not obvious from the distance. The entire town had a tall fence around it, and as we got closer, I saw that there was a fence within a fence and that it all bristled with barbs, such as you hear about being used on American cattle ranches. And every few yards there were guard towers and armed guards, as though the place was a prison camp. Yet, from what we could see from the distance, the populace, while seemingly industrious, also seemed free to go their own ways.

Frankly I was more than a little confused.

In a few minutes, around a curve and at end of the road, we saw a guard's station and gate with three stout fellows in military uniforms, but of a stripe I was not familiar with.

"Baas, what do you suppose these big men are guarding? And do you see their many brothers with guns on those towers? Perhaps it is gold or diamonds, but then again not even the Bank of Durban has so many guards. What could be more valuable then gold or diamonds?"

"Our skins for one thing," I suggested.

"O, Baas, that's easy for you to say, for you are the great Macumazana, but I am only a shriveled yellow monkey as the Great One never fails to remind both of us, and the skin of a monkey is hardly worth more than a rusty nail!"

"Hans, you are worth more than a rusty nail to me, even if you are shriveled."

"Baas, yes, you are right. I am worth more to you because I have saved your life more times than I can remember."

"Perhaps that is so, Hans, but I have saved your skin just as many times!"

By then we had marched right up to the guard shack.

The tallest of the three guards questioned us, or I should say questioned me, in the manner that all such men question the arrival of unexpected newcomers. I explained that I was Allan Quatermain and that Hans was with me, and that we had come out of the jungle after a very long trek from Central Africa and that we were there only because we had stumbled on the place by accident and insofar as it was the first sign of civilization that we'd encountered, would it be too much to ask to be treated with civility and be offered food and drink at the least?

The spokesman looked doubtful, but at least he was not belligerent, and sent one of his colleagues off with a message. I suppose he would have been within his rights to have sent us packing, so I counted our blessings—at least in the beginning!

Hans and I waited in the hot sun. Hans sat on the ground in what shade he could find, but I was too proud and stood on principle. Literally. We waited thus for almost an hour. I could see that our presence there had aroused the curiosity of passersby on the other side of the double fence, but nobody did more than slacken their walking pace a bit, stare a moment, then continue about their business. My patience was running thin, when finally I spotted two men approach the gate from the inside. The gates were opened for them, and they came through and advanced up to me.

SS—

Remind me to do a monograph on the various races of bees—the better to forge a meaningful dialog with the looming authorities who seem to revel in their ignorance of the apiarian universe. Such thoughts could also be condensed for one of the journals.

—M

Third Prologue Chapter

Maxwell

$$L = 4\pi n2a\{\log e\ 8a/r + 1/12 -3/4(\ \theta\!-\!\pi/4)\cot 2\theta\!-\!\pi/3\cos 2\theta$$
$$-1/6\ \cot2\theta\ \log\cos\theta\!-\!1/6\ \tan2\ \theta\ \log\sin\theta\}$$
$$+ \pi n2\ r2/24a\{\log 8a/r(2\ \sin2\ \theta\!+\!1) + 3.45 +27.475\ \cos2\theta$$
$$- 3.2\ (\pi/2\!-\!\theta)\sin3\theta/\cos\theta + 1/5\ \cos4\theta/5\ \sin2\theta\ \log\cos\theta$$
$$+ 13/3\ \sin4\theta/\cos2\theta\ \log\sin\theta\} + \&c$$

—James Clerk Maxwell in *The Dynamical Theory of the Electromagnetic Field*

The man who seemed to be the leader was about my size, that is to say, rather small, but he had a high forehead with a slightly receding hairline, long swept-back grey hair and long extremely bushy grey mutton-chop whiskers, which were quite the rage back then. His hair and beard were so profuse that they connected with hardly a trace of facial skin showing except a little on either side of his nose and around his eyes. The other man was about the same age but had a rounder face, that is, they both seemed about 40 years of age, though the second man sported a trim beard, rather like mine, in fact. This first man came right up to me and held out his hand, which for the sake of politeness I took and shook in the accepted European manner. I make this specification because when one lives in Africa as long as I have, one learns that the common handshake is not by any means a common method of greeting, and, in fact, how one presents one's hands at the beginning of an acquaintance could well spell the difference between life and death . . . but, Luna, I suppose you of all people know this! Also, I had reservations about simply greeting the man, particularly after his having made us wait in the sun for an hour. He spoke and I was surprised by his strong Scottish accent:

"Allan Quatermain! I have heard of you. Yes, I dare say, that there are few who reside on this continent who have not heard of the great white hunter!"

I often hear this sort of remark, or compliment as I suppose it is intended to be, but learned long ago not to take it seriously, for if I did, my head would swell and I could not fit into any of my hats again! But more than that, such things that are heard about me are usually second or third hand and generally not representative of the real me. Thus I chose to ignore his remarks and said, "Sir, I am afraid that you have me at a disadvantage."

Naturally this always embarrasses the speaker, which put me back on top of the social order, and indeed, this is exactly what happened. Blushing, he said, "Forgive me, Quatermain, but my name is James Maxwell, James Clerk Maxwell." He stopped and showed every sign that his name ought to have been familiar to me and that I ought to have been impressed. But since neither was the case, I merely looked back at him with a blank face. Then he quickly motioned toward his companion and said, "And this is Giovanni Schiaparelli," and seemed again to wait for some sort of reaction.

Of course, this second name meant as little to me as the first. Schiaparelli didn't speak, so I could only guess that he was Italian. I nodded to him and said to Maxwell, "Mr. Maxwell, obviously I can't help but wonder what all this is about. None of this is supposed to be here, or certainly I would know of it."

"Yes, yes. We are involved in some research of a scientific nature, and we established this laboratory only a few months ago. Just a moment, please." Here, he and Schiaparelli moved off and whispered together for several minutes. Then Schiaparelli went back in the direction they had come, hurrying through the gate without saying a word to us, and Maxwell returned. "You know, Quatermain, we don't normally have callers, as you can imagine, and I wish I could be more gracious, but I must cut this interview short. I'm terribly glad we had an opportunity to meet, however briefly. Where are you off to now?"

Taken aback by both his attitude and the question, I think I sputtered some sort of response that I cannot recall. Hans took me by the elbow and said in Dutch, "Baas, I don't understand why these men are being rude and did not invite us inside so that we could rest our feet, have some cool drink, and even offer us a place to lay our poor heads." I couldn't have agreed with him more, and was about to say so, when his bloodshot eyes grew round and his wrinkled old face beamed and he smiled, whereupon he said, "Say, Baas! That merciful Spirit of which your Reverend father, the Predikant, never ceased to remind all us poor servants who manned his station, has looked down from his throne, or up from the Place of Fires, I know not which, and has seen our sad case and has come to our rescue!"

"Hans," I responded, "stop your nonsense and let us make ready to leave this inhospitable place."

But the little Hottentot continued his gaping, and said, "It may be nonsense, Baas, but I think you will think otherwise when I tell you that I see someone who will make this sick looking white man swallow his thick tongue. See over there, through that crowd there, there is a face we know well, very well, indeed, leaving that building."

***

Shaking my head in befuddlement, I followed Hans' pointed finger, and, indeed, spotted not only a familiar face but a dear one as well.

"Maxwell," I said to the man, "before my servant and I turn around to go, having been turned away by a degree of insensitivity rare, indeed, nearly unprecedented, in a civilized man, please note that I see an old friend inside your fence whose attention I would like to catch, if you don't mind."

He looked off in the direction I had indicated and seemed puzzled. "Excuse me?" Maxwell said.

And seeing that she was about to round the corner of a building, I called out loudly, "Maria! Maria Mitchell! Professor Mitchell!" which succeeded in getting her attention. She looked our way, double-took, stared, smiled, no, grinned broadly, waved, and rushed over to the gate.

"Allan Quatermain! My God! It is so good to see you! How did you know to look for me here? It is so good to see you! And Hans! Neither of you look one iota different since our Abyssinian adventure last year. Well, perhaps it is closer to two years." Then to Maxwell, "Well, Doctor, what is going on here? Don't you know Allan Quatermain?" There followed

96

an awkward exchange between the two, with Maria finally putting her foot down and demanding, "What are you waiting for? I insist that you escort these men through immediately!"

You see, dear Luna, early in the previous year, I had been hired by several British gentlemen to take them to Ethiopia, which at that time I had never visited. It would be a couple of years later that you and I and Lord Ragnall would travel over that hellish desert to finally come to the little port where we then embarked on separate vessels to return us to our respective homes. It was while on that earlier expedition that our path crossed with Professor Mitchell and her party, and it worked out that the two expeditions were merged before we plunged south into that desert for reasons it's not necessary to go into now. The point being that Maria is an American astronomer, and we were well-acquainted, and it was the purest serendipity that Hans had spotted her just at that particular moment. If he hadn't, if he had been busy yawning or being otherwise distracted, there would be no tale to tell now, and we would be discussing other things!

Well, there was a bit of give and take, with the guards pointing out some particulars of their bylaws and about the minutia of our arrival, and Maxwell holding quite firm.

It was pretty much of a stalemate, when another man approached the gate from the inside and, muttering something to the guards on that side, passed through just as Maria attached herself to him, so that, in a flash they both had come outside and she began exchanging affectionate greetings with me, and also Hans.

SS—

My word, the charming Professor Mitchell takes the stage. My recollections of her are most vivid. A different sort of woman, SS, insofar as she was knowledgeable in the makeup of the heavens. What woman in a million . . . nay! . . . 100 million can rise to such heights! What a shame! Maria has been gone these many years and the world is poorer for it!

—M

Fourth Prologue Chapter

Barbicane

"It appears to me by its rocky and barren character to offer all the conditions requisite for our experiment. On that plain will be raised our magazines, workshops, furnaces, and workmen's huts; and here, from this very spot," said he, stamping his foot on the summit of Stony Hill, "hence shall our projectile take its flight into the regions of the [Lunar] World."
—Impey Barbicane in *From the Earth to the Moon*

This new fellow was yet another with a beard, not as full as Maxwell's nor as well-trimmed as Schiaparelli's. However, he seemed utterly out of place as he was attired formally in tall shiny top hat and tails and smoked a cigar.

"Hello, Maria, won't you introduce me to your friend?"

"Where have you been Impey?" replied Maria, not responding to the inquiry. "I have been looking for you for days."

"Didn't anyone tell you, I was tying up some loose ends 'over yonder.'" This was the first reference that I heard to the mysterious "over yonder," which while not mentioned often, would occasionally slip out in hushed tones, succeeding in rousing the curiosity of both Hans and me at the outset of this adventure.

"Well never mind. You're here now. Impey, this is my old friend Allan Quatermain. You cannot imagine the scrapes we've been through together!" Here she winked at me, and in my mind's eye I saw her swinging and jabbing a glass sword—decapitating a Danikil tribesman two years before! But that is another story, Luna!

"And Allan, this is Impey Barbicane! He sent a missile to the moon five or six years ago. You may have read about it. He is the world's greatest engineer—the chief engineer and architect of all this." Her hand gestured in all directions.

"Maria, that's not entirely true. Isambard Kingdom Brunel's work inspired much of what I have done!"

Now there was a name I had heard of and was impressed with, even having been isolated at the bottom of Africa from the stream of technology that Britain seemed consumed with. Brunel had built some of the greatest ships of his day, the *Great Western* and *Great Eastern* among them, and the *Great Western Railroad*, not to mention gigantic tunnels that crossed under rivers, and enormous bridges that crossed over them. Now that I had heard Brunel's name, a little of the mystery I was feeling faded, as Brunel was quite adept at building the impossible. Though Brunel had died some years before, it was clear to me then that this man Barbicane must have been a protégé.

Anyway, the end result of this exchange was that Maria won the day and Hans and I were shepherded in.

Before long we were established in the tall building that we had seen from a distance, which, while not a hotel in the normal sense of the word, nevertheless served a similar function and we called it that out of convenience, and Hans and I had the grand opportunity to bathe and refresh—or rather, I did, for water seldom touched my manservant except when it was necessary to ford some wild stream or another. This building was typical of the rest of the structures in this so-called laboratory, as Maxwell had called it, that is, the building was made of freshly sawn lumber and other rude materials and had clearly been thrown together in great haste. Indeed, the whole laboratory was *being constructed* in front of our eyes!

When we, that is, Maria and I, met again, it was in what passed for a sitting room of the hotel. Hans was there of course, but he preferred to plant himself unobtrusively in the corner as he was wont to do, as you know, your having known him so well. Maria and I did not just then have the opportunity to converse in private as Maxwell soon joined us, and then it was time for tea.

During that ever-so-civilized ceremony, Maria suggested to Maxwell, "James, Allan's discretion is second to none. In fact, there are things that we have experienced together (here she looked meaningfully at me) that even you have never dreamt of, and of which neither he nor I can ever speak, as we have given our oaths."

"That may well be, Professor Mitchell, but we have a responsibility to discharge, and until such time that is accomplished, there is no room for any who were not invited and who have no professional credentials to speak of. And besides, we ourselves have all given our own oaths with regard to *our* project."

"Well, then," she said, "I suppose my services and my specific areas of expertise are not needed." She stood, and said to me, "Come, Allan, please wait for me to pack some essentials and I will join you." Maxwell also stood, a courteous reflex I suppose. Maria walked up to him and stood eyeball to eyeball!

"Professor, that is not acceptable!" Maxwell said. "If for no other reason, I cannot allow a woman to trek through that horrid wilderness outside our gates!"

At that, Maria laughed heartily! "Ha! James, I assure you that that 'wilderness,' as you call it, is nothing at all compared to the places that Allan and I have shared! That jungle beyond our fences and those desert sands are as formidable as this tea-party, I assure you!" As she spoke, she stared into the man's face.

Taken aback, Dr. Maxwell could only gulp air for a few moments as he composed himself. "Maria, notwithstanding the dangers outside, this project needs your experience and abilities for good reason, and it would be a great disadvantage to our group if you were to leave us."

"Wonderful, then I want your promise that, in due course, Allan will be allowed to know what we are doing." Then she looked at me, embarrassed.

"Allan, I'm sorry, but I assume too much! I was so happy to see you that it didn't occur to me that you only happened upon this place by chance and that you have your own plans. I don't mean to impose on you or force information upon you that you would rather not know."

"Professor Mitchell," I said, "no plans I have are so important that I can't delay them to spend time with a charming dear friend." Here she blushed and I regretted my impertinence.

[Lady Luna Holmes Ragnall: Here, Allan is pausing to reflect, I think, and I don't want to lose momentum, thus I am writing these words to keep my pen moving . . . ." Allan," I say, "you romantic devil! I can see that your fondness for Professor Mitchell transcends mere acquaintance." This stirs him out of his reflection, and he says to me, "My dear, don't be foolish. I am impervious to such designs." And I say to him, "Bosh!" and now he is getting back to his narrative.]

"Very good, it is settled!" Maria had said. "James, until which time as Allan can be told the essentials, please let my friends" (here she turned and looked at Hans pointedly for Maxwell's sake) "have the freedom to move as they please through the laboratory."

"Why do you call this place a laboratory?" I asked.

Maxwell responded: "Well, rightfully, that is what it is. It certainly doesn't have any claim to permanence, though. This is all a temporary arrangement built to support our special studies. It is indeed a scientific laboratory."

"I cannot wait until I know something more about your purpose here, Doctor Maxwell. Professor Mitchell called you thus. I should hope I'll avoid getting ill during my stay, as I would not wish to impose on you."

"Oh, no, Allan," Maria exclaimed. "Doctor Maxwell is the world's greatest living physicist."

Now it was Maxwell's turn to blush. "I wouldn't go that far, Professor Mitchell. Certainly I learned from the great Faraday himself."

"Don't be modest, James." She turned to me and said, "James is the world's authority on electricity and magnetism, and has shown that they are interrelated in what he has called the electromagnetic field. James' brand new tome, A Treatise on Electricity and Magnetism, was published only this year, and there are those that say that it will transform the world!"

"Maria, please!" groaned Maxwell.

"Furthermore, James is this laboratory's chief scientist and all aspects of the work here not related specifically to building and engineering are his responsibility."

And that was the beginning or our adventure, dear Luna. Do you find it interesting thus far?

[Luna: "Allan," I say, "I am thunderstruck and amazed. What on earth could two renowned astronomers (for I am worldly enough to know that that is Giovanni Schiaperelli's field) and the world's greatest physicist plus the world's greatest living engineer, all be doing in an isolated and well-guarded facility on the west coast of Africa?"]

***

Well, there is so much more to tell. In the coming days, I met many famous and notable scientists. (Or so I would determine them to be in later years as I happened across their names in newspapers, or in other sundry manners. Among them were some astonishingly bright young men who had been drafted right out of school to aid in this endeavor—youngsters named Edison, Hertz, John Thomson, Nikola Tesla, Max Planck, and others.) The core of the team consisted of a number of absolutely dedicated astronomers, physicists, and engineers, all specialists in the narrow fields of electricity, magnetism, and electromagnetic waves. It was quite a select group. It seemed all the world's most brilliant men in these fields had been brought to this one small area. Of course, you are wondering, dear Luna, why this was so. What on earth could possibly have prompted all these geniuses to have come together in this manner? Well it took some time for me to glean any part of it, with Maria's help; still I am not at all sure that I really had any idea of what went on there during all the time Hans and I were detained—yes, detained, for in the end, once we were let in, we were not allowed to leave, much to Maria's chagrin.

SS—

It's a shame that Q doesn't tell us more about Tesla et al. But, of course, he had no way of knowing during his stay that they would add so vitally to the great repository of essential knowledge. Lest I forget, we must sort out the pros and cons of moving the robber hives away from the productive ones! Let's revisit this when Mrs. H visits next week. She has learned much on the subject during her holidays here. I would hate to make a major decision without the benefit of her guidance and common sense, which I admit I have found most useful as the years creep up on me.

—M

***

Hans and I had been there only a few days when the first thing of consequence, from our perspective, occurred.

Remember that during this time we were never told anything other than what I have already told you, nor could I even imagine what was going on all around me. The excavation of the pits and the construction of the laboratory went on ceaselessly. The constant smoke and dust made breathing difficult. There was a sort of class structure in place. The scientists and their assistants lived and worked in the main laboratory grounds that we knew from first hand knowledge, but the laborers and skilled craftsmen lived in separate areas and were transported by trains.

As I've already said, there were trains everywhere. And these were of three types. There were the ordinary trains with carriages of the type that you see coming into and leaving a busy urban train depot, though these were neither ornate nor plush and largely utilitarian—spartan I think is the word. The one that almost ran us down was of this sort. Then, of course, there were the dozens of work engines that hauled away the debris deposited by the huge excavators busy at the two pits.

And then there were also the miniature trains that I mentioned before. These were utterly unique, and, frankly, captivated both Hans and me. The entire laboratory, or at least the part we would inhabit for the duration, was crisscrossed with a web of tiny tracks on which traveled this miniaturized railroad system, which, as I had seen earlier, you recall, carried people from place to place. Instead of horse-drawn hansoms and carriages and omnibuses, this place had small electric trains pulled by tiny smokeless locomotives on which there was installed a kind of saddle to seat the drivers, both men and women, who had available an array of levers and knobs and wheels—and best of all, bells and whistles that they used to warn pedestrians and which neither Hans nor I ever ceased to enjoy hearing.

Behind the engines, there were attached a dozen or so small open cars, each holding fifteen or twenty people on benches. And of course these trains had regular stops, though one could always wave one down or ask the driver— engineer?—to make unscheduled stops.

***

By the way, eventually I learned, and was astonished to find out, that the population of the laboratory and its work crew and their families, all of which required this complicated transit system numbered somewhere in the neighborhood of 40,000! Most of whom we never saw, as they were busy out of sight.*

During breakfast of our fourth or fifth day there, with Maria, Maxwell, Barbicane, and myself at a table overlooking the Atlantic Ocean. I ventured, "Professors, Mr. Barbicane, as we approached this . . . laboratory . . . from atop the hill, we thought we saw something odd off in the distance to the south. It seemed to be a columned structure, a sort of temple,

---

* Editor's note: The rapid growth of the laboratory as described by Quatermain is not as uncanny as it might seem at first reading. A comparably scoped but more recent effort was the Manhattan Project. On September 17, 1942, U.S. Army General Leslie Groves was ordered to build an atomic bomb. At that moment in time all that existed were a few equations and some small experiments done in universities. *Two years and ten months later,* on July 16, 1945, the Trinity bomb detonated in New Mexico. In between, there had sprung into being—literally from nothing—the plutonium plant in Hanford, Washington, with a workforce of 45,000 and the Uranium 235 plant at Oak Ridge, Tennessee, with a workforce of 24,000, and, of course, the bomb development facility at Los Alamos, New Mexico, with several thousand more.—T.K.M.

or at least that is how it registered in my humble mind, through the mist or smoke."

Maria and Barbicane looked at one another and smiled, then Maria said, "Allan, what you saw is an interesting aspect of this place. Come, and Impey and I will show you." They looked at Maxwell, but he said he was needed at the workshop.

In a few minutes, Barbicane, Hans, Maria, and I were waiting outside for a westbound miniature train. We boarded and rode it through the main part of the laboratory.

When our conveyance reached the outskirts of the place and began its return leg, Barbicane asked the engineer to stop, whereupon we got off and strode through a guarded gate much as the one by which we had entered several days earlier and I was reminded how heavily guarded the facility was! We found a gravel path that we continued on for a half mile or so ducking in and out of stands of trees. Very soon we heard a roaring very like a waterfall, and smelt a tang in the air. The path entered a glade, and there in the middle of the glade stood the totally anomalous sight of a temple, for want of a better word. It was circular and comprised of ten columns. It stood 35 or 40 feet high with an inside column-to-column diameter of about 20 feet. It looked Roman or Greek, I'm sorry but I've never been educated to tell the difference. It stood in the middle of a broad circular pool with half a dozen shooting fountains.

The path we were on led to a footbridge and we crossed over the pool to the temple itself. There squarely in the middle between the pillars was a sort of circular well comprised of a wall about four feet high, and when we looked over the wall into the well, we saw and heard and smelled huge volumes of water spouting from two pipes in the well's sides. The sound was thunderous! I'm sure that millions of gallons a day must have crashed out of those pipes mingling and plunging down the 20-foot-deep, blue-tiled well. I cast my eyes downward, savoring the power of the raging waters. I stood entranced and wrapped in spray, delighting in the wonder of it all.

"Maria," I finally asked, "what is this place? What is the meaning of all this?" By which I meant the whole massive enterprise, of course; but I was not yet to receive a direct answer. Instead Maria looked at Barbicane who said: "Quatermain, you have not seen anything yet, as you have been here only a few days, but you will soon see and learn things on a scale never before conceived by the mind of man. What we are doing here makes my experiment of sending a manned projectile to the moon and back again look like a mere backyard romp. Let me say for now that we who are involved in this project are performing an experiment that requires an enormous amount of energy. Vast amounts! As a consequence, we . . . well . . . *invented* a system that creates

The sound from the well was thunderous!

electricity in quantities inconceivable before now except perhaps by the mind of God. Where, you ask, does such electricity come from? Well it so happens that electricity can most conveniently be produced by the downhill rush of millions of gallons of water. Thus our engineers, to the purpose of diverting and harnessing immense quantities of water, built a titanic dam high up in the Loma mountains 200 miles to the east, damming the Rokel River and turning a convenient valley into a reservoir. They are the Columbiad Dam and the Columbiad Reservoir, respectively (named after the cannon that was central to my Luna project). To control the flow of the water released from the reservoir a huge gravity-driven network of 11 further dams and reservoirs, tunnels, pump stations, aqueducts and water conveyance pipelines were also built, all of which move 300 million gallons per day and generates over 2 billion kilowatt hours per year of hydropower electricity, which is transmitted here via a 200-mile long network of power stations housing generators, transformers, and dynamos—machines that never previously existed—not to mention the power lines that funnel it all here.

"So, to answer your question," Barbicane continued brightly, "we built this temple—we call it the Atlantis Water Temple—as a monument to that effort. Right here, this very spot, is the terminus of the underground water pipe that begins near Mount Bintumani. This is the final destination of the Rokel River water, water that is spawned by the dense rainforests water skirting the Loma Mountains. When it flows out of this well, you can see that it is expelled into the ocean, for it is not the water that is needed, but the electric power it generates. It was all completed just a few months ago, even though, amazingly, it was only conceived and designed two years ago!"*

---

*Editor's note: The whole gargantuan enterprise described in these pages took less than two years to complete. The construction of the vast energy production system, of necessity, commenced months in advance of the main laboratory. A fascinating analog to this system is the controversial Hetch Hetchy Aqueduct System in northern California, which became operational in October 1934. Requiring 30 years to plan and 20 years to build, this mammoth engineering project still provides fresh water to the City of San Francisco by diverting, storing, and transporting Tuolumne River water from clear across the breadth of the state. The difference here is that the production of enough electricity to run the city's services was its secondary priority, not its true *raison d'être*.—T.K.M.

"Two years!" I cried. "Surely something so vast would require decades of effort and more money than I can begin to conceive of."

"Yes, Allan, that is so . . . unless there is a well-to-do patron, sufficient motivation, and a clear deadline," Maria said.

Well, Luna, what can one say when confronted with such staggering information? Standing there I literally shook from the shock. My companions seemed to understand and gave me a moment to pull myself together. Then I spotted a legend that had been carved into the stone above the columns. It was Latin and read:

IN ASTRIS ES VESTRI POTENTIA ET GLORIA

I asked Maria what that meant and she told me: "In the stars are found your power and glory."

After a pause, I said, "A moment ago, I asked what all this is about? Mr. Barbicane has answered in a manner I could never have imagined in a hundred years, but what I meant to ask was: What is this place? I mean the whole laboratory? Why are you here?"

She looked at Barbicane who could only shrug. Then she said, "Allan, notwithstanding my having taken your side recently, let me say that the details are not for me to share. For now, I can say that we are performing some electrical experiments that include an aspect of astronomy, which of course, explains my presence . . . . Come, let's take a walk so I can hear myself think." She needed to raise her voice over the din of the roaring water. Just then Barbicane made his excuses and went off, leaving me alone with Maria. We then continued on the trail on the farther side of the temple.

Of course, Hans was there, too, but unobtrusively as was his tendency when discussion ascended into realms beyond his comprehension (and frankly beyond mine, as well, if truth be known, but I had the knack of being able to look interested or at least to keep a poker face)—but I was saying that Hans kept to himself.

When we had walked to a spot on the trail that was quieter—and drier, too, as the air around the well was forever filled with a cool mist—Maria began to fill me in: "I was asked to join this project not long after my return to Vassar College from Ethiopia, and when I arrived here, construction of the buildings had only just begun. I've been here at the laboratory now for only about eight months, but when I arrived here, there were only a few shacks and a beach."

Frankly, what she had just said was far more than I could comprehend, but then an image flashed into my head that helped me grasp the vastness of what she was saying.

"I suppose," I said, "it wouldn't be far different from Field-Marshal Lord Napier's Ethiopian campaign—the history of which you recall was an important factor in our last experiences together: 280 ships, 32,000 men, 20,000 mules, and vast amounts of materiel and they set up shop on a beach and—boom!—a small city sprang into being overnight. Locomotives were hauled in, and elephants, and huge piers were built . . . . Remembering that, it doesn't surprise me at all that so much has happened here so fast!"

"Excellent, Allan. Frankly I had not thought of that, but it is an excellent analogy."

Now that I had a picture in my head that worked for me, I continued, "I have so many questions. What are the pits that are being dug? Is it more construction, or are they looking for something? What is it all for? Something to do with astronomy, but how could anything require as much energy as you tell me is being generated. And the aqueduct you described would take years and millions to plan and build. It is all impossible, yet here it is before my eyes!"

Maria looked very serious and then said, "Well, what I can tell you is that we are building a telescope, a very special telescope, one like the world has never seen."

"A telescope!" I cried. "All this for a telescope!" Of course, Luna, the telescope I saw in my mind's eye was a tube such as one held up to one's eye.

"Actually, Allan, we are involved in a project as big as the world, quite literally. The instrument that is being built here has no comparison. And that instrument, that is, the telescope, is at the heart of this project."

"That is all well and good, but why are you here, Maria?

"Well Allan, after our adventure in Abyssinia, I returned to Vassar, where, as you know, my role has been to teach something of the stars and planets to inquisitive young women. However, because of the

SS—

On the subject of journals,
I must finish that monograph
on the bees' dancing language
It ought not be so difficult
to finish as that slippery
Chaldean paper of mine!
—M

meteorite specimens I brought back, I became a bit of a celebrity and received many invitations to present at schools in Boston, Pennsylvania, New York, and the like. Also I wrote and submitted, and had published, half a dozen papers to scientific journals, and I was quite pleased with the response from the science community. Of course there were a few naysayers who accused me of everything from carelessness to outright fraud. However, I'm happy to report that on balance, my supporters were legion. I had been back about six months, and then one day I received by courier an unexpected proposal. That letter alerted me that I would soon be invited me to join a special project. There was no description of either the project or my proposed responsibilities. Though I ignored the note, a few weeks afterward another courier appeared at my door, and this time the message offered some particulars about comets that grabbed my attention. It seemed that these were of particular interest to the people who wished me to join them. Of course, they could not have chosen a better ploy: I became fascinated, but still hesitant, as my responsibility lay just where I was, especially as I had only recently been away for a prolonged time.

"Here is where they offered an inducement that could not be ignored. They offered to build a new observatory on the Vassar Campus on the condition that the experiment they were conducting achieved the desired result. Well, what was I to do? I believed that these people made the proposal in good faith, as the college board was already meeting with their representatives by the time I made up my mind to pursue the invitation. In time I had boarded the steamship *de Grandin*. My destination was the Greenwich Observatory. When I arrived, I received the surprise of my life. At the observatory I was received by James Clerk Maxwell himself! He told me that he had selected me especially and that I had been brought over for the sole purpose of his asking me personally if I wanted to join a select group of physicists and astronomers who were gathering in west Africa to conduct a vital experiment. Allan! James is probably the most esteemed living scientist. Whatever residual concerns I still had about this enterprise, regardless of what it truly was, evaporated on the spot, and I became a dedicated member of the team. Very quickly after my arrival here, machine shops were built with the ability to produce the most sophisticated, delicate instrumentalities imaginable with complex components, even devices for computational work based on the engines of

Charles Babbage." She was quiet and merely gestured all around. "I am anxious to see what will become of it all."

By this time, our little walk around the temple had concluded and we passed through the guard gates and returned to the laboratory. Once inside, Hans, who had accompanied us on this whole astonishing tour, but who had not said a word, and thus I had almost forgotten he was with us, spoke quietly in Zulu to me, "Baas, I have seen and heard this day much more than I could ever care to. And, as you know, I understand nothing this fine lady ever says. Whenever we are around her, my head feels stuffed with babble and pains me, and it seems to me that she is about to tell you still more that will undoubtedly be far more than your poor old Hottentot servant would ever want to hear. Thus I will occupy myself looking for what passes for square-face in this poor place!" At which point he scurried around the corner of a building before I could put in a word one way or another.

Maria noticed Hans' exit and looked at me questioningly, but I only shrugged. Then a messenger ran up to her with a note in an envelope. She read it, seemed delighted and said, "Allan, you are being invited to the workshop. Maybe they will now explain rather more to you."

Maria took me to a low building that didn't seem to

have a door or windows at ground level, or none that I could see, and we descended some stairs to reach an entrance. Once inside, there were more stairs going down and then we were far below ground. We went down a hallway and through some double doors, and thus entered a room—a room they called the workshop—wherein Maxwell was in the midst of writing some mathematic calculations on a large board and lecturing to the many men in attendance, including Barbicane, but stopped when he noticed we had entered.

Maria didn't waste her time nor her breath. "James, I hope you intend to give Allan some information so he doesn't stew in his curiosity. Allan needs to understand what we are doing here. I just explained how I was lured here against my will." She smiled as she said this.

"I see," he said, looking rather unhappy and looking at Barbicane, who nodded. "Well, Mr. Quatermain, since you are here and a close friend of Maria's, we'll let you in on what we are doing. I can give you an overview now. It is an exercise in astronomy that is quite well-funded by an agency that would prefer to keep its identity secret for now.

Then, Luna, Maxwell paused and reflected and seemed confused. "Well, Quatermain, I hardly know where to begin or how to explain it all."

Fifth Prologue Chapter

The Star of Wonder

Τοῦ δὲ Ἰησοῦ γεννηθέντος ἐν Βηθλέεμ τῆς Ἰουδαίας ἐν ἡμέραις Ἡρῴδου τοῦ βασιλέως, ἰδοὺ μάγοι ἀπὸ ἀνατολῶν παρεγένοντο εἰς Ἰεροσόλυμα λέγοντες· Ποῦ ἐστιν ὁ τεχθεὶς βασιλεὺς τῶν Ἰουδαίων; εἴδομεν γὰρ αὐτοῦ τὸν ἀστέρα ἐν τῇ ἀνατολῇ καὶ ἤλθομεν προσκυνῆσαι αὐτῷ.... ̀ Ἰδοὺ ὁ ἀστὴρ ὃν εἶδον ἐν τῇ ἀνατολῇ προῆγεν αὐτούς, ἕως ἐλθὼν ⸢ἐστάθη⸣ ἐπάνω οὗ ἦν τὸ παιδίον. Ἰδόντες δὲ τὸν ἀστέρα ἐχάρησαν χαρὰν μεγάλην σφόδρα. καὶ ἐλθόντες εἰς τὴν οἰκίαν εἶδον τὸ παιδίον μετὰ Μαρίας τῆς μητρὸς αὐτοῦ, καὶ πεσόντες προσεκύνησαν αὐτῷ....

—Matthew 2:1-2, 9-11

"Where to begin . . . ?" Maxwell repeated, mumbling. He looked at Maria. "Have you mentioned anything of the mechanical nature of our work?" "Well," Maria said, "I said that we were building a kind of telescope."

To which Maxwell said to me, "Well, but of course that probably wouldn't mean much to you, I suppose . . . so I suppose the easiest thing to do is to explain the whole thing chronologically." Here he stepped over to one of the many bookshelves in the room, and took down a Bible. (Incidentally, you know, Luna, that I pride myself in my knowledge of the Old Testament.) Anyway, he opened the book to where there was a ribbon bookmark and opened his mouth as if to begin to read, but instead he looked at me first and said, "Matthew, chapter two."

Then he read, "Now when Jesus was born in Bethlehem of Judea in the days of Herod the king, behold, wise men from the East came to Jerusalem, saying, 'Where is he who has been born king of the Jews? For we have seen his star in the East, and we have come to worship him.'" His finger ran down a few lines and he continued, "'. . . lo, the star which they had seen in the East went before them, till it stood over where the child was. When they saw the star, they rejoiced exceedingly with great joy; and going into the house they saw the child with Mary his mother, and they fell down and worshipped him.'"

He slapped the book shut and looked at me. I shrugged and said, "Yes, the Nativity . . . and . . . ?"

"The point of interest here is the star—the Star of Bethlehem. It is astonishing how many myriads of men have devoted unfathomable amounts of energy into trying to understand the nature of that star." Here Maxwell sighed deeply. "So very much time and energy and effort has been dedicated in attempts to understand those few words that are mentioned almost in passing in the gospel. Of course there are those who claim that the author of Matthew (you know, of course, that the apostle Matthew probably was dead and gone when this gospel was composed late in the first century and, therefore, the gospel can be thought of as a kind of forgery) simply made it all up and there was never any star or magi or any of the rest." He paused and shrugged before he went on.

"I don't pretend to know one way or another; nevertheless, we have been charged to conduct this experiment under the assumption that it is true. In a nut shell, all this is intended to study the Star of Bethlehem, and we are building a special kind of telescope in order to do just that." Here he paused.

Frankly, I did not know how to respond. I certainly was never one of those men who expended much on that point. I had never given the Star of Bethlehem any thought at all. It simply was part of the festivities that made up Christmas, along with trees and ornaments, ribbons, toys and children. The star was always shiny with rays of light, usually depicted by a circle of pointed beams. I certainly had never considered that it might be something that anybody would want to study. But instead of saying any of that, I said, "And?"*

---

*Editor's note: At this point in the narrative, Quatermain attempts to recollect details of astronomical hypotheses as presented by Maxwell to him in the laboratory workshop. However, either due to Quatermain's blunted recollection of unfamiliar concepts or Luna's lack of comprehension—probably both—the next several passages (four pages of Luna's diary) are, for all practical purposes meaningless gibberish. There is no point reproducing those remarks here, but I was confronted with a problem: How to determine the gist of what Maxwell was trying to convey without having to guess what Luna's scribbled notes were, in turn, trying to say. It was at this point that I had, what I thought, was a clever idea. Insofar as I knew that Maria Mitchell habitually made daily entries in her diaries or journals, it only made sense that somewhere there must exist her own words that could help give us some sense of the information presented to her old friend Quatermain. Without going into details, after months of inquiries (both digital and traditional), I succeeded in obtaining copies of her journal pages from that period and from the exact days in question—but these particular entries cast no light whatsoever onto the astronomical concepts that Maxwell was flinging about. Nevertheless, Maria's entry on August 19 adds significantly to the texture of this tale, particularly because of its insights regarding Hans the Hottentot, and thus I am grateful that I have been given permission to reproduce her entries in the next chapter, the first supplement to the prologue. Nevertheless, regarding my quest to discover what precisely Maxwell had told Quatermain that day, I did in fact strike gold because I was concurrently investigating another interesting vein of inquiry, the results of which will be offered in the subsequent chapter, the second supplement to the prologue.—T.K.M.

First Supplement to Prologue

Heavens Above!
An Extract from the Journals
of Maria Mitchell

August 14, 1873

Oh heavens above! Allan Quatermain appeared out of nowhere today! He and Hans would have been turned away if not for my fortuitous arrival. I am so delighted!

August 19, 1873

After completing a chapter of my comet probability analysis for James—more than 500 pages so far—I joined him and Allan and Impey for breakfast. Later we gave Allan a bit of a tour, as he had asked about the Atlantic Temple.

We showed Allan (with Hans in attendance) the temple and explained the power needs of the laboratory and how we generate it. He seemed impressed with the classic form of the structure itself and also the enchanting waters as they thundered into the well of the temple, but he seemed pretty nonplussed by Impey's description of the dam and the reservoir and all the rest. But what other reaction could there possibly be, since he had no idea about our real work here— no context.

In time, Impey left us to run some errand, and knowing I could not put off poor Allan any longer, I suggested we take a walk. He, Hans, and I followed the trail around the temple and before long we found ourselves heading east, going in the direction of the Lomas Mountains, which is the source of the electricity that James and Impey have so ingeniously tapped. Of course we couldn't see them as they were 200 miles away over the horizon. At some point I suddenly realized that the ground was no longer jungle nor forest, but dry and sandy. It was a very odd experience to be marching over another desert landscape with Allan and Hans. It seems that we three had been doing this just yesterday, though of course, it was almost two years before, which, come to think of it, is not such a long time after all. I explained to Allan how it was that I was here at the laboratory, and he made some cogent observations. Then he grew silent and slowly pulled out his pipe and filled it with tobacco from a little pouch. Since he seemed lost in thought, I quickened my step and joined Hans. Though usually shy and reticent with people he didn't know especially well, he didn't seem uncomfortable with me alongside. He kept his eyes focused on the faint trail we were following. Hans had picked up a stout stick, I supposed to fend off venomous snakes or spiders or whatever indigenous creatures crossed our path. His dried, dark body was covered by a pair of baggy, brown trousers, a plain woolen shirt, and his battered, stained hat. The invisible wind, or rather breeze, bore away the sweat that beaded on our brows. Our regular pace of walking had become hypnotic, so I was all the more surprised when Hans addressed me.

"Lady Baas, you are a school teacher. Tell me about school, as the only school I have ever known was the bench on the porch of the station which was the Predikant's, the Baas' Reverend father's, in the Cradock district. I remember that we all sat there, the Predikant's servants, like myself, and field workers and any others from the nearby districts that could be persuaded to listen, and the Predikant then told us about the word and laws of the Great Baas in the sky, and talked about the Great Book a lot. How is the school where you teach different?"

Glad for the fellow's curiosity, I explained, "Well, Hans, my school is a very great one full of young women eager to learn, and also older ones like myself, who seek answers to all the world's mysteries, and then try to share the answers that they find with others, such as you just described."

He seemed to think about my response for a few moments, after which he spoke again: "Ah, so. As wise as Baas' Reverend father was, and he was very wise, he did not know anything about, say, my own father and grandfather and what they taught. But of course, everything I ever learned from them was wrong, as the Reverend Predikant never let us forget. And when we failed to pay attention he would first be patient, but after a while he wasn't so patient with us. He scolded me much, especially when he caught me drinking square-face, of which there was always a supply at the station, as the Predikant used it as medicine."

I asked, "What sorts of things did your father and grandfather teach you, Hans?"

He glanced up at the sun, and through squinting, jaundiced eyes seemed to weigh everything about the environment around us, or so it seemed to me. Then he continued:

"They, who were old and smart and told us about the thousand white and yellow sparks that fill the sky, and of the spirits, and of times past and how the world came into being.

These are the things of my blood. But they are all wrong, and my father and grandfather lied, but what would you expect from a pair of worthless old Hottentots, anyway?"

This last statement took me aback, and I asked, "Why would you say that, Hans?" Then he answered that Allan's father, who, it was obvious he held in the highest esteem, was clearly wiser than his own father or any of his own kind for that matter, but then he added, "But, Lady Baas, what I mean is that all these stories, regardless of who said what, can be only so much mist, and who's to say what the truth really is?" Here he looked at the ground pensively and then indicated that he was inclined to think that "the opener of roads," whoever that might be, knew more than anybody, but that on balance, probably Allan's father was closer to the truth, though of course, he, Hans, couldn't say for sure. What a fascinating person is Hans! No matter what he says, it always sounds like he is arguing with himself to the degree that in the end he says nothing at all or comes to no real conclusions. Still, I was truly touched by his opening up to me after his own fashion.

But then I remembered that Hans always spoke deprecatingly of himself, but that once you got to know him you discovered that all that was just show, and in fact he thought very highly of himself and his abilities and his family. I looked over at him and reflected on this and studied his leathery hide and his face, which was a network of deep furrows. He was certainly loyal and a good shot and had much common sense, to the degree that he often got Allan out of otherwise avoidable scrapes. Just as I was thinking this, the earth shook a little. It was a momentary earthquake, I think, or maybe one of the excavators had dumped an especially large load on the ground. Whichever was the case, Allan, who had caught up with us, and Hans too, seemed to take it in stride and said a few words to one another in one of the African languages they so often use.

When we returned to the laboratory, Hans scampered off.

Then I learned that I had got my way! James and Impey had broken down under my onslaught of common sense, and they invited Allan into their inner sanctum to explain what we are doing here at the laboratory. Of course, the Great Physicist needed to simplify virtually everything for the benefit of the Great White Hunter, and James chose his words most carefully and was in fact quite eloquent. After reading Matthew as a sort of required preamble, he went into some of the simpler theories revolving around, and interpretations of, the Matthaean passages and some other particulars concerning the Star of Bethlehem. When James had concluded his rather pedantic explanation, Allan merely stood riveted, his eyes wide. When he spoke, he stammered, "But the cost . . ." and James responded, "Oh, our sponsor can afford it."

[Editor's note: Please see the next chapter to read a summary of the theories Maxwell doubtlessly laid out to Quatermain— as, astonishingly, rendered by Pope Pius IX himself in 1871 in a secret encyclical letter.]

Second Supplement to Prologue

Deus Infinita*

Secret Encyclical Letter of Pope Pius IX,

December 25, 1871

Introduction

Deus Infinita—whose ways are eternally wise and whose cup is infinitely full of truth and mercy—to the extent that everything that was, is, and will be are but your divine whim and whose being is infinitely more than the entire existence of man from Adam through the Four Horsemen on this planet and the planet itself and of the wide and various and ever-changing space occupied by that planet.

All-knowing God, you bestowed on your earthly

---

* Editor's note: From the hints and clues dropped by Maxwell, it was easy enough for me to determine that their mysterious benefactor, or sponsor, was probably Pope Pius IX, which led me to formally request an examination of the so-called Secret Archives of the Vatican, which were, in 1881, made available to scholars. The trip to Italy was a blur, of course, because I am very focused when researching. I spent several days in the cavernous Archives and, children the ability to learn and grow and then decipher your handiwork. In the fullness of time, at the same moment that you created the universe, you created Mary who would bear your son—Mary, who of all persons was the only one to be conceived immaculately, who in herself would be conceived your most precious son—thereby equating for eternity, Father, Mother, Son and the Holy Spirit: Perichoresis of the Holy Four. Thus, following the great news offered to Mary by your angel, she gave herself with infinite humility so that a boy child was born by the working of divine fate, in the time of Augustus Caesar, in Bethlehem. All the world knows that you made signs in the heavens to accompany the birth of your son, which Matthew in his perfect holiness later documented, for he showed us, all your earthly children, the miracle of the Star

---

with the help of some enterprising assistants, laid my hands on the Secret Encyclical Letter of Pope Pius IX, issued Christmas Day 1871, that sparked everything that resulted in the laboratory and all its associated marvels. I present here the Pope's declaration as a separate chapter. You will note that it was written in an unremittingly stilted and formal manner; nevertheless, as it is at the core of Quatermain's tale, and therefore of this book, I am pleased to provide here the first English translation of this historical document.—T.K.M.

in the East, which went before the Magi and stood over where the Child was and which caused them to rejoice exceedingly so that this sign would forever be known and open to all peoples. No other Child was ever born to woman who was heralded with such infinite distinction.

This sign you placed in the heavens to make clear to the lamentably wretched thing that is the human race that your wisdom is all embracing and triumphant over the armies of the Evil One and to guide the Holy Men from the East and then be promulgated by Matthew to the whole world for the rest of time. During recent centuries, at the request and urgings of our predecessors, various learned of our order have scoured the literature both classic and modern to better understand the infinite plan of the ineffable God. Thus were old closed doors opened and old decisions reevaluated.

Being mindful that the College of Cardinals of the Holy Roman Church in 1822 declared that the "publication of works treating the motion of the earth and the stability of the sun, in accordance with the opinion of modern astronomers, is permitted" and that in 1835 the Holy Roman Church went further by allowing to be read the work *Dialogue on the Two Great Systems of the World* by Galileo Galilei and which reevaluated man's position in the universe, we humbly admit the centuries old error of assuming that the heavens revolve around the earth. Galileo was preceded by Nicholas Copernicus, contemporaneous with Johannes Kepler, and followed by Isaac Newton and others whose observations and calculations enriched the world both physically and intellectually, and when these factors have been weighed on balance and compared to both classical knowledge and extrapolations of possible inevitable advances, our committee, which wields vast classical and contemporary knowledge and which is led by His Grace, His Eminence Alberto Cardinal Cigliutti, whose fields include Physics, Astronomy, Electromagnetism, and Communication at a Distance, has concluded that it is possible to make a clear determination of the nature of Matthew's star, which is Mary's star, which is God's star for all space and all time, and which shone upon the place where the immaculately conceived Mary gave birth to the most holy perfect being—part god, spirit. and man.

The Root Divine Reasoning

It is widely known that there have been many theories concerning the nature of the Star that guided the Magi. There are arguments in favor of various celestial phenomena, such as a planet or planets, or a conjunction of planets, or a triple conjunction of planets, or a massing of planets, or an occultation of planets, or a comet, or a nova—or even a combination. Each of these ideas and more has received attention over the centuries. Of special note are the observations of Johannes Kepler, whose mathematics and access to pertinent, and even rare, written records were second to none and who was able, by the Grace of God, to calculate the positions of the stars and planets within the various constellations and nebulae going back in time millennia or, in truth, going forward for millennia. Therefore, Kepler showed that it is simple enough to describe the appearance of the skies during the birth of Jesus, which information has aided incalculably to the absolute determination of what the Star truly was, proving its nature as a physical, measurable phenomenon.

Kepler, though blessed with divine skill and faced with astonishing truths, published unwarranted conclusions (likely due to the tenor of that period and hoping to avoid the fate of his acquaintance Galileo), ignoring his own discoveries and choosing to deny the real, physical, and measurable nature of the Star. Rather, he elaborately conjectured in *Opera Omnia* that the Star could only be a divinely produced miracle, a miraculous light placed but a comparatively short distance above the heads of the Magi, for their benefit alone. We reject such naïve conclusions. We say it is a great pity that the times dictated the circumvention the self-evident truth!

Conjunctions and Triple Conjunctions

First, as to the phenomenon of conjunctions. It is now commonly known that insofar as the planets are in different orbits, some closer to the sun than ours, and others more distant, then it is clear that they will appear to move across the sky at different speeds and at changing intervals, each making one full orbit in the course of their own prescribed years. Thus, when it is said that two planets are standing in conjunction, that means that from our perspective as God's divine creatures inhabiting our Earth and peering up into the night skies, it appears during the period of conjunction that one planet is passing another in the infinitely black sky while close together, much as in the manner of two ships at sea, which, we are told, is a common enough experience. However, very infrequently a triple conjunction* occurs. In

---

*Editor's note: The term "triple conjunction" is often erroneously applied (even by those who should know better) to a quite different celestial event—the triangular massing of three planets, discussed next.—T.K.M.

this case one planet appears to pass another planet three times in a row, with the central passing appearing to be backwards.

This happens thus: Jupiter, for example, appears to be moving westward in the sky from night to night. But when Earth, which is nearer to the Sun, passes in front of Jupiter, there is a period of a few days when Jupiter looks for all the world as though it is moving backward in the sky, or, indeed, eastward. Now, a triple conjunction of, for example, Jupiter and Saturn occurs this way: First, Jupiter appears to pass Saturn in the normal course of events, but then the Earth continues in its orbit so that the line-of-sight shifts, causing Jupiter, which is closer to Earth, to appear to, uncannily, reverse its path and pass Saturn a second time. Naturally, though, the Earth simply continues on its path, and the two outer planets resume their original westward motion, which causes Jupiter to appear to pass Saturn a third time.

By virtue of the mathematics, inspired by the aforementioned Kepler, we can say with assurance that a triple conjunction of Jupiter and Saturn occurred in 7 B.C., the dates of each passing being May 29, September 29, and December 4.

Massing of Planets

The massing of planets is when three planets are in such a position that one can see three all at once, close together, forming a bright triangle in the blackness. There is no more awesome sight in the heavens than a massing of planets. It is an event to quicken your pulse and cause you to hold your breath—an unforgettable sight. *And does not this massing, all at once and so close together, prove the infinite wisdom and ability of God to symbolize His three natures— father, son, spirit?* But let us not forget that such a sight is made manifest to us (such humble beings) only by virtue that we are standing on Earth, that is to say, the Mother, who is always with us, yet is seldom recognized or seen.

Kepler famously observed during the autumn of 1604 the triple conjunction of Jupiter and Saturn—and then only 13 days later the massing of Jupiter, Saturn, and Mars.

Furthermore, Kepler himself was able to calculate that in February of 6 B.C. those self-same three planets formed a tight triangle and could be seen plainly in the twilight.

Regarding the Nature of the Magi

It is important to determine the nature of the wise men

from the east who saw and followed the Star so that Matthew could record for all time that most holy event. It is common to think that there were three wise men, and that they had names—Gaspar, Balthazar, and Melchior—or many variations on those names. However, in the spirit of truth, the gospel doesn't say anything about their number or their names. These features have come down to us through tradition, variously attributed to histories and embellished scriptures dated from 1,000 to 1,500 years ago.

Also, in the spirit of truth, there is no historical evidence that these Magi ever existed; however, for the purposes of this Encyclical Letter, we suggest that Matthew reported accurately. Therefore, the consensus of informed opinion from a whole spectrum of authorities is that the Wise Men may well have been Zoroastrian astrologers.

These men would have hailed from Persia and have studied the night sky. They would have carefully watched the constellations, stars, and planets at all times, constantly alert for celestial signs that would foretell events to come. Both triple conjunctions and planetary massings, being singular events, would have been most distinctive and full of meaning for them.

These priests, for they would have fulfilled that role within their religion, would have noted these planetary groupings—the triple conjunction and the planetary massing—either of which in and of themselves could have seemed as divine heralds to the Wise Men of Persia. Thus both events, that is, the cumulative events of 7 B.C. and the other of February 6 B.C., occurring in sure succession (the former in the constellation of Pisces, the fishes, that relates to the Hebrew people), would have had still more terrific meaning. Could either of these celestial events or their close proximity or juxtaposition in time be considered the Star of Bethlehem?

Considering Novae

Again being mindful that the great Danish celestial observer Tycho Brahe saw and recorded at length and in detail his famous "brilliant nova" *[Editor's note: That is, a supernova, a term not coined till 1931]* of 1572, that which the Chinese before him had termed "Guest Stars," and which he described in his volume *de stella nova*, thus coining the word *nova*, there is merit in remembering that his protégé Kepler, when studying the remarkable triangular massing of Mars, Jupiter, and Saturn in Autumn 1604 (having also studied a triple conjunction of Saturn and Jupiter during Christmastime 1603), observed on October 10 the birth of a brand new star—never known, never seen, never recorded, a star, as bright as Jupiter between Jupiter and Saturn—his own brilliant nova!

Kepler, being inquisitive and logical, wondered whether this new star could have been created by the triple conjunction and the massing, or by just the massing. Certainly, this new star could easily have passed for the Star of Bethlehem if it had sprung into being 1,600 years earlier. So, Kepler, who was among the first humans who had the skills and tools to make this determination, wondered if any similar celestial events had transpired at the time of Christ's birth. And, lo!, his instincts were correct. He discovered both *the* massing of 6 B.C. and *the* triple conjunction that had preceded it. But instead of yielding to incautious vanity and claiming that he had discovered the nature of the Star of Bethlehem, he published instead that, despite these unique phenomena being clustered in time, he believed that the Star of the Magi was nevertheless a true miracle that originated in the upper atmosphere and had nothing to do with the observed and calculated celestial phenomena.

On a New Miracle

In 1871, John Williams, Assistant Secretary of Britain's Royal Astronomical Society, published his voluminous list of comets—*Observations of Comets, from B.C. 611 to A.D. 1640. Extracted from the Chinese Annals.* The Chinese were more observant than their Western counterparts for centuries, and the list contains data that is in answer to our prayers. There are two points of considerable interest. A comet that Williams lists as number 52 appeared for some seventy days in March and April of 5 B.C. near the constellation of Capricorn. The records show that the comet moved westward across the southern sky. As far as can be told, this was a typical member of the comet family such as we all think of, a ball of blue light with a sparkling tail pointing away from the Sun.

But more important was Williams number 53, which is referenced as a "tailless comet." It appeared in the constellation Aquila in March and April of 4. B.C.—almost exactly a year after 52, but this was no ordinary comet. This was infinitely more spectacular, an exploding star so bright that it hurt the eyes to view it. Could Williams number 53 be the star that appeared to the Magi to shine over the Holy

Family that first Christmas season? Could 53 have been Kepler's hypothetical brilliant nova that he then disparaged?

Therefore, following the careful weighing of the afore listed information over the period of time granted us by the Divine Father, we are not in a position for mere speculation and conjecture, but we do declare that the publication of John Williams' holy book at this particular moment in time* stands as divine proof that number 53 is in all reality the One Star. We further declare that the consequent revelation is that the Star of God that illuminated the world was born in the constellation Aquila and gives us cause to rejoice and to accept a charge from God that we must now peer into his mind. Thus we make bold plans.

---

*Editor's note: This expression *"at this particular moment in time"* needs some explanation and some of Maxwell's words, as recorded by Professor Mitchell elsewhere in her journals help us understand. "In terms of our chronology, we must veer away from the sky to note that our sponsor, who has a natural interest in these matters, became quite ill in 1868 and thereafter, his death seemed imminent; however, he lingered, and his dearest wish was to learn about the

The Charge

After much deliberation through both lone meditation and conference, we have decided that, just as John preceded Jesus in the hills and streams of Galilee, His Star was the true herald of his birth—a spectacular event not to be ignored, which, like vast legions of angels with trumpets, would be seen and honored as no event before or since has ever been honored. Yet the herald itself would have its own heralds, and thus we can state with assurance and as fact the following:

The new star or brilliant nova in Aquila during March-April of 4. B.C. called Williams 53, was and is the true Star of Bethlehem, the Star of God, the Star of Christ, the Star of Mary.

---

nature of the Nativity star. But he couldn't do more than just wish simply because there was no information. But when the Williams catalog was published, he and those close to him felt the finger of God had given them a sign that they could then do far more than merely wish." In fact, Pope Pius IX died on February 7, 1878.

—T.K.M.

Furthermore, fittingly, the Star itself had heralds, which we declare were as follows:

• The triple conjunction of Jupiter and Saturn in 7 B.C., that gave the Magi cause to believe that something vital would soon happen amongst the people of Israel.

• The great massing of Jupiter, Saturn, and Mars in February of 6 B.C., that formed a tight triangle—an arrowhead pointing to the birth of a new era.

• The comet of March-April of 5 B.C. (Williams number 52) that would have further emphasized the import of that which was due.

And whereas all these heralds of the Herald Star were transitory and meaningful through their clustering in time, and have moved on and have lost their meaning, the Star itself, the celestial Herald of Christ, we now know to be fixed in the sky. We have conferred and are in agreement that that which *was* must *still be* and if we are ever to understand the mind of God we must look in Aquila, for this is our opportunity.

It is therefore decided that every effort must be made to do whatever is necessary to learn of what is now in Aquila. Though the Star that flared brightly over Bethlehem 1,900 years ago cannot be seen with the unaided eye, we can rest assured that it still remains and that a thorough study of its divine presence cannot help by benefit mankind. That which was must *still be*.

The Declaration

Therefore it can only be viewed as infinitely wise and useful to paraphrase ourselves and draw upon our own words from the definition decreed seventeen years ago concerning the Immaculate Conception. What we said then we can say again for the Truth is the Truth, and divine language is divine and deserves to be restated as necessary, and there is no value in assigning qualitative differences, for the one is as infinitely perfect and divine as is the other: The Blessed Virgin is the uttermost perfection of being and Her Star is uttermost perfection, and the one is the other and the other is the one, and we here state again that which needs to be said again. These words have proven their merit and, through the majesty of the college of Bishops, have been declared the purest words of God, of the Holy Spirit, of the Christ, and of the Blessed Virgin:*

"Wherefore, in humility and fasting, we unceasingly offered our private prayers as well as the public prayers of the Church to God the Father through his Son, that he would deign to direct and strengthen our mind by the power of the Holy Spirit. In like manner did we implore the help of the entire heavenly host as we ardently invoked the Paraclete.

"Accordingly, by the inspiration of the Holy Spirit, for the honor of the Holy and undivided Trinity, for the glory and adornment of the Virgin Mother of God, for the exaltation of the Catholic Faith, and for the furtherance of the Catholic

---

* Editor's note: In essence, Pope Pius IX is saying here that his wording from this point will in part be a repurposing (or borrowing) of perfect language he had already promulgated in 1854 in his historic document *Ineffabilis Deus*, which was his Apostolic Constitution on the Immaculate Conception, in other words, his declaration that the Immaculate Conception was a matter of fact and no longer something that could be argued about. The sections where he deviates from the earlier text are here bracketed and italicized.—T.K.M.

religion, by the authority of Jesus Christ our Lord, of the Blessed Apostles Peter and Paul, and by our own:

["We declare, pronounce, and define the gleaned wisdom that the Herald of God that we call the Star of Bethlehem and the Star of the East and the Star of the Magi and other names was, in the first instance of its conception, by a singular grace and privilege granted by Almighty God, in view of the merits of Jesus Christ, the Savior of the human race, made the most glorious star in the Universe and has confidently been revealed by God and therefore to be believed firmly and constantly considered fact, and that furthermore, God the Glorious is awaiting our supreme effort to meet Him through His Star which is located in the constellation of Aquila and is there now awaiting our attendance.]

"Hence, if anyone shall dare—which God forbid!—to think otherwise than as has been defined by us, let him know and understand that he is condemned by his own judgment; that he has suffered shipwreck in the faith; that he has separated from the unity of the Church; and that, furthermore, by his own action he incurs the penalties established by law if he should dare to express in words or writing or by any other outward means the errors he thinks in his heart.

"Our soul overflows with joy and our tongue with exultation. We give, and we shall continue to give, the humblest and deepest thanks to Jesus Christ, our Lord, because through His singular grace he has granted to us, unworthy though we be," *[the wisdom and knowledge of how to proceed in this most urgent matter as timing is of uttermost import and God Ineffable has granted us the vision at the auspicious moment in time wherein and so that we can, with effort and expense, forever pull off the veil of mystery that has surrounded the Blessed Star for nearly two millennia and finally see forthrightly and unobscured the Might and Mind of God His Father and finally understand the point of all life and matter and soul and space and spirit, the sun, moon and stars, and all else that claims descent from the Most High.]*

Given to the Select at St. Peter's in Rome, the twenty-fifth day of December, 1871, in the twenty-fifth year of our pontificate.

Pius IX

Sixth Prologue Chapter

Hans Finds the Diamond

Just as Maxwell was concluding his ridiculous business about the Star of Bethlehem, I noticed that Hans had made an appearance. He was standing by the door to the workshop, trying not to be noticed in his typical chameleon manner of blending into his surroundings—yet at the same time gesturing frantically to me. When I felt I could politely withdraw to the side of the room where he was, I excused myself to find out what sort of trouble my servant had got himself into. I found him to be sopping wet!

"Hans, how on earth did you find me, and what happened to you?"

"Never mind that, Baas! You know I have my ways! Baas! Listen. This will not be the ordinary sort of chatter, chatter by reason of which the Great One takes great pleasure calling your servant a little yellow monkey, or dog, depending on his mood. Again, listen! Not finding any square-face in this place which is so like so many army barracks, and I admit I didn't look that hard because I knew that if I was lucky enough to find some, I would doubtlessly do something foolish and then you would find cause to be angry with me, and of course I didn't want that to happen—"

"Not that that ever stopped you before!" I interrupted.

But he seemed not to notice and rambled on: "I decided to visit that place that our teacher lady friend and that tall fellow with the tall hat who spoke funny [referring to Barbicane's American accent I supposed] took us, the place of the crashing waters. I was looking into the waters and then thought I saw something sparkling down at the bottom. I looked and I looked again and again and I felt certain that there was really something shiny down there—not like the visions I sometimes swear to have seen when I've had too much square-face, which as you know all too well is truly seldom."

"Get to the point, man, or I will find reason to get angry with you right here and now," I said grinning all the while, but also being conscious that my absence from the group was causing some looks to be cast our way.

"Well, Baas, my curiosity got the best of me and I decided to take a look, but I knew that if I jumped into that whirlpool that I would be instantly swept out into that hole high in the cliff that dumps into the sea, at least we were told of such a hole and I doubt not its existence or the fact that if I were to be swept out of it, I would be dropped far into the ocean and you would never find me again, or if you did I would most certainly be broken and crushed and have joined your Reverend father, the Predikant, in the Place of Fires. So I hurried back through the guard gate as they knew me and I found a stout rope and returned to the spot, made the rope fast to the thick tree branch you saw me pick up this morning and which I used as a staff such as I've seen pictures of Moses do in the Book that your Reverend father, the Predikant, showed often to all those on the station when they had the time. Then I placed the pole across the top of the well, secured myself as I know that Baas would want me to and climbed down where the current nearly swept me away, but luckily I had wrapped both ankles and wrist securely to the rope and was able to get my balance. Then I held my nose and went deep into the water head first and felt around with my hands in search of whatever the shining object should be. Well, after a time and trying several times, in the end, and seeming like I had half-drowned, I caught hold of it and climbed back to safety. When I saw what I had caught, I forgot the rope and all else and raced back here to find you."

"Well, what is it? What was worth all that trouble?"

"Just this, Baas." Then his hand dropped into his pocket and he pulled out an object palm up. My surprise was total, and what can I say but this was like life—my life, the tree of my whole life—had just been topped by a shining star! A star unimaginable! Hans was holding out to me a huge natural diamond—far, far larger than a hen's egg!

From the sketchy details that Quatermain provides Luna, it is likely that the diamond found by Hans in the temple well was the famous Jonker Diamond, which was found 60 years later in the Elandsfontein region of South Africa *(see "Select Bibliography")*. How the stone got from Quatermain's pocket at the laboratory on the west coast of Africa to Elandsfontein, some 4,500 miles away— well, therein lies this story.

Immediately I recognized it as probably the largest diamond ever found. I quickly grabbed it from Hans' grubby hands and slipped it into my own pocket. I was speechless. Perhaps I even cried. I could hear my heart pounding in my chest. Hans looked frightened.

"Baas! What are we to do? I didn't think that anything so shiny could turn my belly so! I think, that now that you have seen it, it would be best to throw it back where I found it."

"Are you out of your mind?" I asked harshly through my teeth, trying to be inconspicuous.

"Baas, is there something wrong with your mouth suddenly? It is all twisted?"

"Well, what do you expect? Suddenly we are millionaires and set for life. It's the most outrageous and wonderful thing that could ever have happened."

"Well, perhaps you are a millionaire. But for myself I would rather be the trusted servant of a good shot, and if I had to, then I would prefer to be the servant of a good shot who happens to be a millionaire. I still say we ought to throw it back where we—that is I—found it."

"Stop being so foolish!"

Luckily, by this time the sun was getting low, and, since Maxwell's lecture seemed to have reached a conclusion, I could naturally plead exhaustion. It was dark and we went off, with Hans trailing behind, to the hotel where we had long settled in.

***

The next morning, we were both up early, which is normal for us. Hans insisted on taking me to the temple to show me exactly how he had found the stone. However, just as we were passing through the gate, Maria caught up to us, to my dismay, as I wanted just then to hear Hans' story alone. However, she and I fell into conversation. As we approached the temple, which commands a view of sea, Hans ran ahead to the cliff's edge,

SS—

I swear, SS, Hans' brain was keen. As much as I admire the adventurer, his sidekick interests me more. Now that I say that, I realize that the two of them together display the qualities of a group mind not so different from hives!

—M

160

as he forever does when there is the possibility of something exciting ahead.

"Baas! Baas! Lady Baas! Over here, You must see this!" Suddenly he was shouting, and the whole scene gave me a weird sense of *déjà vu*! We rushed around the temple and through the forest where there was a path and joined my servant.

"Baas! Look, do your eyes see what mine see?" And he was pointing and gesticulating wildly. When I looked in the direction he was indicating, frankly, I couldn't believe my eyes.

"Baas! The whale we saw the other day, there it is again, or its twin brother. And its game has changed. It has risen and is asleep on the water's surface."

Sure enough, I looked down and saw that the sea waters were calm and devoid of ocean surf, and there it was, that marvelous gargantuan whale we had spied at the outset. It was down below and it did seem to have come to rest.

"Surely it is exhausted," said Hans. "In fact, I too, in its place, would need to rest after such sport as we saw, Baas! Can you imagine its weight? But look: it seems to have died. Yes, already it is stiff. As still as a ship at anchor. Death must

161

have come quickly. Our monstrous friend must have been a fool for a whale or a very old man!"

Dumbfounded, I could only lamely mutter, "Yes, but in either case it clearly over-exerted itself." I turned to Maria, who was by my side. As her reaction was only to wear an inexplicable smile, I turned back to the scene with the whale.

"Oh, you have spotted one of our little toys! Gentlemen, meet the *Nova*, the king of the seas!"

I looked at her hopelessly, my jaw dropped open. "What? Toy? Toy? What do you mean?" And then I suddenly realized what the truth must be. "You mean that's a ship? A ship that you built?"

"Well I didn't build it personally, of course, but Impey supervised its construction based on some documents that were . . . well, uncovered." Here she seemed to hide a smile.

"Is *that* what all *this* is about?"

"No, of course not!" Luna, here Maria almost looked at me pityingly. "Do you forget so fast that we are bound to study Christ's star. The Nova is merely a tool to help us build our telescope."

Frankly I could not speak, and for once in his life, neither could Hans!

"Come, Allan, your seeing the Nova was probably premature, and I think that Maxwell will need to explain this part of the puzzle as well!"

Seventh Prologue Chapter

All the World's a Stage

"Perhaps you are entitled to know about our submersibles, too." The scientist hummed and hawed and seemed tortured, but then he finally spit it out. "The fact is that this complex you see all around us is only half of our project. There is a similar facility 4,500 miles west on the coast of Ecuador on the west coast of South America and, of course, we must stay in as close communication as possible. While we have successfully—through veiled buffer agencies—persuaded various governments that the establishment of a trans-Atlantic telegraph cable linking the two continents is vital, that link hasn't been completed quite yet. In the meantime, our urgent requirement for fast communication and transportation forced us to improvise."

Vividly aware of the huge diamond that was burning a hole in my pocket, I wasn't able to pay attention as I should have. Clearly Maxwell was frustrated that I didn't have more to say, so I forced myself to say something.

"Doctor, geography beyond southern Africa is not my forte, but I do seem to recall that Ecuador is on the other side of South America, that is on the Pacific side. If I stretch my imagination, I can conceive some sort of a cross-Atlantic communication line, but it's impossible to see how any cable or ship, no matter its shape, could easily move back and forth between Ecuador and Sierra Leone without being forced to navigate the Straits of Magellan at the bottom of South America."

"Oh, that is easy. We simply utilize the cross-Nicaragua underground river."

"The what? I don't understand," was all I could venture.

Maxwell said, "I can best explain by means of an illustration. Please step over here." We walked to a far corner of the room where there was a large table, and I only realized when we were right on top of it that the table top was a very large map. More specifically, it was a map of the Atlantic Ocean with South America on one side and Africa on the other side.

"Yes, that is exactly what it is. Now look at it closely. Do you see anything peculiar?"

I looked again and went over it with some exactness, but there was nothing that jumped out at me. When I delayed in responding, Maxwell said, "Look especially at the two coast lines."

I did and then I did see something. "The coasts almost look as though they could fit together, like two puzzle pieces."

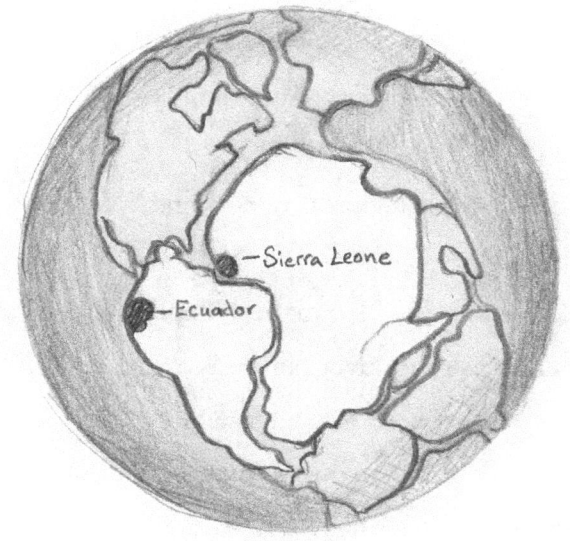

The positioning of the continents as postulated by Abraham Ortelius (1596), Lilienthal (1756), DeBrahm (1771), Snider-Pellegrini (1858), and Alfred Wegener (1912), though it wasn't recognized generally until the 1960s, following the acceptance of sea-floor spreading as a mechanism.

"Yes, that is exactly what I hoped you would notice. Quatermain, there is in fact every reason to believe that in the distant past, the two coasts were connected, and that some unthinkably titanic convulsion millions upon millions of years ago split that landmass into two pieces and that the two continents have been drifting apart ever since.

Well, Luna, frankly that was the most wild and preposterous claim I had ever heard, and, being in a sour mood, I said as much, instantly being regretful of my outburst, but Maxwell went on probably because he didn't hear me in his enthusiasm.

"Well then," he continued, preening like a peacock, "let us go on to the next point. As you see, if there had been in the distant past a large deposit of a mineral, say silver, and whatever force split the landmasses happened to bisect that deposit of silver, then it stands to reason that if such a deposit was located today on the west coast of Africa, that one could find a comparable deposit along the northeast coast of South America."

Here he took a stick and pointed to the two areas just mentioned.

"As it happens," he continued, "the experiment we are performing here requires, in fact, two masses of silver that are some thousands of miles apart. We chose this location for our laboratory partly because of the proximity of one such silver mass (undiscovered to date of course and thank goodness or it wouldn't have lasted long). We sent some of our associates to South America to seek the other half of the silver lode in Brazil, but they were unable to isolate any such deposit, a fact we found perplexing. However, applying their geological and geographical knowledge, they did in fact find the deposit we were seeking in Ecuador."

"I still don't understand," said I.

"If we can agree that the two coasts seem to fit together like puzzle pieces, then here is another perspective that is not so obvious."

Here he pulled the continent of South America off the table (as it turns out that they were in fact pieces of a puzzle rather than a drawing as I had first supposed), and turned that continent 90 degrees and set the top of the continent adjacent to west Africa. I was amazed to see that this was an excellent fit as well!

"Thus you see that there are other possibilities," Maxwell continued. "This agreement of geography may well have preceded the more obvious one by some millions of years and it is this configuration which interests us."

Here he pointed his stick very deliberately. "You can see that Ecuador, then, would have abutted right up here to where we stand on the coast of Sierra Leone!"

Interestingly, this general configuration was suggested more than a century after Quatermain's adventure by Jerome E. Dobson in "Spatial Logic in Paleogeography and the Explanation of Continental Drift" in *Annals of the Association of American Geographers*, Vol. 82, No. 2 (June 1992).

When Maxwell had finished, I pondered his remarks and privately thought his thinking was flawed and that the whole thing was coincidence and it was preposterous for a noted scientist to take any of it seriously, but this time I kept my feelings to myself and merely nodded sagely. I don't recall now, but I may have also asked a few questions, enough

169

to give him the impression that I understood what he was talking about.

"Thus," he went on, "just when it was becoming clear that we needed to somehow transport to and from, and to communicate with, the other laboratory 'over yonder,' which we would build in Ecuador, we began to cast about looking for a solution, and when we found it, it was two-fold! We found convincing evidence in a recently discovered document that a submersible had been built and was perfectly operational some two millennia ago. We also in the same document learned of the subterranean river under the southern portion of Central America that connects the Atlantic Ocean with the Pacific Ocean.

"But where did you get the plans? How could you even imagine that it was possible?"

"The solution came from an unexpected place," Maxwell said. "The British Museum, it seems, has a cache of codices and scrolls recovered from Ethiopia a few years ago, scrolls that had been saved from the Library of Alexandria 16 hundred years ago."

Luna, I cannot tell you the shock this man's words sent through me. Remember that Maria Mitchell and I had trekked in Ethiopia a year or two before. Well, in fact it was during that expedition that I had heard much about those self-same scrolls that had been rescued by Richard Holmes, the curator of the museum, who had accompanied Field-Marshal Napier during the 1868 Ethiopian campaign. But that is a wholly different adventure and needs to wait for another day. (Actually now that I think about it, I did already tell that story in the presence of two notable gentlemen in New York State of all places, shortly after I settled into the Grange.

One of them, my friend Dr. Watson, took ample notes and, in fact wrote up the whole story and posted it to the other gentleman, the landscape painter Frederick Church.) *[Editor's note: See volume two of this series,* The Great Detective at the Crucible of Life*].*

SS—

Ha! Quatermain tells us of his shock! His shock couldn't be more than mine—seeing that I was also on that expedition! Since my brother can accomplish virtually anything at all that he desires that has to do with the British Government, I must see these millennia-old plans for a submarine boat myself! After all, after that B-P affair, am I not within my rights? I'll have him send me photographs!

—M

[Luna: Frederick Church! Allan, you never cease to surprise me!]

(Ah yes. I know John kept a copy—a copious thing, I fear. I'll see if I can borrow it to show you.) In any case, it was at this point that Maria turned to me there in the presence of Maxwell and Barbicane and winked, whispering, "Isn't it interesting how these things happen?"

I couldn't just let that go. "Maria, I distinctly remember that you used the word "uncovered" earlier! Uncovered indeed!"

She winked again. "I didn't think it was my place to tell you . . . and besides, I wanted to see your face when you were told."

Maxwell, meanwhile, ignoring our little tête-à-tête, was continuing: "The scrolls telling of the submarine boat described an astonishing design that incorporated great speed. That was our inspiration, and so we challenged Barbicane, who was well underway with the planning of both laboratories."

I exclaimed, "You mean to tell me that the Ecuadorian laboratory is as immense as this one with the same energy requirements?"

Here Maxwell looked meaningfully at Barbicane, who answered, "Yes. Pretty much insofar as it was necessary to dam the Sumatara and Chambo Rivers, and develop the same sort of reservoir and power complex, though it was somewhat simpler to build the gravity driven aqueduct system due to the rivers' descent down the Andes being significantly steeper compared to the equivalent descent from the Loma Mountains here." Here he vaguely pointed in the general direction of the mountains 200 miles east of where we stood.

Then Barbicane cleared his throat and continued on the subject of submersibles, "When our sponsor, who had learned quickly of the British Museum's new Ethiopian acquisitions, approached us with a possible solution to our long-range transportation and communication problem, in the form of the 2,000-year-old papyrus scrolls, I was intrigued. And the part of my brain that is irrefutably an engineer began to spin plans instantly. But I had a second exceedingly important advantage that I had not consciously connected with our problem. You may remember, of course, that six or seven years ago, the newspapers were full of reports of sea monsters destroying ships—" He looked at me for affirmation, but I had none to give him.

I said, "Doctor, I haven't heard anything about sea monsters, and even if I had, I wouldn't have paid any attention!"

"But surely the furor—"

"I spend months at a time in back country. A hunting expedition to the Chobe River or my trading among the tribes of Nala and Wambe would have coincided with that time frame. It is not uncommon to be on safari for a year. Thus your furor may well have come and gone while I was trying to earn a living."

I admit I was a little put off by Barbicane's remark because I had become bored with the cosmopolitan style of the man who was assuming that everybody must know just what he knows and who can hardly fathom that there are some people whose livelihoods don't conveniently intersect with newspapers and magazines.

He went on, unfazed, "As I was saying, in any case, the United States government became determined to hunt the creatures down or know why not! The upshot is that accompanying the naval task force was a Professor Aronnax, a French naturalist. Their mission had considerable success, though it was not the sort of discovery and resolution that the government could allow to be reported. Nevertheless, through mutual friends I was able to meet with Aronnax, and he described in detail the true nature of those so-called sea monsters. It turns out that there was only one of the creatures and that it wasn't a creature at all, but an armored submarine boat named *Nautilus* that was designed, built and commanded by one Captain Nemo. In the end, I pumped the professor for every scrap of information and data he could recount as it interested me immensely. Remember that our meeting was *before* the singular nature of the papyri scrolls had been discovered and, in fact, *before* our sponsor had any notion of what the future held for him. So, you see, I was the right man for the job. They had hired me in the first instance to build the laboratories. Building the *Nova* and the *Stella* was merely an adjunct to the larger project, but a most useful one. My principal contribution, I think, was the adaptation of the submersible's motive power from steam to stored electricity."

"*Stella*!" I had gulped, I remember, then cried forcibly. "You mean *there are two of them*?" (Mind you, Luna, it was as difficult then as it is now to say that one special name aloud.)

"Certainly," Barbicane said. "Since we had all the infrastructure in place, the dry docks and so forth, it only made sense, and they have both been immensely useful. In fact, I have just returned from 'over yonder.' Everything is coming along fine, I'm happy to say!"

SS—

Drat!! I received the package from my brother! Disappointment!! The world has been robbed! All he could send me were photographs of the few bits of charred remains of the document. The original scrolls and the detailed, annotated English translation, along with a multitude of other treasures, simply burnt—burnt away, vanished, destroyed, along with an entire wing of the museum during the fire of 1902! Destroyed! What he was able to send is lacklustre at best, only some disconnected phrases that mean nothing in and of themselves. I can't even say that these remains are tantalising: "whore and the devil's own bitch," indeed!; "hitting home in the middle of Frigga's quivering abdomen"; "doors overlooking a narrow dock constructed of grates also of iron"; "the propulsion system will take two days to" . . . Bah! A dead end. Too bad, Quatermain! At least I have learned of your adventure these 30 years later. That is something!

—M

Third Supplement to Prologue

The Twelve Scrolls of Xulê*
(Fragments)
As Translated from the Original Languages
and Edited by Angelina DeMars and Geri Wills
University of Kansas

---

*Editor's note: Reading of M's disappointment, naturally, I was also disappointed and discouraged. I, too, wanted to see the translation of those precious scrolls. A submarine boat as early as 1873? Amazing! Now, of course, I knew of the remarkable Confederate Hunley of the American Civil War, but a full-fledged operational submarine capable of crossing the Atlantic in mere days! Impossible. Ludicrous! Then, on a whim, I began to search the Internet using the phrases that M's brother had provided—"whore and the devil's own bitch"; "doors overlooking a narrow dock constructed of grates also of iron"—and within 40 minutes, PDFs of photographs of papyrus fragments written in Latin and Greek and called by scholars for convenience *The Twelve Scrolls of Xulê*, plus an English translation, were sitting on my computer desktop! The simple facts chronologically are these: As discussed in volume 2 of these memoirs, *The Great Detective at the Crucible of Life*, the proprietors of the Great Alexandria Library had the foresight to copy some of its holdings and send them elsewhere for

177

safe-keeping, some of which wound up in Ethiopia, thus avoiding a total loss, at the end of the fourth century A.D. when the Christian Emperor Theodosius ordered it all burned. In 1868, as a result of the British sending an expeditionary force into the highlands of Ethiopia and the subsequent death of the Emperor Theodore, 900 ancient documents from Theodore's library were sent to the British Museum. Apparently among them were some scrolls that included the information that inspired the laboratory's secret benefactor to suggest to Maxwell and Barbicane that they plan and build their amazing submersibles *Nova* and *Stella*.

However, by the time M had asked his brother, who seemed to have had a high position in the British government, to send copies of the scrolls to M, he was informed that the museum fire of 1902 had destroyed the scrolls except for the few fragments already noted. Then when I followed those same breadcrumb-like clues, I completely unexpectedly discovered *The Twelve Scrolls of Xulê* and the terrible circumstances that led to their discovery. *It must be emphasized here that while the Ethiopian scrolls and the Twelve Scrolls are linked only by conjecture,* still I am convinced that the former must be a copy, or a copy of a copy, of the Xulê documents that had somehow crossed the ocean or oceans from South America and had been deposited in the Alexandrian Library sometime during the 300 years prior to the library being destroyed. Once found, as the reader will see, an international team of experts led by Professor DeMars of the University of Kansas spent two years translating and interpreting the Latin and Greek originals.

Given these documents' (seemingly) vital connection to the laboratory, scientists, and engineers who are, or were, pivotal to Quatermain's narrative, I have decided to include the translation here, just as I included similar supplemental material in my previous book, *The Great Detective at the Crucible of Life*. The volume *The Twelve Scrolls of Xulê* was a scholarly work intended for scholars and was not much known beyond its core audience. Dr. DeMars and the University of Kansas have graciously permitted me to include here portions of the work (which are in any case fragmentary to begin with) for which I am grateful.

Lastly, I ask the reader to indulge me. Upon reflection, it seems to me that the following almost prescient lines from H.P. Lovecraft are both note-worthy and thought-provoking when considered in the context of the discovery of the scrolls:

"I was confronted by the richly ornate and perfectly preserved façade of a great building, evidently a temple . . . . Neither age nor submersion has corroded the pristine grandeur of this awful fane—for fane indeed it must be—and today after thousands of years it rests untarnished and inviolate in the endless night and silence of an ocean chasm."

—H. P. Lovecraft in "The Temple

(Manuscript found on the coast of Yucatan.) 1925"

—T.K.M.

Introductory Note
By Angelina DeMars, Ph.D.

The discovery of the twelve ancient and priceless papyrus scrolls of Xulê, maid-servant to Julia, daughter of Caesar Augustus, will, while fragmentary, I'm sure prove to be as notable a discovery as the Rosetta Stone—not only changing our entire interpretation of history, but radically shifting the thrust of science as well.

The importance of this discovery is three-pronged. While the scrolls give us a heretofore unexpected portrait of Julia, they also offer a glimpse into what was likely a pre-Tierradentro empire that rose and fell in the northwest quadrant of South America during roughly the same period as the Roman Republic and Roman Empire combined (less a century or two at either end). Also, we can now surmise, on the strength of the scrolls, that there existed then well-established trade routes that penetrated well into North America, at least as far as Yucatan, spreading culture in both directions.

Mention should be made at this point that the story of Julia as told by Xulê does not adhere particularly to the records of antiquity which historians have, until now, taken as fact. As co-translator and co-editor of the following chronicle, which was composed in the Latin of the period with some Greek annotations in a different hand, I can only testify that the scrolls appear to be authentic in every detail. Doubtlessly, scholars will be arguing for decades in this regard.

Finally, it is known that Julia was exiled in the year 2 B.C., which dates Xulê's narrative to the nascency of the first millennium.

Note that period measurements and nautical terms have been rendered into modern forms to allow for accessible reading.

University of Kansas, February, 1988

Prefatory Note

Though many fine men were lost that terrible May night, it cannot be denied that the destruction of the super-submarine *Leif Erikson* has proven instrumental in turning a fresh page of history of incalculable value.

The following newspaper clippings were compiled to show the reader at a glance the tragic circumstances through which the scrolls of Xulê came to be located.

Since the details of the *Leif Erikson* disaster are well known and on public file, these few clippings are intended to only briefly recount the highlights of the calamitous incident in chronological sequence, thereby putting the finding of the scrolls in proper perspective.

A.D.

The New York Examiner

VOL. 134 NO. 290—NEW YORK, WEDNESDAY,
MAY 3, 1985—-40 CENTS—FINAL

Giant Trident Sub With 209 Lost In Depths Off Mexico; Navy Denies Triangle Link

LEIF ERIKSON
SEARCH GOES ON

Checkerboard Hunt
250 Miles Off Yucatan
On Tropic of Cancer

By Raymond Brown
Special to the
New York Examiner

WASHINGTON, MAY 3 —— The U.S. ballistic missile submarine Leif Erikson, with 209 men aboard, submerged last night in the Gulf of Mexico and failed to surface as scheduled, the Navy said today.

The Leif Erikson is a Trident submarine of the Ohio Class, the largest class yet built, and carries 24 armed ballistic missiles, which have the power of destroying 1,300 Hiroshimas.

183

The vessel, which was making a routine run, is "presumed to be lost," according to Vice Adm. Robert M. Reuben, Chief of Naval Operations.

Two dozen surface craft and as many aircraft are searching the area of the last dive approximately 250 miles northeast of Campeche on the Yucatan peninsula in southern Mexico.

No oil slick or debris has yet been sighted in the search area that includes an undersea valley.

Hope of finding the submarine is centered on the Navy's three deep-sea submergence research and ocean engineering vehicles, NR9, Treiste III, and Long John Silver, which are hastening to the 9,400-foot deep waters.

Loss of the $3 billion Leif Erikson, with its 18 officers and 191 enlisted men, would be the Navy's worst peacetime disaster since the loss of the Thresher with 129 men in April of 1963.

Originally launched one year ago as the Alaska on April 11, 1984, the renamed Leif Erikson is 585 feet long and displaces 18,000 tons.

Reuben firmly denied "ill-informed" rumors that the loss of the submarine is connected with the infamous Devil's Triangle associated with Bermuda.

"This tragedy is doubtlessly linked to some mechanical failure," the Navy chief announced to reporters from his Pentagon office at 11 p.m. last night.

Admiral Reuben went on to say that there was "no possibility whatsoever of nuclear explosion or radiation hazard from either the ship's reactors or from its 24 ballistic missiles."

The Leif Erikson submerged last night at 6 P.M. EST near the reef of Triangulo Oeste for a routine deep-diving test accompanied by the submarine rescue vessel Switcher with which contact was maintained through underwater telephone for 27 minutes.

Communications from the Leif Erikson were broken in mid-sentence during a routine depth report that gave the submarine's depth at "approaching its maximum classified capabilities," Adm. Reuben explained.

The Navy has sent destroyers from its Galveston facilities as well as specially equipped aircraft from its Houston air station into the search area with the hope of picking up signals that will aid in obtaining a fix on the missing jumbo submarine.

The Chief of Naval Operations emphasized that the accident would be thoroughly investigated by a court of inquiry headed by Vice Adm. Samuel Ashley, President of the Naval War College....

LEIF ERIKSON HUNTED

Rescue Craft Search Area Of Last Dive In 9,400-Foot Deep Waters

---

By Allan Sunshine
Special to the
New York Examiner

WASHINGTON, May 4 —— The Navy said today that its giant atomic submarine Leif Erikson and its crew of 209 "appeared to be irrevocably lost" in the Gulf of Mexico.

Debris consistent with the makeup of the submarine was reported to have been sighted in the area where the vessel took a deep dive test at about 9 p.m. two days ago in water 9,400 feet deep, 250 miles east of Mexico.

"At those depths," said Adm. Robert M. Reuben, Chief of Naval Operations, "rescue would be impossible—even if we were to find the vessel."

The Navy still denies that any sort of nuclear leakage or contamination is to be expected following this tragic incident....

NAVY RULES OUT
REACTOR FAILURE

———

Leif Erikson No Radioactivity
Hazard, Navy Says

———

By Allan Sunshine
Special to the
New York Examiner

WASHINGTON, May 6 —— Naval officials ruled out today the possibility that the loss of the atomic submarine Ohio Class Leif Erikson had been caused by any problem in her nuclear power reactor.

Officials also gave assurances that the vessel's power plant was "in absolutely no way a danger to either people, the environment, or sea life...."

HOPE ABANDONED FOR 209 ABOARD LOST JUMBO SUB

Board Of Inquiry Launches Investigation Into Mysterious Disappearance

---

NO SIGN IN 72 HRS— OIL SLICK UNRELATED

Bathyscaphes Continue Search Relentlessly

By Allan Sunshine
Special to the
New York Examiner

WASHINGTON, May 7 —— There is little possibility that survivors will be located from the lost atomic submarine Leif Erikson, the Navy said today.

"We have officially abandoned hope," Adm. Robert M. Reuben announced to reporters from his Pentagon office at 11 p.m. last night....

Reporter Claims
Sub in Collision

GALVESTON, Tx., May 8 (AP) —— A Russian submarine collided with the Leif Erikson and caused its destruction, the Galveston Lone Star Tribune reported yesterday.

A reporter for the newspaper claims in a copyrighted article to have heard the recording of the last message from the Leif Erikson before it disappeared.

The reporter, Ashley Neville, indicated that the source of the "bootleg" tape was to be kept confidential. The recording clearly reveals that more than one submarine was involved in the tragedy.

The Navy has gone on record calling the report "ludicrous and an example of someone's imagination running wild...."

The New York Examiner

VOL. 134 NO. 297—NEW YORK, WEDNESDAY,
MAY 10, 1985—40 CENTS—FINAL

Sub Lost In Collision With Russian Counterpart

NAVY BRASS
COMES CLEAN

Russians Silent

INQUIRY BOARD A SHAM

By Lloyd Overholtzer
Special to the
New York Examiner

WASHINGTON, May 9 —— The nuclear submarine Leif Erikson was destroyed in a collision with a Russian missile-firing submarine in the Gulf of Mexico, Vice Adm. Samuel Rankin, the Navy's Director of Undersea Warfare, admitted today....

Following the revelation of the collision and the resultant brouhaha, the following small article and later equivalent science and archaeologically oriented stories were relegated to the back pages of the world's press.

GEOPHYSICISTS HELP IN SEARCH

Will Map Sea Floor
Echo Soundings To Pinpoint The Submarine

A LONG TEDIOUS JOB IS FORESEEN

By Allan Sunshine
Special to the
New York Examiner
ABOARD U.S.S. SAND DOLLAR, May 11 ——
A team of geophysicists is on the way to the scene of the Leif Erikson disaster tonight.

The experts will help to mark the approximate spot where the nuclear submarine went down and map the ocean floor with echo sounding equipment.

The Sand Dollar, the fastest destroyer that is based at the Naval facility in Galveston, Tx., was expected to reach the scene by first light. However, rough seas may slow the operation....

The New York Examiner

VOL. 134 NO. 297—NEW YORK, SATURDAY,
MAY 13, 1985—40 CENTS—FINAL

LOST ATOM SUB FOUND

No Survivors

Navy Bathyscaphe Spots Wreck At 9,400 Feet

By Allan Sunshine
Special to the
New York Examiner

WASHINGTON, May 12 —— The bathyscaphe Long John Silver photographed an object yesterday that has been positively identified as a section of a conning tower instrument panel of the type installed in the Leif Erikson, the Navy announced today.

Other debris, mainly bulkhead sections, hatch covers, and misshapen tubing, was also located in the same vicinity.

"There seems to be little doubt that the remains of the Leif Erikson have been located," said a Navy spokesperson....

192

MYSTERY DOME FOUND NEAR SUB WRECKAGE

5,000-Year-Old Structure

Special to the
New York Examiner
CAMBRIDGE, Ma., May 14 —— The three Navy bathyscaphes photographing the wreckage of the submarine Leif Erikson yesterday stumbled upon the submerged ruin of an ancient dome-shaped structure, possibly an observatory, predating the Preclassic Mayan period by at least a millennium, the Navy disclosed today in a special news conference.

Found at a depth of 9,400 feet, the structure "precedes the Classic period Maya by millennia," according to Harvard University archeologist, Dr. Bruce Edwards. "We estimate it to be at least 5,000 years old," Edwards said.

"The edifice was originally built on dry land, probably a very narrow peninsula that unaccountably subsided geologically recently," the scientist said. "For convenience's sake we call it a dome, but the fact is that its shape and size are somewhat elusive."

A Navy source, who spoke on the condition of anonymity, said that "there seems to be some sort of sonar anomaly. If I didn't know better, it's like the structure is surrounded by an invisibility shield, like a Romulan Bird-of-Prey," referring to a type of....

PAPYRUS SCROLLS
FOUND IN DEPTHS

Special to the
New York Examiner
CAMBRIDGE, Ma., May 20 —— Among the artifacts retrieved by Navy bathyscaphes from a sunken pre-Mayan dome-like structure are a series of sealed jade jars containing papyrus scrolls, Dr. Bruce Edwards of the Harvard University archeology department announced yesterday.

The dome, discovered May 13 by the three Navy bathyscaphes making a photo-reconstruction of the debris-littered sea floor following the Leif Erikson disaster, appears to be a 5,000-year-old observatory.

Since the temple sank into the depths of the Gulf of Mexico at least 1,500 years ago, this startling discovery "gives a shot in the arm to the diffusionists' theories that the American empires were influenced by Mediterranean contact," Dr. Edwards explained.

"The scrolls were preserved in watertight jars made of a type of white jade found only in proximity to Colombian and Ecuadorian volcanoes," he said.

After being properly treated with preservatives, the scrolls will be turned over to University of Kansas philologist Dr. Angelina DeMars for translation.

"The text is written mainly in the colloquial Latin of Augustus' time, with some Greek annotations," Dr. DeMars told reporters.

Dr. DeMars hopes to have the translation prepared for publication in two years....

THE TWELVE SCROLLS OF XULÊ
Prelude

Dying

I am Xulê, and I am dying. I am from the woodlands of Strobe and my skin is black as the coal of Britannica; I am sick, and my dying will be slow. The sword thrust I received in my belly last month at the hand of a skull-faced Taaxipalkul barbarian will be my death. Even as I write, the pain is comparable, I think, to the worst that the cyclonic fires of the Phlegethon, River of Hades, could inflict in several score incarnations. A fortnight I have been delirious, or so Campachix the Surgeon informed me upon my awakening from the swirling greyness. For greyness is all I remember following the moment the barbarian miraculously sidestepped my driving battle-axe and plunged his glass long-sickle through my loins.

For many hours after my emergence from the delirium I lay weak and gasping upon my pallet, seeing nothing but the planked ceiling of an adobe hut, listening to old Campachix prattle on and on about how fortunate I am to be such a giant of a woman; how a lesser woman, sheathed in less substantial muscle than I, would have died instantly from such a wound. Campachix, while a dedicated man of medicine, has the misfortune, however, of being a totally honest man. His string of lies, though uttered with marvelous fervor, became more transparent with each word he spoke.

After I had lain still for some time, feeling a measure of strength finally return to me, Campachix came to my side to change the hot compresses he periodically applied to my throbbing, hairless scalp. Yet once again he was making further assurances that my life was as good as eternal when finally I grew tired of his mutterings and abruptly reached up and grasped his wizened, red throat with one hand and declared that if he insisted on insulting my intelligence for one second longer, I would send his soul as herald to my own arrival at the steps of Hell.

Being not only a man of dedication, but also a wise man, he instantly perceived that my desire for the truth was sincere and that, even in my considerably weakened state, I could easily snap his throat with but a twist of my wrist. Presently, though his eyes had snapped shut at the touch of my fingers, they now bulged open like great yellow moons threaded with red, and a thin, gurgling sound proceeded from his ashen lips which I took for a plea for mercy. I released my hold and pushed him gently aside, at which point he took in a prodigious draft of air, his one hand rushing to his throat while the other pressed against his middle.

"Xu...Xu...Xulê!" he ejaculated. "Mercy, my friend. For well over two years I have served you and your mistress with unswerving affection. I have ministered to your wounds, and on platters of quintessential gold I have given you my counsel. You, who have the strength of ten jaguars, have been as mother, daughter, and sister to me. All this you know well, yet you come within the space of a snake's tooth of murdering your devoted servant. Whatever slight cause you may have had for such an act I honor and respect, yet I deem that, similarly, your respect for me, Campachix, should inspire you to treat me with measured discretion at the very least."

I gazed up at his thin, long-chinned face, stared into the brown irises of his eyes, all the while listening intently to the nervous jingle of the tiny bells on his elaborate, feathered headdress, and regretted my action. I considered the possibility of avoiding apology by feigning a relapse into coma. Instead, following a deep breath, I let a great ponderous growl emerge from deep within the corded muscles of my throat, a sound that has shocked many an adversary into fatal hesitation. Campachix involuntarily took a long step back, then caught himself and stood his ground.

"My physician, ally, and trusted friend," I began unconfidently, "in the course of defending this fair land of Yokatix-Mezel,* the Nation of White Jade, I have contracted a wound, which, despite your maternal prattling, I sense will be my death. Admittedly, I am not a surgeon, yet I detect a contrived note in your ceaseless optimism. I insist, therefore, that you confide in me your honest appraisal of my injuries. If, having only just wakened from a fortnight of sickness and delirium, I lost patience at your interminable hawking of my goddess-like health and allowed my more bestial nature to predominate, I ask your forgiveness."

I swallowed thickly then, for only twice before had I ever admitted to fault, one of those times at the prodding of a full century of Caesar's legionaries!

---

* Editor's note: Probably a pre-Tierradentro civilization between Olmec (1200-300 B.C.) and Early Classic period Mayan (A.D. 300-550), known to be situated in the vicinity of Colombia, mainly, and Ecuador, somewhat south of the area traditionally associated with the Maya and somewhat north of the Peruvian Incas.—A.D.

Campachix then admitted that the barbarian's serrated blade had opened my innards in such a devious fashion that, though the outer wound appeared healed, there remained a continual, slow bleeding on the inside for which there was no available remedy. Picking each word with finesse, he explained that death was inevitable. It may take many months, but it was certain that I would progressively waste away and die.

Though, as I have said, much of this truth I had already perceived, Campachix's words, despite their silken delivery, stung nearly as badly as the bite of the blade itself. I do not fear death, or, better, I cannot look upon death disdainfully, yet the sure knowledge that my path thenceforth was to be unswervingly guided by the haunting specter of slow death caused all the muscles of my body to go tight as stone. I closed my eyes and, with a wave of dismissal, begged Campachix to leave my side so that I might think—and reflect alone upon my direful fate.

**

But I get ahead of myself. It was three days ago that I first wrote that I awoke from the grey delirium. It was somewhat later when I lost my patience with Campachix.

My first thought when I awoke was of Julia. "Where is she?" I asked when I saw that she was not by my side.

"Aboard *Thebes*," was Campachix's reply.

"I would have preferred that she had remained by me."

"Do not fret, Xulê. Your mistress will return before long. For a full fortnight she lived by your side, eating and sleeping on a mat laid on this very spot where I stand. She would only leave after the learned Moab prevailed upon her the urgency of the matter."

"Matter? What matter is more important than her concern for me?"

"I know only that the earth shook badly, and Moab insisted that they leave immediately for the bottom of the bay in *Thebes*."

"And what of Frigga, she whom you call the Jade Princess?"

"The Princess accompanied Moab and Julia, my friend. That was three days past—only hours before you awakened."

"Is there more to tell, then?" I asked.

"Only that as they sped away to the mooring of *Thebes*, The Bride (I should say that Julia often claimed to be Nerio, Bride of Mars, in other words, a goddess, and who am

I to say otherwise, I who worship her!) charged me with your care and bade me tell you, when you awoke, that a crisis of unutterable singularity has sent them to the floor of the Great Bay of Mezel."

I lay quiet then and knew in my heart that my friends had good reason for quitting this woman's side in her hour of need. After a time, my thoughts turned to the defeat of King Ponamyak and the barbarian army of Taaxipal . . . for doubtless, brooding on this subject of my mistress' desertion could only beget woe for all.

Now I asked, "How is it we stand champion against Ponamyak? Surely we were blessed by the gods that morn!"

The surgeon, who had fallen into thoughts of his own, looked up and answered, "Indeed! If fewer had died I would call it a miracle. As it is, the gods saw fit to stage an epic with a handful of spectators . . . . But you ask how! The answer we learned from the Taaxipalkul wounded. King Ponamyak's warriors, having partaken of the mescal cactus, fought well and as madmen so long as it was dark. But, when the first arc of the sun appeared, thrust out of the sea, these same madmen saw not the sun, but the cruel mouth of a heinous creature racing upon them to savor their flesh. It seems such visions are common to all who are simultaneously drugged."

Now, when I heard this tale, it struck me so funny that I laughed—or tried to—a gesture which I instantly regretted, for the effort caused me a paroxysm of anguish of unparalleled extent.

When the seizure had passed for the most part, Campachix wiped my face of the tears of pain, and I muttered my hate for Ponamyak and his whole infernal breed. Not so much for my wound or the ceaseless skirmishes did I hate the Taaxipalkuls, but for their cowardly attempts at conquering the peace-minded Nation of White Jade.

And for what?

For the amassment of sacrificial victims for the sloshing altar bowls of the ravening, several-headed snake goddess Bemxote!

"By Greenox!" I was finally able to articulate, calling upon the Janus-faced and capricious forest god of my clan. "If only that fierce creature had been real. Perhaps it would have made feast of Bemxote as well!" But, now I dared not so much as smile, but only lay back and stayed quiet as well as I might.

It was at this point that Campachix began his incessant harangue concerning my recuperative powers.

"Ah, Xulê, when you are better, you will be that creature! You will lead Yokatix-Mezel to victory . . ." ; et cetera, et cetera, et cetera.

***

It is two days since I last picked up quill and scroll—that day Campachix confided in me the nature of my ailment.

And the fifth since Julia, girl-child of Augustus, departed for the depths of Mezel Bay on her enigmatic mission. On a journey of mystery she has embarked, and Xulê has no answers! Xulê has no conception of the reasons!

O, Moab, learned captain, take care of her, daughter of empire, daughter of Rome!

Now, as I await her return, and being confined to my pallet fully against my will by Campachix and his pretty wife, Meyexican, I will further exercise my writing prowess—for scribe I am as well as warrior and gladiator—and record on this papyrus for eternity and for all the future worlds of men the journey of Julia across the Great Sea.

Part One

Exile

Most days, having nothing better to do, Julia would climb the only mound that passed for a hill on our insignificant islet and comb the horizon for hours in search of an unwary merchant or fishing vessel to hail. In two years, though several were apt to approach, none could be persuaded to land, their prurient crews always being reminded of, or giving second thought to, Caesar's decree that whomsever sets one foot on Pandateria without his express Imperial authority loses his eyes, tongue, and all four limbs.

It was on such a day, Julia attentively watchful and ripe with hope, the sun high in a typical Mediterranean clear-blue sky, that our fantastic travels and adventures began.

Within sight of the Italian coast, the barren chunk of rock called Pandateria *[Editor's note: Known today as Ventotene]* pokes out of the sea fifty miles due west of the Bay of Naples. Despite its consisting of little else but grey sand and shattered razor-edged stone, it bears signs—dusty furrows and dead hedges—of being cultivated in decades past. The only things that grow there now, however, are an occasional brittle grapevine, a rarer prickly bush with holly-like berries, and a few sprigs of some sort of yellow grass.

Biting winds whirl unceasingly about the seaward crags and meandering dunes, singing and moaning through the burned-out ruin of the old villa on the northern end of the island, driving deeply into the ancient sea-carved grottos and caves which provide the only other convenient shelter.

Here it was that Gaius Octavius Caesar, the August, First Citizen and Pontifex Maximus of Rome, Emperor of all the known world, chose to exile his daughter and only child, the only person he ever truly loved. This was home for Julia for two endless years.

And for what ghastly crime was she convicted?

Adultery!

At the age of thirty-seven, after three husbands and five children, Julia was shown to be in violation of the *Lex de adulteriis*,* evidence of which was brought before her father

---

* Editor's note: This refers to one of several laws framed by Augustus himself in the year 18 B.C. aimed at strengthening a demoralized Rome. In particular, the *Lex de adulteriis* was meant to reestablish harmony and virtue in the Roman family by threatening the unfaithful wife and her lover with lifelong exile and the confiscation of a significant part of their property.—A.D.

by her own horrid step-mother, Livia. It was Livia's plan to cast dishonor upon, and thereby discredit, Julia's two sons—who were also Augustus' adopted sons and Imperial heirs—Gaius and Lucius, by which treachery she hoped to raise her own son, and Julia's husband—Tiberius Claudius Nero—to second person of the empire!

The whole matter was especially irksome to Augustus. That his own child would violate the mandates not only of his own devising but those of Rome herself was more than the old fellow could bear. His heart was broken. He behaved hysterically, exposing her before all of Rome and imposing the mandatory penalty on her!

Now, this affair becomes particularly interesting when one realizes that all the charges brought against Julia were perfectly true—that she was, in fact, involved in, or experimented with, to a very great degree, her own special species of copulation with an assortment of men, an activity she fondly refers to as her "sport."

Though Augustus loved his daughter more than a man can say, he loved Rome more. So, here was a man pitiably torn between the two things of the world for which he cared most, knowing that the mightier of the two must prevail. Doubtlessly, his hysteria turned to madness for a time, and in the end he lashed out at the cause of his torment. Julia must be banished for the good of Rome!

Never again would her name pass his lips!

Thus it was that Julia, my mistress, was thrust from all the civilized world and forced to live out the rest of her life on a bit of rock with nothing but the fishes, seagulls, field mice, and sand crabs for company. That is, except for myself, Xulê, most stupendous woman warrior of all Black Strobe and Nubia combined! How many men has this one woman slaughtered in the arena? More than I can count—and all I have to show for it is a few scars. I don't count the fine scars on my breast, which were self-inflicted. Here is the reason: there had once been in the arena a Northwoman whose flesh evaded my blade by only the smallest fraction no matter how I pressed my advantage. She laughed in her contempt, for the only thing that prevented my blade from contacting her was the impediment of my own body. Her laughter didn't last long though because the next time I parried, my fury was boundless and my short sword came down and whisked off those minor obstructions in the merest blink of an eye. Can you imagine my joy when my thrusting blade curved back up and smoothly entered her far better than any man, the momentum carrying the point straight up with demonic force through her torso, wiping the laughter off her face by piercing her throat and neatly slicing off her jaw? O, the lucky girl who has known the love of Xulê!

Yet, it came to pass that two years of the sentence was all Julia suffered. Two years of anguish and loneliness unimaginable! Two years with little else to do but hate and loathe her father and everything for which he stood.

Nevertheless, those two years were far from wasted. In that time, having little else to do, she and I both fired by ever-growing thoughts of revenge, each day for hours on end, I would instruct my mistress in the use of the Roman short-sword, the Northern long-sword, spear, axe, bludgeon, and the like. Every day we practiced, whetting her skill, and putting muscle on her slight frame. For in all of Julia's life, with the exception of her "sport," her time was spent weaving, spinning, bearing children, and the other household duties considered traditional and proper for aristocratic Roman women. But now, I, Xulê, taught her the cunning of the gladiator. And being that Julia is intelligent and lithe of muscle by nature, her proficiency developed rapidly. At the end of two years, I can say in all honesty that she was nearly my equal in swiftness of thrust and agility of parry. Often, in practice she has succeeded in striking the blade from my hand with deadly precision. In point of fact, when her blood is hot, she strikes like lightning.

So it was, then, that sweet Julia, daughter of Rome, stood atop the sand-hill fronting our cave on the southern coast of the island one bright morning, gazing out to sea. Enchanting it was to behold the figure of this woman standing tall in the distance, her long, tapering legs taut and spread wide, her elbow-length auburn—but prematurely silver-streaked—hair swelling bewitchingly in the gusty-breeze. Standing naked on that high crest of quartz sand, she clutched her long-sword solidly in her right hand, while shielding her eyes from the glare of the fiery sun with her left. Turning her golden goddess-like form toward one end of the small island then slowly back again, she searched for that unsuspecting Greek or Carthaginian fishing boat or trader to hail. For two long years, Julia had not been able to indulge in her sport, and my mistress, knowing her own needs, never ceased to look for man or men who could service those needs—the ultimate heinous fate of those poor souls seeming not to interest her one whit, her need was so great! Though not the noblest of attitudes, I tended to give her the benefit of the doubt and thought of this as her one foible. Fortunately, no man ever took the bait, as I have no doubt that Augustus' spies would have found him out!

***

As I crouched inside the mouth of our cave cleaning our breakfast fish and watching her golden body glisten in the sun, I saw her suddenly hesitate in her pivoting search of the sea. Then she raised her sword high into the air and waved it in a wide beckoning arc.

Knowing something different must be in the offing, I leaped up and ran with long strides all the way to the top of the hill. Reaching my mistress' side, I did not hesitate to fix my attention on the sea towards which she pointed with her outstretched blade. By Greenox! I was expecting nothing less than a fleet of Macedonian warships, but all I saw was choppy waves in our little bay.

"What is it, mistress?" I asked. "There is nothing that I can see."

Julia looked up into my eyes, her freshly washed hair scattering like wind-whipped fire in the rising breeze. "By all the gods, there was something out there, something big, but it has disappeared. At first I thought it was an island rising."

In the end, I impatiently marched back to the cave and that day proceeded just as any day. Shortly after nightfall we wrapped ourselves in pelts and huddled by the blazing fire, and I teased her about her "island."

Julia wasn't happy, and she said, "Ah, my big, beautiful comrade-in-arms, have you so little imagination, no romance for the unique and marvelous things that so seldom touch our lives these days? Can you not believe that I saw something out in the bay?"

I replied that I had more than abundant imagination, but she ignored my sarcasm. Sleep then came over us.

***

We were pounced on in the dark of night and pinned to the ground in our sleep! We had no way to anticipate this outrage. Then we were dragged struggling to the beach. Out there in the bay, we saw a large mass like a floating reef moving rapidly in the bright moonlight—a mass that wasn't supposed to be there! A mass lit with yellowish light *from the inside*. We were so amazed that we both stopped struggling and simply stared. Then we were in for a still bigger surprise. Julia made sense out of the scene before I did.

She cried out, "It has jaws and they are opening! And by the specter of my great-uncle, is that a boat emerging from its mouth?"

Indeed, before our eyes, the thing had come to a rest, agitated seawater splashing against its moon-lit shining blue-black hide. And out of its peculiarly stiff, gaping mouth a spry little boat was being driven by the oars of ten men! As soon as the boat emerged fully, I began to recognize that the great mass resembled a whale—wonder of wonders!—a great fish! The boat pointed its prow toward the beach and cut swiftly through the rolling waves. From atop the hill where Julia and I were held captive and observed these marvelous proceedings, we saw that in the center of the small craft, surrounded by the pumping oarsmen, sat the small, slumped figure of a man dressed in a simple, white Greek robe.

We saw also that the boat would touch the sand of the beach in a short time. Then as one, the men released us shouting with excitement, Julia and I, neither of us wearing so much as a rag around our loins, sprinted into the surf. Side by side we waded out, gleefully waving and calling out all the while. Then, when the boat came between us, we pushed and tugged at the craft till the oars touched bottom and the oarsmen, freedmen I saw now from the manacle scars on their wrists, leaped over the side and leaned their backs to the task, and together we pulled the boat onto the beach. In all the excitement, only the Greek, which we saw clearly now was the case, remained undisturbed and dry.

No man of them, however, uttered a word to either Julia or me during this first encounter, the old Greek only staring fixedly ahead with a faint smile on his lips. But no sooner did the boat come to a rest than he stood up and waited till one of the freedmen, a lieutenant I supposed from the heavy knot in which his hair was arranged, offered an arm, which the Greek took. Clutching up the folds of his robe with the other hand, he stepped from the boat, then casually glanced from my naked form to Julia's.

He lifted his hand to his mouth, coughed slightly, then spoke. "Julia, my dear, daughter of Octavias Caesar, you must pardon our intrusion."

From where I stood, I could see Julia's eyes open wide at the sound of her name. The master of the boat evidently saw this as well, for he said quickly, "Yes, Julia, I know who you are. Indeed, I was sent here by your father on a mission of mercy."

"I do not understand, old man," Julia exclaimed. "My father has publicly stated that he would never again speak my name. Indeed, I was to be exiled with no other human contact but Xulê here, my protector, for the rest of my life."

"Indeed, Julia, that is so. Yet, what Augustus saw fit to tell Rome and that which he held close to his heart were two entirely different matters."

"Then I will be allowed to return home?"

"No, I'm afraid not, but he has gone to great pains to see that your life of exile be less strenuous then he originally indicated to the Senate."

"Less strenuous!" Julia nearly screamed. "Less strenuous than two years of solitude, of loneliness unimaginable! It seems a little late for missions of mercy. How would you like to live with nothing but sand crabs and seagulls for company for two years? If it had not been for Xulê, I would have died for want of companionship. Don't talk to me of less strenuous! Speak no vile hypocrisies to me, old man!"

"Nevertheless, my dear," the old man continued, seemingly unaffected by the outburst, "all these two years past, your father has secretly been the architect of a rather intriguing deception, designed principally to allow you to regain at least a portion of your freedom—a plan which you will doubtlessly accept gratefully once you hear the details.

214

But first, let my men and me be welcomed into your home. A moment of leisure for ourselves after a long sea voyage . . . and a surprise for you."

"But who are you?" Julia finally found the wits to ask. "And what in the name of Jupiter is that monster yonder? Fish or ship or the handiwork of demons? Great gods, man, if you are master of that monster, as I take it you are, are you man at all . . . or monster yourself?"

The Greek laughed, more I gathered from the sudden change in my mistress' expression than from the content of her accusations.

"You need not concern yourself over such matters, my dear. I am quite as human as you, if not so young—and *Thebes* is merely a ship of my own design. Shall we go?"

"It's all beyond words," Julia said as we walked, her lovely limbs swinging gracefully in time with the sea sounds. "It's so good to see new faces again after all this time."

"Yes, so good! I too crave new faces and talk," I said, "especially if that talk deals with freedom—for you, at least, if not for me."

***

"My name is Moab," our guest explained once he had seated himself in the shelter of our cave. "I am a Greek, who but recently was residing in my homeland in a small coastal town called Poros. It was there that I built *Thebes* ever so discreetly so as not to attract attention, directing the efforts of my dedicated men.

"I am a naturalist primarily, but can make do with mechanical devices. In recent years, I have become particularly interested in solar eclipses, which, of course, can be easily predicted through calculation, but, by far, the majority of them occur over open ocean. When I found that there was no ordinary means by which I could quickly cross the seas, I endeavored to develop a fast craft, and while I was at it, I thought I could build it suitable for exploring the vast mysteries of the sea below the surface. As you have seen, I succeeded admirably."

"And you fashioned your craft in the guise of a whale for reasons of camouflage, no doubt," Julia offered.

"Yes, but also to decrease water resistance so as to improve speed. It is the only one of its kind in the world, so far as I know—unless old Job's Leviathan is to be believed!—and quite comfortable I might add. With it I can do my eclipse studies wherever they may happen and travel at depths quite unattainable prior to its construction. Yes, yes, depths absolutely unheard of. It is also, needless to say, your means of escape."

Julia's face still showed confusion. She said, "You say that you calculate the location of eclipses. How can that be?"

"Excellent question, my dear! I can see that your intellect has not been exaggerated to me. Yes, while I do pride myself on my mathematical prowess, I was fortunate to happen upon some plans, in the Great Library at Pergamum, for a mechanism that aids in determining celestial positions. The modified version I built has proven most useful in confirming my own calculations.*

Julia remained quiet far a time, no doubt awed as much as I by both the apparent skill of the Greek and the proposition he offered. Miracles and freedom all at once! It was more than we could assimilate at one time!

"But," began Julia finally, after a long silence, "at irregular intervals an Imperial galley circumnavigates the

----

* Editor's note: Moab's device may have been based on the so-called Antikythera mechanism, thought to be part computer, part astrolabe, discovered in an Roman-era shipwreck off a Greek Island in 1900.—A.D.

island, skirting the shore, making certain that I am still here. Sometimes, knowing they have arrived, I keep hidden to see what they do next. But it's no good, for they always send ashore an armed party of mute women who comb the rocks till they find me. It is the closest I've come to having fresh company. But it is no good at all because no sooner do they find me, they turn around and head back to the galley, which in turn sails off and disappears before long. How can I leave without the whole Imperial Navy raising the alarm?"

"That, my dear, is no problem at all. That is, it is no problem now. Your father has gone to great lengths, great lengths indeed. But, let me explain his entire scheme. In order to save face, it was necessary to prepare for all contingencies. That is why it has taken so long.

"Without making known his motives he sent dozens of specially chosen couriers throughout the empire with instructions to look for innovative inventions, especially sea-going vessels, and new weapons.

"After eighteen months, one of these Imperial representatives learned of *Thebes* from fishermen and, after observing her performance from a distance, immediately impounded her, much to my chagrin, naturally. Within a month, I was told to take *Thebes* to a hidden cove several hundred miles north of here. There, much to my surprise, Caesar himself met me, examined *Thebes*, and explained his needs, which he made quite clear: simply stated, I was to remove you from Pandateria and give you your freedom so long as you never again set foot within the empire . . . and that I was subject to your direct orders and desires—and, of course, even your merest whims so long as we both shall live—which state automatically guarantees my own exile!

"I must say, while sympathetic, to tell the truth I didn't much care for the idea of having to leave all the known world behind, as obviously would be necessary if I agreed to his plan. He made it exceedingly plain, however, that I really had no choice whatsoever in the matter. And whereas I've lived a long and fulfilled life, with great expectations of continuing to do so, I readily saw his point, whereupon I began preparations for an extended sea voyage.

"Caesar then further explained the second part of his plan, namely that he had dispatched a number of mutes across the empire who were to search for a double—a veritable twin—of yourself; then finding such a double, they were to bring her back with them under the strictest guard, by force if necessary, with the intention of training her to mimic your voice and every movement and then substitute her for you—

that is, to pose as you—on this island and thereby fend off the suspicions of the watchful galley."

"But that's horrible!" Julia cried. "I could never allow such a thing!"

"Nevertheless," Moab continued, "It was among the barbarians who dwell in the broken country north of the Danube that a woman was finally found who met the desired specifications. She was seized, as a matter of fact, some time before knowledge of *Thebes* had reached Augustus, and was taken to a secret training center on Sicily where she was instructed in her new role—namely, to be you.

"Mind you, from what I understand, she was not a particularly willing student, but in time she picked up enough of your obvious mannerisms—drilled into her by certain of your own tutors and servants—to fool most casual observers.

"Frigga—that is your double's name—is to take your place here and live out the rest of her life on this island as you would have done—"

The old Greek would have said more but Julia's face grew livid, and she nearly thrashed the fellow right there. The way that tiny, slumped-over old man recoiled from Julia's wrath was quite the sight. I would have laughed but for the fact I wanted to hear what my mistress had to say.

"By all the gods," she began, her small fists trembling with restrained fury, "I cannot allow this to be! It is ghastly! I would not wish such a fate on an innocent. For shouldn't I know what life on this god-forsaken cinder is like? It is bad enough that my own father would cause me to live in torment and despair for two years; I cannot allow this guiltless woman to live out the rest of her life in my place, despising every moment of that life, living only for hate as I have done, with not even a friend such as Xulê to console her in her worst moments. I will not live to see such a fate forced upon another! I will sooner stay than see that! Do you understand, foul worm of a man?"

At that moment, the man with a knot in his hair, whom I had taken for Moab's lieutenant, leaped up from the group of sailors who were stretching and lounging outside the entrance of our cave and raced up to Julia. As he rushed past me, I saw his face draw tight into a mask of hate, a sight which made my muscles convulse, and I found myself confronting the man, my hands on his shoulders.

"Julian bitch!" he cried. "No hell-bound offspring of that demon Augustus nor niece of Caesar the traitor can talk to my master like that! By Jove, I'll wring your poisonous neck till your sharp tongue bloats purple before I'll hear such talk again!"

When I heard this, I think I must have blacked out for a time, for the next thing I remember is feeling pain in my arms as six men pinned me to the ground. I ceased to struggle, at which point the men backed off and I sat up to see that the fellow with the vile mouth had decided to go to sleep slumped against the wall of the cave, which I thought was good for him, for otherwise I would have killed him.

Julia, meanwhile, though calmed down somewhat, still glared at Moab, gasping air. It seemed as though she was fighting violently the anger rising out of her heart. Yet, I could tell her mind was entirely on the subject of her double. She seemed, for all appearances, unaffected by the incident that just occurred with regard to the man who had fallen asleep.

"O, man! Where is this woman now?" she demanded.

"She remains guarded in the submersible."

"Then bring her to me immediately. I would see this twin of mine."

Moab gestured to another of his men. "Erasmus, return to *Thebes* and bring Frigga hither. And take Livinius."

Immediately, the man called Erasmus turned and began kicking and berating his fellows in a comradely fashion, relaying and enlarging upon his master's orders.

In a moment, they were all on their way back to the long boat, two of them supporting Livinius the Blowhard, who was slow to keep up.

"Please, you must pardon Livinius' behavior," Moab began to explain. "He is really quite loyal to me, and easily takes offense far too personally, I fear, when criticism is aimed my way. Furthermore, he was once the personal slave of Horatius Claudius Nero, your step-mother's uncle, and, therefore, remains faithful to the Claudian side of your family—despising anything Julian."*

"In that case, I'll pay him no mind," Julia said. "Perhaps, he will become less of a fool someday. In that event, he may learn to call me 'friend.' Well, old man, you tell me my father, the great Caesar has engineered my escape

---

* Editor's note: Despite the fact that Augustus (great-nephew and adopted son of Julius Caesar, and, therefore, a Julian) and Livia (a blue blooded Claudian) were man and wife, Emperor and First Lady of the empire, the Julians and the Claudians were vehement political enemies.—A.D.

and contrived to retain his honor in the bargain. Yet the freedom I wish is not the freedom that is now offered to me. What is a girl to do, ah, Xulê? We should have thought he would pull some trick as this. My father has many faces. I suppose that's why he is emperor of the world. But I will never understand how even one with a multitude of faces could exile his own daughter to a living death. Then again, I suppose that one such as that is capable of anything— anything at all!"

"True, mistress, yet it was he who brought us together. So, though I hate him for the one, I love him for the other, and now that I know that he did not truly forsake his love for his daughter, I find myself almost respecting the man again."

Here, I strolled to the cave entrance, looked around and assured myself that all of Moab's men had returned to their vessel. Then I faced Moab and set my expression in a serious mold.

"Moab, old Greek, listen, I say, to my words. Bear witness to these words which must be spoken! For two years this woman"—here I gestured towards Julia—"Daughter of Rome and, therefore, of the World—and I have lived alone together on this hellish rock. The frustrations of our heinous imprisonment you can never fathom, never having experienced it, yet through our suffering, a suffering of the spirit which I can tell you from hard-earned and bitter experience is a thousand times a thousand times worse than any physical torment, we, myself and this woman, fallen heir to the world, have come together, and grown so that we share a kinship, a sense of nobility, and a knowledge of well-being while in one another's company that never can two other people—man and wife be damned!—ever hope to obtain, nay, to imagine, I say! You gaze upon us and see two; we look upon one another and see but half of ourselves. Enough! You are witness now to my words. You, who fate has chosen to be our rescuer, have heard the truth of my bare soul. No, say nothing. Merely contemplate a fact as firm as this cursed rock on which we sit. Julia and I are as one and shall remain so till the gods reclaim their own. And I tell you now, that if I have a say in the matter, Julia shall regain this, her rightful world— she shall be empress of all the lands as is rightfully her due— and I, Xulê, with sword and teeth if need be, will deliver it into her hands!"

"Nay! My friend," Julia broke in. "I shall accept no such gift from you. We will take it together, for it is as much yours as mine, for in fact we are joined in soul as you say, and togetherness is our blessed boon. What say thee, now, old Greek, Moab, our redeemer? You are bidden to speak."

Moab, who had been sitting quietly, staring into space, slowly lifted his gaze. Lingeringly, he looked first at Julia, then deliberately shifted his owl-like, bottomless eyes and took in my own near-Olympian figure.

"Solitude!" he began. "How it can distort the mind! How it can make one hunger for one's own kind! I can well imagine the need you both have to talk to a new person . . . . For instance, I have only been on your island for a few minutes . . . not even an hour . . . and already you both are pouring out your souls to me. Can you be sure I am a sympathetic listener? I think I understand your sadness, for I begin to feel it in this vast welling of words, this tide of emotions. It must have been excruciating, your time on this island, yet I gather from your words that, quite unexpected to both of you, you have found something which has almost made the experience worthwhile (that is no doubt the wrong word)—you have found that which is genuinely and finally the truth that comprises your essential selves. You each have discovered within the other a part of yourselves, a part that has always been missing whether you knew it or not. I can state that with the utmost assurance. No one is ever born whole; that missing piece of the individual is always locked away deep inside another person. It is the task of each person, then, to search for that missing piece. Some succeed; some fail. Yet the road is never the same for any two successful unions.

"I am happy to say that it appears you two have succeeded . . . . Only to discover this, to understand this, it was necessary that you suffer the foulest agony of the spirit so that you would each seek succor within the other. The greater the pain, the deeper you must have plumbed the other till at last you found that which you had no idea you sought: your lost selves, that elusive fragment of your mind and personality which the Creator saw fit to sequester in a safe place till you stumbled upon it in the dark (which is the way it seems always to happen). Though you had never conceived that you were lacking some vital part, when you found it, you soaked and bathed in total joy.

"And I tell you now that having bathed, you have confronted your Destinies. From that moment when you found your lost parts within the other, you became whole— complete as too few men and women ever can be—and being whole, there now awaits you a future to be reckoned with.

That I can promise you, but I cannot say more . . . for who truly can outguess Destiny, ummm, my friends?"

Now, I ask you, whoever may someday read this, what would you have done if such a speech had been addressed to you? Julia and I could only sit quietly for a while, the only sounds being the distant roar of the surf and the muffled beat of our own hearts. At times I would, with an effort, look up at Moab, who seemed lost in his own thoughts, or at Julia who would meet my eyes. During the next few minutes, it was as though we could read one another's minds: as our emotions and feelings ebbed and flowed, our eyes were like windows in which we read the softness, the hardness, the confusion, and, finally, the understanding that the other experienced.

After a time which proved to be a far longer time than I had imagined, I realized that I could take no exception to the old Greek's words and was about to say as much.

But then, there came a howl from the beach.

Part Two

Frigga

The long-boat had returned. All at once, Julia and I were on our feet and racing for the crest of a wide sand dune which blocked our direct view. Reaching the top simultaneously, we saw clearly in the moonlight Moab's men splashing and gesticulating wildly at the sea's edge. I sprinted ahead, arriving first at the site of the commotion where I thrust aside three or four of the guffawing oarsmen and beheld in their midst—to my utter amazement!—a blond, lily-white and snarling Julia clothed in snowy linen and brandishing a curving, saw-toothed bronze dirk; and, too, doubled up kneeling in the wet sand was a skinny, saffron-hued freedman who clutched the side of his bloodied head and moaned pitifully.

The next moment, Julia herself came rushing up, stopping dead at the sight of this strange tableau.

"Great Mars! Jupiter and Juno! Xulê, is this real? I cannot believe what I see. It's myself—but a pale version to be sure!"

Hardly had Julia gasped these words than, with the lightning speed that only the hopelessly trapped animal can summon, the woman in white leaped at Julia, and in a flash they were knotted together, rolling in the surf, the crescent dagger lashing furiously through the flying salt foam and churning sea wash. Not once, however, did that driving blade touch my mistress' golden flesh. With one flashing wrist, Julia parried the down-swinging blade over and again, while her other hand grappled ferociously for a fast hold around her foe's alabaster, rock-corded throat.

For a time, I watched the sport with some relish— mindful, of course, of mishap and of possible harm to Julia— but, when I saw that the fracas was not about to end quickly, I took it upon myself to resolve the quarrel by unceremoniously taking up the false Julia by her little waist and ample thigh and holding her high above my head, all the while threatening to crush her spine into pulp if she didn't stop struggling. Needless to say, she had no intention of ceasing her struggles—my threats serving only to add fire to her senseless thrashing. Rather than ingloriously twisting her life out, I chose, instead, to toss her floundering body across the beach (first taking the precaution of disarming her) where she landed in a linen heap amongst a tangle of oozing, red seaweed.

No sooner had Frigga landed, than my mistress, with the speed of a mountain wind, was by her side offering to help her to her feet, there being no animosity on Julia's part. But her milk-like twin scuffled in the sand, then bounded up like an airy sprite in the moonlight with both hands extended and fingers carven into claws, pouncing at Julia's throat. This time, however, Julia was ready, instantly sidestepping so that her twin, of necessity, had to lunge futilely to the side while still in mid-air, a move which put her completely off balance and caused her to crumple headlong into a sand pile. But, in less time than it takes to think of it, she was up again, ripping off her clinging wet garments. In a second she stood naked and white, her feet braced in the sand, facing the equally naked, brazen Julia!

Imagine the sight. Two immeasurably perfect women—Aphrodites both—cast from identical molds standing but a few paces apart ready to pounce on one another, teeth and eyes flashing!

The white Julia's flesh was as smooth and hard as ivory; my mistress' like the finest bronze. They circled, the one snarling, the other watchful. They crouched . . . the globes of their breasts hanging in ideal symmetry, swaying, ripe, and wholesome, as their bodies stepped quickly and agilely over the rocky sand. For a moment, it seemed as though they were dancing, as their hands, legs, and arms moved, weighing the potential of each passing moment, searching for openings in one another's guard.

Before then, I had never seen a more gracefully composed idyll of flesh and limbs and gleaming, glaring eyes than those two women, replicas but for the baking of the sun and the tint of the hair, leaping at once into the air and intertwining their bodies in tight, if inimical, embrace before hitting solidly into the ground. It was uncanny—the pantherish molding of the one mirrored the other, even to the way their forms blended and folded so that their smooth, tight bellies and groins joined as one.

No sooner had Julia's shoulder dug into the sand than she twisted and was on top of her adversary all the while shouting between sobs and gasps that she intended her twin no harm, but she may as well have spit at the moon for all the good it did!

Only now did old Moab arrive at the scene, tut-tutting, coughing and seeming out of sorts generally.

"My, my, Frigga is putting on quite a show today," he said as he moved wearily to my side.

I had never seen a more gracefully composed idyll
of flesh and limbs.

"You mean this sort of thing is a frequent affair?" I asked. "Not 'frequent'," he answered. "'Common' would be better."

"What's the use of splitting hairs, Greek?" I snorted impatiently.

"From the looks of things, I'd say I'm not the one who's splitting hairs," Moab said. "Don't you think it would be wise to break up this . . . uh . . . altercation? Especially since it seems to be for no purpose, your mistress having effectively given Frigga her freedom—at least, that is my understanding. Further hostility seems rather pointless, actually."

"Once already I have tried to break up this game," I replied, alert to any change in the course of the fight, "but to no avail. Now I am content to let things take their course."

And then, Julia launched her knee up with catapulting force, hitting home in the middle of Frigga's quivering abdomen. Things happened quickly then. Frigga, who had been flying through the air at the time, diving for Julia's thighs, crumpled into a ball and crashed into the sand. But even as Frigga's knees touched the ground, Julia's calloused foot smashed into her hard, round jaw, throwing her whole body backwards and twisting. Surely, Frigga's knee would have come disjointed had her body not moved instinctively, flowing with the fall, even as she sprawled unconscious in the liquid sand.

For three breaths, Julia remained poised, muscles ready to attack, before she realized fully that her twin would be no more trouble. Then she, herself, fell headlong into the surf beside her quieted foe.

Instantly, I went to Julia, lifting her up in my arms, as two of the freedmen, responding to a signal from Moab, hauled up the other and carted her across the beach. Within a few minutes, we had both women clothed in dry linen and situated comfortably in the shelter of the cave. Julia had awakened, but lay quietly at my insistence. It was necessary, however, to take the precaution of tethering Frigga's wrists and ankles in case she was still in an ugly mood when she awoke and wanted to display more of her fighting skill.

[Summary: Over the course of the long night, Julia, Frigga, and Xulê learn to trust one another so that by morning they resolve to put themselves in Moab's care. Considering that the absence of Frigga in Julia's stead on the island will surely betray their flouting of the Emperor's will and condemn them, they are cavalier and anxious to quit heinous Pandateria forever.]

Part Three

The *Thebes*

Moab spoke, "Little more do I have to say except that as we are all exiled, under sentence of death by crucifixion should we return home, let us remain together and be friends. It is to our advantage, I think."

Frigga's hard, glaring eyes rolled up white as she threw back her head and laughed a full, deep, meaty laugh.

"Old beetle, do not fear my wrath, for if death should claim you by using my hand as its instrument, you would never know it. But, I do not foresee the necessity for that course of action, for there is value left yet in your withered old carcass, I suspect. Let us then respect one another—you for my splendor, and I for your genius and enchanting craftsmanship. We shall travel together in peace, my father."

"Fine," Moab said, a shining in his eyes. "Then let us prepare to leave—quickly—for the tide will soon be ebbing."

In less than an hour, Julia's belongings, which consisted of a few chests of clothing, body ornaments, perfumes and other accoutrements—most of which she had not bothered with at all in two years—also, along with all our

236

weapons and what few items I possessed, were heaped in the bobbing long-boat, and we pushed off toward the unimaginable! Behind us, Pandateria lay heavy in the sea, its baked sands cooling in the late-afternoon sun, devoid finally of human life, far removed already from the human suffering it had harbored for so long. As we pulled away from the beach, neither Julia nor I looked back at any length, for we saw that the whale's monstrous great mouth was opening wide to receive us.

"Meet *Thebes*, King of Fish!" Moab crowed, extending an arm broadly toward the torch-lit maw which loomed strangely ahead of us.

Our boat glided over the submerged lower jaw into a cavern of hanging bristles and combs that from a distance passed for whale baleen but which I could see now was some kind of sturdy tree bark tinted white and pink. At the rear of this mighty orifice, 25 or 30 feet from the tip of the snout, where one would expect to see the cavernous gullet, were two wide, bolt-studded iron doors overlooking a narrow dock constructed of grates also of iron——iron being the principal constituent of the vessel. On the starboard and port sides of this dock were two small slips just wide enough to snugly accommodate our long-boat and another which in all respects was identical. The oarsmen guided our boat into the empty starboard slip, and, no sooner had this been accomplished, the great doors swung outwards and two men emerged, one tall as myself but pale and blond, the other stooped and brown with straight Ethiopian hair. Hurrying to our side, these two caught the line which Erasmus tossed out and pulled the boat firmly into its notch.

When this was accomplished, all the oarsmen jumped out of the boat and disappeared along with the two new fellows through the portal, leaving only Julia, Frigga, Moab and myself standing on the deck watching the red dying light sparkle on the open sea beyond the cavern-like mouth. Uncanny and eerily lovely was the entire scene—as nearly like the holy, many-hued Greenoxite Caves where Pepumsay-Lemox conversed with the gods, as anything I have seen before or since. So engrossed were we in absorbing the colors and the shimmering light in that extravagant environment that Julia and I, at least, failed to notice the fast growing darkness.

Then, however, I noticed that the ceiling, that is, the roof of the mouth, was dropping fast—that the whole mouth was growing smaller! Involuntarily, I jerked around searching for a means of escape. But Moab, seeing my distress, quickly put his hand on my forearm and said, "Xulê, fear not, for we are preparing to leave the bay, and *Thebes* must secure her snout for this to happen with expedience."

I was still wary nonetheless. Despite the wonder of it all, and the many reassurances, I did not like the idea of being shut up inside an iron fish. Yet, to please Julia, I made a pretense of relaxing my guard and watched the final shutting of the tremendous mouth philosophically.

"Follow me," Moab said, "and become better acquainted with *Thebes*. As its creator, I'm sure you will sympathize that I am justifiably proud of my rather elaborate creation. It is unfortunate that Caesar learned of its existence, thus impeding my unfettered dual studies of eclipses and marine habitats. But, perhaps it is better this way. If I had shown my invention to the world, or if knowledge of its existence had circulated during one of Rome's frequent naval campaigns, then I'm sure *Thebes* would have been conscripted for military service. Its usefulness as a tool for peaceful naturalistic research would have been finished in that event—my submersible would have become a war machine. As it is now, at least, *Thebes* can honestly be called an instrument of freedom, and the warring nations are mostly ignorant of its existence."

Julia snorted, "Ha! Thank the gods for small blessings!"

Moab ignored her, continuing reflectively, "Yet, still a creator enjoys some recognition for his craft . . . ." Then, with a grand sweep of his arm and a profuse bow, he ushered us through the great, bolt-studded doors.

The first thing that caught my notice was a refreshing draught of cool air rushing from somewhere within the bowels of the monster machine. Though curious, I mastered my desire to question the master of the boat right away, realizing even then at the beginning that one question would lead to another, which in turn would lead to interminable others as our tour progressed. In point of fact, I desired to be the least nuisance I could, especially as I was sure to learn all I wanted in good time.

Julia, however, suffered from no such inhibition.

"That cool flowing air feels grand. Where does it originate?" she inquired.

"At the moment, a hatch is open at the opposite end of the ship and all communicating compartments are open for ventilation. It is just an ordinary evening sea breeze."

The room in which we now found ourselves was small, no bigger than the docking facility outside to which it was adjacent, and studded, like the doors, with iron bolts in orderly vertical and horizontal rows, a common sight we would soon learn throughout the craft. The light in this room came from a series of tiny flame-jets that glowed dimly inside red glass globes. The effect was to fill the room with a rubyish gloom. No sooner had we entered, than Erasmus, who was occupied with some strange, notched levers in one corner, ordered the doors sealed. Immediately, two husky fellows, the same two who had helped pull in the long-boat, and who were now busy at some task involving still more levers, moved quickly to obey the order, and the doors were secured with a thunderous clanging. Then, a solid iron beam nearly forty feet long and as thick as my fist and which was fixed to the bulkhead in a sort of hinge arrangement was dropped into place across the doors, holding them firmly in place.

"The seams in the doors are water-tight now," Moab explained. "We have not yet in our journeyings or explorations reached a depth at which the exterior water pressure would prove a formidable risk. Of course, these doors are afforded double protection due to the large space beyond, which forms the whale's mouth and the fact that the giant lips, when sealed, are also air and water tight.

"This compartment, by the way, serves not only as an antechamber but houses the mouth opening and closing controls as well. The mechanism itself, that is the machinery involved, is accessible through floor and ceiling hatches there"—he indicated the locations of the two hatches—"and there. If you are interested, you are welcome to study the controls at your leisure. Only be sure either Erasmus or Livinius or one of the other officers is close at hand, for the instruments are very delicate. You must remember, due to the strangeness of most everything you'll see, to please observe common sense safety precautions at all times. A good rule of thumb is if you don't know what it is, don't touch it. Are we perfectly clear on that point? Good. Then, I have much I want to show you . . . and you have much to see! Come along, come along."

We stepped into a corridor somberly lit with that same disagreeable ruby-red radiance. Frigga then announced, "I'll go to my quarters now, Master Moab. I am acquainted well enough already with your iron whale."

"Yes, yes, go ahead, my dear. Go freshen yourself and rest. We will see you at dinner, then."

But Frigga was already striding off ahead of us, disappearing around a bend in the corridor.

"Till then!" she called out.

Moab now pointed out that the corridor here branched off into six small metal rooms, three on either side, five of which were officers' quarters, and the last on the starboard side being the ventilation and blowhole control room. Glancing inside the latter, we were impressed by a most singular array of iron pipes and valves obscured by a hanging cloud of steam. The two burly, sweaty men who were at work inside turned at the scrape of the opening door, smiled cheerily and tossed up their arms in sloppy salutes, then returned immediately to their labors.

"Our principal motive power is no more complicated than ordinary steam," Moab explained. "Boiling water. But the excess heat, steam and smoke from the furnaces must be expelled. At intervals we allow it to escape through what in a real leviathan would be its blowhole, a trick which helps to maintain the illusion that *Thebes* is a living creature, though a bit of an anomaly, I would wager. . . . The ruse is extremely effective when we wish to avoid unwanted guests, and, I think, the disguise is rather aesthetically appropriate, don't you agree?"

Now we came to the elbow in an L-shaped bend in the passageway and turned right for a short way, then left, where we came to a set of closed double doors. Entering, we found ourselves standing in a dining hall, fitted with six large tables, each table having six chairs—room for thirty-six men at a meal. Each of the tables and chairs, I noticed, too, was securely bolted to the deck.

"Our dining room is equipped to handle half the crew at meal times—the other half maintaining their posts—and is large enough to accommodate the entire crew during briefings and special occasions," Moab explained.

"Wait!" I couldn't believe my ears. "You mean to tell me that your crew consists of over seventy men?"

"Seventy-five, to be precise."

Then we followed the old man into the after-starboard corner of the dining room where he showed us the tiny, but fully equipped galley. He introduced us to Jabez the cook, who we learned was an Egyptian, and who, also, was obviously quite fond of consuming his own plain but palatable preparations. We talked a little, learning that a fresh food storage compartment of considerable size opened off the galley, then we continued on our tour, exiting by the same doors through which we had entered, though we saw that we had the option of using another door should we have chosen.

Then, just as we stepped into the corridor again, there was a sudden sensation of forward movement as though the floor had moved ahead of my feet. Caught unawares, I had to grab at the door jamb to keep my balance. Julia faired better, I suppose since she is smaller than I.

Moab, however, appeared as though nothing at all had occurred, though he smiled at my small predicament. "Livinius," he explained, "is moving *Thebes* out to sea now. We will remain on the surface for a spell to allow the nighttime air to circulate through the vessel. Unfortunately, the one problem I haven't been able to solve as of yet is the build-up of poisonous air and heat while submerged. In fact, this limits our time under water to two hours—no more than four in the event of an emergency."

We followed the corridor directly into the port fin control room. This compartment was fitted with a series of mechanisms that controlled the angle of the one fin, thereby helping to steer and dive the ship. On the starboard side of the craft, we learned, there was an identical room to control the starboard fin, but with the cranks and gears reversed. Also, in each of the two rooms was a great set of spiraling stairs which ascended above the hull—or hide of the whale. Moab now motioned us upward, so Julia and I mounted the stairs, she first. "Jove preserve me! Moab, you have a tidy set-up here. From the beginning, I wondered how you saw to steer this thing. Now I know! You are a wizard!"

Now I, too, saw what Julia perceived. The stairs wound above the ceiling of the fin control room ending in a sort of platform wide enough for two people to stand. And at this point the metal hull of the upper part of the craft was broken by what at first I thought was a circular hole through which I saw the moon and a few bright stars. But on closer inspection, upon reaching Julia's side, I realized that it was no hole at all, but some sort of solid transparent covering in the form of a hemisphere or dome. It was there because I could feel it with my fingers and knock on it with my knuckles, yet I could indeed see the sky beyond.

"By Greenox the Merciful! What kind of witchcraft is this, Greek?"

"'Tis nothing but glass, but of exceedingly high quality, melted from the purest quartz sand, made to my specifications by the most skilled glass-makers in Alexandria."

Though I had no reason to doubt the man, the material I touched for the first time that day resembled not in the least the alabaster-like substance I had learned to call glass. In any case, the configuration of this strange window was such that, while standing on the platform, one's head protruded above the hull allowing perfect visibility in all directions but down. Looking forward, I saw *Thebes*' blue-black snout driving through the dark water, bits of foam glittering white in the frosty moonlight. Turning around, I looked down the length of the titanic beast-machine and saw that we were at a point less than a fifth of the way from the prow. Greenox, such size! Yet, of even greater interest, I was able to see in the distance the tremendous tail flukes of the machine rising above and slapping the surface of the sea with eruptive, powerful strokes—with a slow, regular rhythm—propelling *Thebes* towards uncharted worlds!

Julia coughed, and I realized that my bulk was blocking most of her view. I climbed down and faced Moab squarely.

"Master, how by all the gods do you move this enormous contrivance?"

But he only smiled and said, "You will understand when you see, my friend, in due course, for the propulsion room is the final compartment in the vessel. Patience, Xulê."

We left the port fin control room, following the corridor to the right. We stopped for a moment to inspect the crew's quarters which was a spacious area furnished with crude but adequate wooden bunks. I had seen many such bunks aboard the quadriremes and quinqueremes of the Roman Navy. The difference here being that these bunks had no chains or manacles attached.

Across the hall from the crew's quarters was a storeroom filled to the ceiling with an assortment of salted and dried meats, nuts, and fruits, and barrels of fresh water, which we learned was a by-product of the power generation. A little farther along, the passageway divided, one branch jogging off at right angles to the left. Moab explained that in that direction lay the starboard fin control room. Adjacent to this compartment, just at the point where the hall veered to the right again, was a door quite unlike the bolt-studded, iron-grey doors and hatches we had already grown accustomed to. This door was solid bronze, shining brightly even in the dim red light of the colored globes. Moab made no move to stop here, mentioning only, "This is the Master's Stateroom. You will find that I am frequently there." I thought that the second part of that remark was rather odd, its meaning, by rights, being self-evident. Yet, Moab, as I learned as the days progressed, had his own notions about his personal conduct. As we passed by the door, I noticed a small copper plate was attached a little below my eye level. Emblazoned on the plate was the single word: MOAB.

Next, our host pointed out the guest rooms, two on either side of the passage.

"These will be your rooms, my friends. I'm sure you will find them suitable at least, if not comfortable."

I opened the metal door of the room that he had designated as mine—Greenox preserve me! The place was hung to the hilt with combed lion skins and carpeted with antelope pelts of every brown imaginable. Above the bed, two bronze-headed spears crossed through the heavy, black mane of an especially large lion, while two razor-sharp and bone-handled axes crossed on an adjacent wall. And the bed! The bed was obviously soft! And covered with leopard furs!

By the goddess' fountaining . . . ! A tub! This was a room more properly assigned to a senator or visiting dignitary than to a weathered and much-scarred gladiator veteran like myself.

"Greenox's gushing . . . !" I exclaimed. "Old Greek, what am I to do in a room like this? I'm more used to wooden pallets and flat rocks."

"Xulê, a woman of your obvious worth and loyalty deserves far more than rock to sleep on. I ask you to try it . . .

then, if after honestly trying to develop a taste for the simpler comforts of life, you still find the room unacceptable, then we'll make other arrangements."

"That sounds fair, old man. I agree to your terms. I'll try to grow accustomed to the plush comfort of it all. But, mistress, let's see your room. If mine is fit for a king, what must yours be like?"

Julia stepped over to the door of her room, which we learned was the room next to Frigga's, pulled the latch down and slowly pushed the door open . . . . Gods! This was no room! This was a palace! Rubies and sapphires and a myriad other gems—and braided gold hung in clusters and ribbons from each of the four dark wood posts that supported the embroidered silken canopy. The bed itself was strewn with rich velvets and exquisitely colored fabrics from the four corners of the empire. The carpets were of brightly dyed wools—wine red, amber, cobalt blue, jade green, orchid violet, and more—and woven thick as hawsers. Silken draperies covered the walls, and yard-high mirrors of polished copper set in frames carved in the likenesses of a phoenix, a griffin, and a sphinx adorned the three walls opposite the door. A bureau and stool of solid cast silver sat nicely in one corner, and an ivory-inlayed acacia-wood tub filled another. Even the clothes hooks were of gold!

Quoth Julia, "Moab, my friend, you certainly know how to do right by a girl! You spoil me nearly as much as I was used to!"

To which Moab humbly replied, "The daughter of the Caesar deserves no less, my dear. Your personal belongings will be brought to you shortly. Then you may arrange things just as you like. But shall we continue? There is only a little more."

Our next stop was the library, which was comfortably arranged with hammocks and several stuffed settees. Cushions, too, and vividly hued pillows were cast about to the number of a dozen or more. Built against the walls were numerous scroll-racks and shelves heaped with ancient and modern writings—everything from the Sumerian epic Gilgamesh to Livy's latest works. Of course, the walls were hung with bright material of varied and expensive sorts, and the floor was of rich, dark rosewood. The finishing touch was several white marble busts—of Homer, Hippocrates, Philolaus, the Egyptian Amenhotep, Socrates, and others of the same sort—securely fastened to raven-black pillars at various strategic spots around the room. Altogether, it was certainly a formidable chamber, to be utilized by the best-honed of the world's great minds. I imagined, in fact, that I would pass many a pleasant hour there.

Once Moab was certain we were duly impressed, he led us through one of the library's two communicating doors—the other being to his own cabin—to the main control and navigation room, the nerve center of the entire ship. Here, there were seven or eight men busy at some of the most peculiar instruments I have ever seen: arrays of hanging balances, swinging hour glasses, delicate glass yellow-and-scarlet-liquid-filled tubes, and other paraphernalia which defy my powers of description, and which, to this day, even after living with them for as long as I have, I do not fully understand except to say that they dealt with matters such as the level of the ship, its depth, speed calculations, and increments of time. Some of the devices were even able to determine the position of *Thebes* at all times relative to the sun and stars. From this room the course of *Thebes* was directed. Orders were sent from here to the fin control rooms and to the aft propulsion room via flexible copper tubes which—wherever else they might lead or branch to—all began at the captain's station, a raised lectern which overlooked the entire room. Radiating in all directions, the tubes disappeared into the bulkheads where they led to every compartment and corridor, thereby giving Moab complete control over his vessel. He explained that all he needed to do to communicate with any other compartment was to talk into one or other of these hollow tubes and his orders were conveyed by echoes the length and breadth of the ship, either to individual compartments or to the entire ship, as he so pleased. Naturally, these tubes allowed communications in both directions.

And, of course, the control room was fitted with a spiral stair leading to a glass observation chamber above.

Then we came to the featureless catapult room, a bare, iron space in the center of which were two giant wooden catapults that, we learned, were constantly manned and ready for any emergency, especially wise given our soon-to-be renegade status. Nearby was a store of boulders and barrels of oil placed within easy reach of the artillerymen. This is where they also stored their other weapons—bows, arrows, swords, and suchlike.

"But, Moab," Julia queried, "how do you launch your missiles and flaming oil? The ceiling and hull seem completely solid."

Moab smiled and made a motion to the two freedmen who were standing at attention nearby, and they strode over to a length of rope which hung from a large pulley suspended near the ceiling and began to pull down in swift jerky movements. Then, with a great squeak and rumble, the ceiling moved back slowly and slid up onto the whale-ship's back, revealing the great starry expanse above.

Julia turned and gazed at the old master with an expression of reverence, a feeling I easily shared. Moab coughed, blushed, and hurried out of the catapult room, signaling to his men to return things as they were.

Finally, we came to the end of the passageway, stopping before a door which Moab explained led to the main propulsion room. He pushed the door open and let us through.

Instantly, we were enveloped in an oppressive heat and stench, and blinded by an intense flickering light. Yet, despite the discomfort, the area was filled with song . . . not the knell-like droning of galley slaves, but the lilting chanty of a happy, well-fed crew. Sitting on two benches were twenty men wrapped in towels and rolling dice, laughing and swearing loudly at one another. Another twenty sweating filthy fellows—the ones who were singing—were occupied pushing a massive horizontal wheel. This wheel was about

20-feet in diameter and designed like a chariot wheel with the exception that the twenty thick-beamed spokes protruded out past the rim, providing plenty of leverage for the laboring men.

As they heaved the wheel around, a series of gears, pulleys, and rods were activated that alternately stopped and unstopped two steam vents, which were the heart of the entire propulsion system. The power itself was created by, as Moab had said, nothing more complex than boiling water. In an uncanny way, Moab had devised a means of funneling steam from comparatively small boilers into narrower and narrower pipes and tubes, which steam then emerged at tremendous speed and pressure from the two vents in scalding streams aimed at a circular paddle device that spun and whistled first in one direction then the opposite direction as the two vents were alternately closed and opened. The whirling paddle-wheel, in conjunction with other gears and rods, then lifted the monstrous flaxen and bronze tail-flukes high and then lowered them an equal distance, thus propelling the wondrous craft through the seas. The speed of travel was determined by the speed with which the men turned the great horizontal wheel, thus increasing or decreasing the rate of flow from the vents.

All the excess steam and smoke from the boilers was continuously sucked out of the atmosphere with gigantic bellows and then piped to the front of the ship where the smoke was eliminated through the all-too-realistic blowhole and the steam was recycled into potable water. Then, just as soon as *Thebes* surfaced, other bellows forced in fresh air, replenishing the stagnant air. When the craft submerged, however, it was necessary to dampen the fires, slow the ship down to minimum speed, and send snorkel tubes to the surface whenever possible. The depth to which *Thebes* was able to submerge was limited only by the length of these tubes, though towards the end of our adventure, we were able to circumvent that limitation and descend to depths even unimaginable to venerable, old Moab. But more of that in its place.

This entire propulsion system proceeded smoothly when the vessel was in motion, but a major problem had to be dealt with at all times in order to maintain the safety and integrity of *Thebes*. The hazard was a mechanical one which resulted from the constant motion of the various moving parts—the gears, pulleys, and such. If not continuously lubricated, all these moving parts would quickly wear out. To combat this, four men were specially detailed with heavy brushes and thick grease to circulate among the moving parts, slapping them thick with the stuff. And since nearly all of these parts were suspended in the air between the bulkheads with beams, three of these men worked on catwalks and scaffolding installed over and around the thrusting beams, creaking hinges, and whirling wheels.

The noise level was far too intense to allow normal speaking, so after watching for a time the amazingly coordinated activity, we finally exited through a second door which opened opposite the captain's library. No sooner than the heavy iron door shut behind us, Julia put her arm around Moab's shoulders and exclaimed, "Pluto's den, I have been there now, by the gods! Your men must be paid well to slave in there voluntarily, Greek."

"You are quite correct, my dear," Moab responded, "though 'slave' is hardly the right word. It has been long since any of these men were slaves or worked for a slave's pittance. In fact, it has not been many years since most of these men were marked for the games—some as gladiators, some as fodder to sate the bellies of starving beasts—but I was sufficiently well-to-do to purchase the most able men I could find, men who could help me build and guide the vessel of my dreams. And having bought them as slaves, I immediately gave them their freedom, offering them a good wage to remain and work with me.

"And such was their faith in me and the project that would culminate in *Thebes*, they stayed to a man. Furthermore, each and every one has pledged himself to our forthcoming adventure. And despite their affection for me, and their willingness to stay with me, I have promised them that should we find a new and hospitable land in which to settle they all have the right to chose to stay or leave as they desire."

"Master Moab," Julia piped, "right now, I want only to wash the sand and sun from my body . . . to lie in a soft bed . . . to swim in cool silk . . . and to decide which of your men I'll first bed down with. I must admit, you seem to have chosen a fine crew . . . a fine crew indeed! Whatever else our voyage might hold, it certainly promises not to be entirely boring . . . no . . . more than likely not boring at all!"

And with this last remark, she turned and strode spritely down the passage to her room, which she quickly entered, pulling the door shut after herself.

Beaming—that is to say, beaming as well as a face shriveled like a raisin can—Moab turned to me and said in a clear, quiet voice: "Julia, darling that she is, will claim a world someday, Xulê. But somehow I feel it will not be this one. One thing I can tell you is that more worlds abound than meet the eye." And with that enigmatic comment he excused himself and stepped into the library.

Left alone, I followed Julia's example and went to my own room, filled with thoughts of immersing myself in a tubful of scented water. But once inside, the sight of a platter of steaming roast lamb and a flagon of crimson plum wine shoved all thoughts of a bath from my mind. Lustily, I sat myself down on the bed and attacked the meal to good purpose. I ate as I had not eaten for two years! As you can well imagine, fish and clams and coarse brown bread are no fit diet for one such as I. Aren't I the most cunning and vicious and able fighter of all Nubia, Black Strobe, and Rome combined! No! Fish and bread and the occasional stringy sea-fowl were not my fare. Give me a shank of roasted meat and a villain to brain, and I'll be content!

Finishing this sumptuous feast, I finally bathed—an elegant experience which I could write about for many feet of papyrus, but will refrain from—and eventually lay my naked, sore body on the down mattress, drinking in its feathery caresses.

I was just drowsing off, thankful for our good fortune and blissfully considering sleeping the night away, when the ear-shattering toll of a gong resounded mercilessly through my skull, quite effectively voiding any such self-indulgent fancies. Then a full, rich resonant voice—not loud, but terribly earnest—filled my compartment:

"Submerge *Thebes*! Down! Submerge! Emergency!"

***

Hardly had I become aware of the urgent cry, having thrown on a garment, I found myself in the corridor beside Julia and Frigga. Inside of a breath, Frigga took the initiative.

"To the control room," she cried, and we raced down the corridor, men running before us and behind us as they hurried to their stations. My only thought as we ran was—How does one fight a decent fight when surrounded and protected by thick iron walls?

In a moment we burst into the control room. Moab and Livinius were there already, directing five men who were busy pulling controls and cranking wheels.

"More water!" Moab bellowed with a force I hadn't suspected he could muster. "More water! We must submerge faster! Now!"

Submerge? Only now did I realize that the whale-ship was off the level, slanting gradually downward. Great Greenox! We were under water and sinking deeper with each passing second! Of course, I understood intellectually that *Thebes* was designed for just this purpose, but to accept it emotionally was quite another matter. As I stood there in the control room beside the two women, not for one minute did I really believe that we were completely underwater.

"But how?" asked Julia, as soon as she too realized the full implications of Moab's order. "We never did learn . . . how do you control the vertical movement of *Thebes* in the water? What makes it sink, then rise to the surface again?"

She was not questioning anyone in particular, seeing that Moab and the control room crew were working frantically, but merely thinking out loud. Frigga, however, replied confidently, "You see, Julia, *Thebes* has not one hull, but two—a slightly smaller one inside a larger one. The space between the two hulls is completely empty when *Thebes* is on the surface, but when she must submerge, cranks are turned which open vents in the outer hull and water floods in with enormous force causing the craft to sink. The more water that fills the space between the hulls, the deeper and faster *Thebes* will sink. When it is time to come to the surface again, some of the steam from the boiler is diverted from the propulsion system into the space between the hulls and forces the water back out of the vents. When we have risen to an acceptable height the vents are closed and we're back at the surface."

"Ingenious, even if I do say so myself," we heard Moab say. "Thank you, Frigga. Your explanation was quite concise."

We turned, but Moab was already busy consulting one of his men, passing out instructions and inquiring into the moment-by-moment state of the ship.

Livinius, I saw, was engaged in supervising the four men who worked rapidly with the mechanisms set into the forward-starboard corner of the room. At one time, he happened to look my way, and the concerned expression on his face bent into a grim frown. Then he glanced at Julia, but his attention did not linger, turning quickly back to the problem at hand. I didn't need a tutor to know that I had an enemy in Livinius. But, by the looming sight of Greenox, what was life without enemies to slaughter or be slaughtered by?

Just then, a man we had not at first seen rushed down the stairs from the observation chamber above and busied himself with more instruments that I did not understand. Seeing that the transparent dome was not at that moment being used, I glanced at Moab, who looked my way only long enough to nod authorization. I clambered up the steps and saw, when I reached the top, that *Thebes* was indeed under water, that there was nothing but water over and around me, and that I could actually see fish being tossed about, illuminated dimly by the eerie, distorted moonlight that penetrated into the madly swirling sea. Yet, the surprise this vista inspired in me was as nothing compared to the jolt I would experience the next moment.

As I watched, thrilled by the insane beauty of it all, the wooden prow and keel of a 75-foot long galley cut the surface overhead, propelled by the stark rhythm of forty long-oars. Without doubt those on board her who saw *Thebes* slip right under her nose were startled by the momentary sight of such a great whale—but not for an instant could they have realized it wasn't a whale they suddenly saw in the darkness. Even now, the officers and men on deck were probably gawking in wonder at the last bits of white froth that had marked our presence a moment before.

The next instant, the man whose place I had taken in the glass dome returned, pushing himself past me, peering in all directions, then yelling down: "All clear! Ship clear off the port beam." Then, he was back down the stairs again, only to be replaced in a flash by Julia.

"O, Neptune!" she cried. "So it's true then! The sea is now my home . . . below as well as above!"

"Apparently," I responded, "that is indeed the case. If this machine truly works . . . and without killing us . . . it would seem that we, like the fish, will call the great seas our home."

"How I wish Quinctius Crispinus could share this with me," she went on, "or Cornelius Scipio. He too would have thrilled to this sight as too few men can. But, alas! They are dead or are somewhere in exile, aren't they, dear Xulê. And Appius Claudius Pulcher and Sulla Validus and the rest. All they had offered me was their love, and they all died or were banished for it! Mars above!"

The next instant, there came an ear-splitting crash and the terrible rending of wood and iron being torn like parchment, and the whale-ship lurched wildly to starboard, throwing Julia clear to the deck below. Not having sea legs, I too was left hanging by my fingers to the handrail. Dropping to the deck, I pulled Julia to her feet, and together we lifted up Moab who lay stunned against a bulkhead. He shook his head, putting his hands to his temples, then remembering, he cried, "Full about! Overtake that galley! She's been broadsided! All hands to rescue stations!"

Suddenly, I felt the ship swing about. Once again, both Julia and I were caught off balance. Enviously I watched Frigga strutting around the control room, not seeming to notice the frequent sudden movements of the ship at all. And thankfully, she seemed totally unconcerned with Julia's and my unfortunate awkwardness, as she went around watching and, as I found out later, studying the activities of each of the men working the control mechanisms and aiding them as she was able.

When I regained my footing, I, with Julia right behind me, raced to get another view through the dome. Straight off the bow I could just make out not one, but two ships' hulls. As we moved closer, it became obvious that the two galleys were aligned perpendicularly to one another, and that one was stoved in.

Moab bawled out from below, evidently getting his information from the forward observation domes via the communication tubes, "It looks to be a Persian warship.

Probably pirates. And the Imperial galley is sinking fast! Bring us alongside! Full speed!"

So absorbed was I in this drama that I didn't at first notice that we were surfacing. No sooner did I realize this, than the dome broke water and the sky was full of stars twisted by the seas running off the glass. Both vessels were aflame, and many men with sword, spear and crossbow were intertwined, jabbing and slashing. The Roman defenders fought bravely and fervently but their crumpled ship was sinking fast in a vortex of rising flame, and their screaming foes were a horde of demons reaping a plentiful harvest. Yet there would be little pillage, it was sure. There would be little enough time for the victors to regain their own ship and put out the fires before she, too, was lost. The Persians this time would have to content themselves with glory only, for the baubles they sought would soon be food for the fish.

Then, as I watched, *Thebes* came around and picked up speed, moving some distance out. Then she turned and sped back the way she had come, faster and faster, ramming speed surely being her goal. She crashed through the dividing seas on a perfect collision course broadside to the raider. Moab was going to ram the pirates! I couldn't believe this!

Why would he want to help Romans?

Julia gasped as the flaming, groaning vessels loomed ever closer; then, with a horrible shudder and a crack which made the original sound of the two galleys colliding seem like a whisper, *Thebes* smashed into the raider, the whale-ship's broad snout acting as a perfect battering ram!

Quickly, we submerged, only to surface right under the broken hulk of the offending vessel, which was lifted into the air and capsized back into the cadaver- and debris-ridden wash.

We dived once more, than came up again close to the Roman vessel which was all but gone. I could see several men and children clambering about the awkwardly sloping deck, trying to get into a small boat that was bobbing furiously in the water. Suddenly, the galley rolled over and slipped beneath the waves, carrying many flaying forms with it. Though the smaller boat was tossed around a great deal, it weathered this last great upheaval and remained afloat. Amidst the pools of flaming oil and debris, the eyes of all the occupants of the small boat follow their galley as it pursued its unexpectedly defeated enemy deep into Neptune's domain.

As *Thebes* came abreast of the overloaded little boat, Livinius pushed himself between Julia and me and peered out at the survivors of this catastrophe—what looked to be about two dozen souls, mostly children.

"Out of my way, cupids!" he said roughly as he shoved. I was minded to make some comment or other appropriate rejoinder but then thought better of it considering the circumstances and only smiled at him, my teeth gritting like two stones being rubbed together.

Then, as we passed them by quite closely, some of the children saw our faces peering out at them from the innards of the crazed whale and pointed at us with looks of paralyzing fear. Never have I ever seen such faces distorted and twisted so by such terrible apprehension. Even as we observed and began to recognize their intensely overwrought state, at least two children appeared to collapse.

Moab brought *Thebes* about one more time, circled the boat, then, again surprising me, headed far out to sea as though leaving the frightened children to their fate. Then, just as unexpectedly, *Thebes* came about and directed its snout directly at the small craft for all the world as though to ram it!

As we drew nearer, the looks on the children's faces—as on the older survivors—were no longer human but mirrored those most abysmal pits of Hades that even demons fear. Here, I glanced at Julia. Her entire frame had become a single knot of fury, every muscle taut, ready to leap down into the control room and somehow avert the impending disaster, to divert the steaming monster even if she had to kill to accomplish this.

Part Four

The Imperial Novices of the College of Augurs

Yet, the next moment, I saw the great whale's maw begin to open. Steadily, the monstrous upper jaw lifted till it blocked my view. It was evident, however, that rather than ramming the little boat, Moab intended to take aboard the survivors, while on the run! No doubt, he assumed, as I would have, that there were other marauders in the area and he had no intention of making their acquaintance.

Even without touching her, I could feel Julia relax.

"Never again! Never again!" she moaned, gulping. "By the great gods' bowels, never again do I want to know such suspense! Mars only knows how close I was to killing that old Greek, damn him!"

Thebes continued moving ahead slowly. Then the jaw began to drop into place, and simultaneously the whale-ship put on sail, so to speak, quickly leaving the remaining wreckage burning and smoldering behind us. The sharks would have their fill this night.

Julia and 1 jumped down into the control room just as Moab and Frigga rushed out from his stateroom and I caught a glimpse of its ornate, brass and tapestry filled interior. We caught up with our friends, then the four of us legged it down the passage till we faced the double doors which opened into the whale's mouth. Moab gestured to Erasmus who moved to the doors, pushing aside a small metal plate at eye level that revealed a tiny window against which the lieutenant put his eye. Evidently seeing that all was safe, he summoned another man to his side, and together the two of them pulled on a rope, which, via a pulley, lifted the bracing beam out of the way. Then Erasmus cautiously opened one door. Peering out again, double checking that all was safe, and satisfying himself on this account, he kicked open the other door, and immediately the two women, Moab and I stepped through, squeezing Erasmus against the doorjamb as we passed.

There, afloat under the false-baleen ceiling was the small boat with fifteen occupants, thirteen of whom were children. Of the other two, one was a surprisingly neat (considering. the trial he had just endured) young fellow of about twenty-five years dressed in a sea-green linen robe. The other was a battered, bloodied, great-bearded, war-hardened centurion of about twice the age of the younger man. The children, all of whom seemed to be about nine or ten years, and who also were dressed in plain raiment, seemed no less frightened to death than they had when seen through the glass observation dome.

The moment we appeared through the doors, the centurion began to yell and wield a short sword.

"Where in Hades are we?" he bellowed. "What kind of wizardry have we met with? In the name of sweet Jupiter! by Mars the damned! What is going on here? Who are you and what is this thing?" By this last he meant *Thebes*.

Moab cried back, "All is safe! Bring your boat here."

"But we have no oars!" volunteered the younger man.

"Wait! We'll throw you a line."

In a few moments the boat had been pulled alongside the deck, and the children were standing, shivering from both fear and cold, by our sides.

The centurion, grimly facing Moab now, asked: "But who are you? Who is the authority here . . . wherever here is?"

"You are now guests aboard *Thebes*," Moab answered plainly. "And I am the authority here—Moab, builder and Master of *Thebes*. We are happy to have you as our guests, however, accommodations may be a little cramped."

"Thebes? What does Thebes have to do with this monstrous conveyance?" inquired the younger man. "Thebes is a city of my own country—Greece. What does one have to do with the other?"

"Thebes is also the Greek name given to the Egyptian metropolis of Waset, the very same city the Romans call Diospolis. 'Hundred-gated Thebes' is older by centuries, if not millennia, than its Greek counterpart, my friend, as you should well know, from the looks of you."

"But what is this hollow fish?" demanded the centurion.

"This hollow fish, as you call it," answered Moab, smiling, twisting and contorting his permanently bent body so that the smile could be seen by the taller centurion, who was only average height. "This monstrous conveyance is but a boat—a boat which I designed and which was built under my instructions. Simply stated, it is a submersible. You have already seen, I'm sure, its ability to run submerged. It was built so that I might study my starfishes in peace."

"Starfishes!" the Roman and the Greek cried at once.

"Well, the whole marine habitat, actually, but starfishes are my joy."

"If I understand it, then, you built a craft which will sail under water simply so that you can study starfishes," continued the Roman.

273

"Essentially, yes."

"Then you are mad, and it is any wonder that you tried to kill us just now."

"Madness is a relative state of mind...uh...uh...I don't believe you have properly introduced yourselves, yet.... In any case, you were picked up quite gently, I assure you, centurion. And, as for that other service I have done for you today, I believe you owe me a word of thanks for having saved you from those murderous pirates."

"Yes, I suppose we do owe you at least that. I am Publius Flavius Germanicus, last surviving man of the Special Guard assigned to protect these children, the Imperial Novices of the College of Augurs. Mars knows, we did our best. Eighteen good men slain, and to what purpose? Phooey!"

We were all looking at the children, now. Could these bedraggled, shivering, and frightened babes be in fact the omniscient heirs to that divine, nearly omnipotent institution which guided the Destiny of Rome?

"In any case, we do thank you for saving our lives." This was the young Greek. "Publius' manners are not the best—but neither are they meant to be. I am Herodotus, tutor to these spawn of the gods. We were traveling in secret, without escort, to avoid suspicion to the Imperial Palace in

Sardinia, where they had hoped to study for the winter. If you could be so kind to just drop us off at any convenient spot where we could get word to the Pontifex Maximus"—here Julia flinched—"of our imperiled situation, I'm sure that you will be well rewarded."

Publius was standing opposite Julia, and I saw that he had ceased fuming to some degree and was eyeing her in a peculiar manner. All the while that Herodotus talked, the centurion's eyes roved over the mostly bare body and face of my dear mistress. To be sure, Julia offered much to see, but it occurred to me that simple arousal was not at the bottom of his sudden interest. Then, much to his own surprise, he took notice of Frigga, the perfect double of Julia except for her coloring. His expression changed so drastically that I thought I would burst out laughing.

"By the gods!" he ejaculated. "You're twins! And if I didn't know that she was imprisoned on Pandateria, I'd swear that you were both Princess Julia! But wait! Pandateria is less than a day's run from here! Jupiter's harlots! What kind of damnable plot have we stumbled on? Who are you? Both of you! But first the darker wench, who I swear is the traitress Julia to her last wanton hair!"

Now, for the first time, one of the children, a boy who all this time appeared somewhat less concerned than the others, and who was dressed differently only insofar as his plain robe was fringed with red embroidery, chose to speak up.

"You are so right, Publy. This one"—here he pointed to Julia—"is indeed the Princess Julia, an observation which I believe you would have done better to keep to yourself."

Here, I saw Herodotus' eyes start. It seemed he was about to squall something; then, thinking better of it, he quickly recovered his aplomb.

"Excuse me," Herodotus said. "I haven't introduced the children. This impetuous lad is Pliny. His powers of divination are somewhat more sensitive than the others, and for that reason the other children are under his authority in regard to most things. Of course, the High Priest of the College and any of the adult augurs have authority over them all and myself as well. I am merely a humble teacher. Then, of course, the Pontifex Maximus has final authority....as you well know, Julia, daughter of Augustus, daughter of the Pontifex Maximus. Yes, I have no doubt that you are Julia, for if you live and work with these novices for as long as I have, you learn they are seldom wrong, and Pliny is never wrong. Wait! Let me introduce the others."

And the young Greek teacher slowly walked by the ragtag children, scolding them into forming into some kind of rough formation. Then, when they stood in two lines facing us, some still scared, some turning shy, Herodotus walked back slowly tapping each child softly on the brow and running through their names.

"This is Sataspes, Jason, Loot, Pambasa, Titus, and 'Isaac — fine boys every one. And the girls...this is Helen, Semele, Ana, Pomona, Livinia, and Mariam—each one a goddess in her own right, as I'm sure you can see."

"And I am Xulê," I volunteered, "Julia's most trusted ally. We are as one, in fact, and he who does Julia wrong faces death at my hands."

All faces turned towards mine, but I saw there would be no argument. I simply looked as fierce as I could and hoped that would be sufficient to forestall any needless rhetoric on Publius' part, for Herodotus I hardly took seriously.

"Ah, well stated, my delicious love," Julia offered in response. "Yes. The child is quite correct. I am Julia, famous for my debauchery and whoring, the scandal of the empire, disowned by my own father. All that may be true, but I'll tell you, I had fun doing it, and I wouldn't change a thing if I had to do it over again. That is nothing except the exile, but that is a long story I would rather not go into. The point is, I'm no longer imprisoned on that miserable little island. I am free again, though I might as well still be in exile...as I'm afraid you all are as well from this day on!

"But I'm forgetting myself. It appears everyone knows everyone else now except for this fair beauty." Julia wrapped her arm around Frigga's waist. "This is my new sister, Frigga of the North, enchantress of the heavens."

But Frigga chose not to speak just then, only raising her eyebrows and making eye-contact with all those standing on that hard iron deck in that cold and bizarre mouth.

Publius now chose his words very carefully. "Princess Julia, I heard you say something to the effect that we too"—he made a sweeping motion with his arm toward Herodotus and the children—"were in exile from this day on. Could you clarify that statement, please?" Despite the flowery wording, it was obvious that poor Publius was at the end of his tether. I braced myself, expecting him to wrench his sword from its scabbard again at any moment.

"I'll answer that," Moab broke in. "But first let's get inside. It is awfully uncomfortable out here. Let me show you to your new quarters where you can freshen up. Then we will eat, and afterwards we will discuss our future...objectively and with open minds, I hope, since I dare say you realize this whole business is a rather touchy situation. Now, please, please, come with me, come with me."

Evidently, something in Moab's words—possibly the mention of food—or the manner in which he spoke was sufficient to calm the centurion down, for I saw his fists unclench and his shoulders loosen.

Part Five

Master of the Boat

So, with Moab leading, the fifteen castaways stepped through the double doors into the belly of *Thebes*, the fabulous whale-ship.

Even as this strange company passed through the great doors, exclamations arose from the youngsters' throats. I could see that their fear was quickly changing to wonder and admiration. One of them, Pliny, called out to Moab who was some distance ahead, demanding in a shrill voice, "What powers her, old man? For such a large craft, you must have many slaves?"

"There are no slaves aboard this ship, my boy. Only earth, air, fire, and water...and many friends."

"In that case, steam must be your primary source of power."

"Quite right, quite right. I'm surprised that you should be aware of such things. Surely that is fairly worldly knowledge for a child, despite your rank."

Pliny closed his slack jaw and stared wide-eyed at the old Greek as they walked down the corridor. Finally the boy responded, "Old man, you forget to whom you are speaking. I am Pliny of the Imperial Soothsayers."

Moab smiled patiently and said quite sincerely, "Excuse me, Master Pliny, but we have only just met, and I was not yet cognizant of your amazing powers of perception."

"Well, now that you know, Greek—ah yes, I can tell by your clothing—I suggest you not forget."

As well seasoned as Moab must have been, as old as he appeared to be, even he was taken aback by the insolent tone in Pliny's remark. His jaw snapped shut audibly and he stopped in mid stride, his wizened face turning pink behind his whiskers.

"Now, just one minute...!"

Here, Julia, who had been walking beside me following behind the knot of excited children, pushed herself forward through the whole company and stopped before the small boy who was only a little more than half her height and smacked him hard across the face with her open right hand. Pliny whirled around and crashed face-first into a bulkhead. Then, instantly, Publius fell upon Julia and restrained her by the arms, though I doubt she had proved her point to her satisfaction. Even Herodotus, though at first stunned beyond words by Julia's action, launched himself into the melee, hanging onto Julia's thrashing legs for all he was worth.

At this point, naturally, my vision clouded with blood and I dragged the two knaves off my lady Julia and smashed their heads together, not so hard as to kill them, but sufficiently to teach them that I was annoyed by their actions. And, of course, I punctuated my attack with some appropriate palaver: "Sniveling bovine tripe! You dare lay hands on Julia? Is this how you serve your empire? May you rot in the nethermost sties of Pluto's yawning chasms...forevermore!"

But the centurion Plubius Flavius was no slouch. He recoiled instantly from my smashing attack and showed that he feared neither advantage by weight nor height and rammed himself into my middle knocking my breath out, so that I gasped horribly for all to see and hear. But now, Julia was back in the midst of the affair, falling upon Plubius with a vengeance, clawing, thrashing, and tearing wildly. Poor Herodotus was quite unconscious, he not being as fit as Plubius in the arts of combat, and lying queerly against a bulkhead.

All this time, which I suppose was little more than a few moments in reality, Moab and the children stood back and watched. Though Old Moab took it all in stride, the Imperial

Novices were quite shocked. It was only when Julia drew her dagger and was about to push it into Publius' heart that Moab leaped into the action, thrusting himself between the blade and the battling soldier, thus shocking Julia into the realization of what she was about to do.

Dazed, but not in the least repentant, Julia detached herself from the soldier, an action which he utilized to his fullest advantage. Somehow he managed to kick one of my feet out from under me and we both fell crashing to the floor. It was only on account of several of Moab's men rushing to the scene, attracted by the noise and commotion, and pulling us apart that I suppose Publius lived. It is just as well, for in the end I learned to like the man and we parried many an enemy's bludgeoning offence together; but that is another tale, in another time, indeed, in another world!

But, at that particular moment, hate—a dripping and seething loathing—consumed our souls and contorted our countenances. As we were forcibly restrained, the thick air of that close corridor was filled with our maniacal curses.

Moab stepped between us and spoke: "Enough! There has been too much sacrilege and fighting born of ignorance this day. It seems that I somehow inspired the derision of a son of the College of Augurs. Yet, he, in point of fact, offended me, an old man who I believe gave no cause for such impudent behavior, even from one of such illustrious background and tender years. So Julia, the princess of the empire, naturally took it upon herself to defend my honor and punish the boy. But the boy, of no small account himself, was immediately defended by those to whom he was entrusted by the very highest authority. But Julia, the progeny of that very same authority, is not without a staunch protector of her own. So, noble Xulê here too became embroiled in this fast growing web of enmity. Then, of course, Julia, who prides herself as being no man's inferior, fell back into the fracas, and to what avail, I ask you? For honor? But whose honor is it that needs to be defended by a common brawl? Please! This is a small boat, and we are much cramped as it is, and we may need to spend a great deal of time in one another's company. Therefore, it is imperative that we patch up our differences!

"Since the trouble arose, I believe, from the misimpression that he child has that his authority is greater than mine—on my own ship!—I think this is the time to make clear that I am the commander of this vessel. I am the highest authority aboard *Thebes*, and my word is absolute. I will not have children telling me what to do. If they have something to say, then they may ask to speak, is that clear? Furthermore, I am not ignorant of the talent these particular children possess. Indeed, before our journey is finished, we may have more than enough opportunities to test their skill. And for that reason I will give them the respect they truly deserve. But I will not tolerate an insolent attitude or tone of voice directed toward myself. Is that clearly understood?"

This last question was obviously meant to be answered. Yet, poor Pliny, who was clearly thunderstruck, probably having never been spoken to thus, could only open and close his mouth and gibber a few spittle-flecked syllables. It was little flame-tressed, clear-skinned Pomona who replied on behalf of the startled and uncertain troop of prodigies. Stepping forward, she looked up at Moab and then at the rest of us. Her voice was soft and gentle:

"Master...Princess...fair Frigga of the North...Xulê — the thirteen of us ask you to understand and forgive the indiscreet and apparently arrogant remark by which our fellow, Pliny, hoped to make clear our own singular status within world affairs. It was not his intention, I assure you, to insult or give injury. I realize there is doubt in your minds as to the truth of this matter, but as Master Moab has mentioned, we are only children, and it is expected that we will spend much time henceforth in one another's company, so let us make amends all around, shall we?"

Though the perception and wisdom in the little girl's remarks were indisputable, Publius' and my own frames of mind were not so easily reconciled, for we snarled and growled at each other like two beasts defending their respective broods. It is even conceivable, I suppose, that we two looked ridiculous but I don't think it likely that there was man or woman living who would have laughed at us at that particular moment.

"Why, thank you, Pomona," Moab responded. "Your remarks are quite sincere, I have no doubt, and I am impressed by your extraordinary felicity. You can rest assured that I will not give the matter any further consideration so long as everyone here fully understands that the authority on this vessel will be properly respected at all times. That includes the officers of *Thebes* as well. And all of you who are guests aboard *Thebes* will be accorded the respect and privileges that guests are due. I ask for no questions or debate, for I am the law here, and none of you have any choice if you wish a degree of freedom aboard this ship. At the first sign of insubordination the guilty party or parties will be locked away in their rooms to be released at my pleasure. Now, if this is clearly understood by everyone here, I'm sure that internal harmony will be the rule aboard this vessel from this time on. Are we agreed?"

Somewhat reluctantly—for autocratic authority is seldom admired completely—all the children, including Pliny, Julia, and Frigga nodded or muttered assent. Only Herodotus, Publius and myself refrained from answering. On Herodotus' part it might have had something to do with the fact that he was still unconscious, but the centurion and myself were not about to make any further commitments until we could rest assured that one or the other of us had successfully embarked on his Last Journey to the Land of His Fathers, regardless if that land be a place of joy or not!

"But as I see that the heat of passion still rages in two of our fellows," Moab noted, "now would be a good time to set an example. Metellus, see to it that these two gallant contenders are safely locked away, won't you?" This last order was issued to one of the several sailors who were actively restraining Publius and me, with some success I have to admit.

Then Moab jerked a thumb in the direction of the guest rooms, and I was dragged away. Someone opened the door to my room and I was thrown inside like a sack of meal.

Behind me, the door was slammed clanging shut and bolted from the outside. From somewhere nearby there came similar metallic crashings, so I assumed that Publius Flavius Germanicus had been dealt with in like manner as myself.

Fury unimaginable consumed me. Consciously, with an effort worthy of the gods, I tried to dampen the fires raging inside me, and I had begun to think that my maddened brain would sheer through the normal confines of sanity when I spotted a slip of parchment being pushed under the door!

Pouncing on it, as though life were dependent on my action,

I read the few hope-preserving words that swam before my eyes:

RELAX, DEAR, XULÊ. YOUR RELEASE IS IMMINENT. IT IS ONLY A RUSE FOR PUBLIUS' SAKE. YOUR SWEET J.

Relief has come to me in many forms in many situations in my day, but never did relief feel so good as it did when I read that note in dear Julia's hand. In a flash I regained my composure, and waited out the next hour in high spirits, wistfully conjuring up visions of poor Publy's plight somewhere in a nearby room. Finally, the door of my compartment opened slowly and noiselessly, and I, just as silently, slipped out to meet the relieved and divinely lovely face of my mistress Julia, daughter of empire, Princess of Rome!*

*Editor's note: Unfortunately this is the end of Xulê's twelve scrolls. We are grateful that they conclude in a satisfactorily upbeat manner with a self-contained sense of resolution. For the time being, this must suffice, as we don't even know if Xulê wrote anything more before she eventually died of the stab wound described in her prologue. Also, we may never know whether the Ethiopian scrolls recovered from Emperor Theodore's library and taken to the British Museum and referenced by the scientists and engineers at the secret laboratories in Sierra Leone and Ecuador were in fact facsimiles of the Twelve Scrolls, which were clearly venerated by the local population of the time since they were found encased in white jade jars under a most uncommon dome-like structure. Furthermore, as I mentioned earlier, the two sets of documents (one from Ethiopia, the other from the depths of the Gulf of Mexico) being in any way related, as I have unconcernedly attempted to make them appear here (I fully admit), is nonetheless only the purest conjecture; still, the points of similarity are strong, and I hold to my opinion, or theory, that they are one and the same. However, if the Ethiopian scrolls were sufficiently detailed that they served as some sort of blueprints that Barbicane and Maxwell followed, then it follows, if they were copies of some previous iteration, as we are supposing, that Xulê's twelve scrolls were either originally much more detailed in a technical sense, or perhaps whatever it was that was copied and sent across the Atlantic to the Alexandrian Library millennia ago was another set of documents altogether—*almost* Xulê's scrolls but *different*. We may never know.

—T.K.M.

This haunting image is an artist's conception of how Moab's *Thebes* appeared at the time Xulê was writing her narrative. Notice that the submarine boat, or its master, appears to have an objective, the nativity star—that self-same star that Pius IX, Barbicane, and Maxwell strove to attain two millennia later. Though Barbicane says he improved the ship's propulsion system, Xulê's and Quatermass' descriptions are so alike that there is no reason to assume Barbicane altered significantly its structural integrity or appearance, thus this image could stand in for the *Nova* herself.

Eighth Prologue Chapter

Synchronization and Calibration

Thus it stood, Luna, for several weeks, our being housed pleasantly enough in the laboratory—though effectively against our will—though I, for Maria's sake, chose not to make an issue of the matter. After all, it was not as though Hans and I needed to be anywhere in particular and it was not as though our hosts were belligerent or indisposed overly much to our presence once they got used to our loitering around. They, however, quite ably diverted any suggestion or effort of mine to quit the place. (Well, I say that, but, of course, they would have given much to be rid of us; they simply didn't seem to have much of a choice; they were damned if they did and damned it they didn't.) And truth be told, I found that my curiosity had been piqued after I learned that the hoped for culmination of all this enormous work was expected in an unspecified "short time."

In fact, as you can imagine, Luna, I was torn. On one hand I truly enjoyed spending time with Maria. Though our backgrounds couldn't have been more different, I found I enjoyed the honest and straightforward interest she showed in Hans and me. I'd spent some time with her the year before, as I've said, and she certainly showed her intellectual side then, especially when propounding about the stars and comets, and I was affected then, as I was again in this instance, by her down to earth and straightforward and reliable manner— unlike so many of your sex, who are experts in deceit and prevarication and falseness generally—and I think I can say with some certainty that her affection for me was also sincere.

But on the other hand, I had a fortune burning a hole in my pocket. That diamond was enormous and I have no doubt, looking back on it, that its value would have been far greater than the value of all the diamonds Sir Henry and John Good and I brought back from King Solomon's Mines, which have made us all wealthy, and my life so comfortable here in Britain in my new home, the Grange.

[Luna: Here I had to interject and ask what became of the diamond, as it was clear that the story he was telling occurred a dozen years or so before he in fact became wealthy.]

Ah, Luna, you are the one who asked to hear my story, and if I were to tell you that now, I would have no finish to my story. But since you insisted and I am now well along, I am having fun recalling it all, as I haven't had any need to reflect on these incidents and circumstances to any degree before now. Now, where was I?

As I was saying, beyond my affection for Maria, I'd become interested and now I wanted to see how it all played out in the end. What could all this effort and material and money be for? Can you imagine the fortune all this must have cost—tens of thousands of workers, two 200-mile-long aqueducts, vast dam complexes arresting the flows of mighty rivers high in the mountains, power plants, and not one but two inconceivably large laboratories on opposite sides of the earth, the submersible boats . . . ? Aside from the vague awareness that it all somehow had to do with learning something about the Star of Bethlehem, Hans and I knew nothing and we had no choice but to cool our heels.

The huge pits we had seen being dug on either side of the lab as we approached it had reached a sufficient degree of completion that the scaffolding had by now been dismantled and removed. The excavating equipment was removed, too, and it was then that I realized just exactly what the many plants with chimneys were producing—they were smelting silver, and the insides of the pits, or bowls, were being covered with silver leaf. Thousands of square yards of pure silver. So you see, while Hans and I loitered, we saw a vast fortune in silver coat those two fantastically huge bowls—and there were two others presumably just like them all the way over in Ecuador. The more I learned, the more preposterous it all became. A telescope indeed! I was not so stupid to be fooled so easily any further . . . or so I thought just then, dear Luna.

Eventually in the middle of the bowls grew arrangements of tubing and wires and scaffolding of a different sort and from which all manner of unfamiliar equipment was suspended, all shaped into a pattern I cannot begin to describe other than to say that it was complicated to the extreme.*

----

* Editor's note: Quatermain's description of the mysterious bowls sounds similar to the Arecibo Observatory in Puerto Rico (as seen in the films *GoldenEye* and *Contact*) at least in terms of shape if not in composition. Thus one need imagine four such radio telescopes

At any rate, it was now about eight weeks after we had arrived at the laboratory gates. Maria and Maxwell told me over breakfast that they were ready to calibrate the machine to, in effect, connect both laboratories and the vast machines that they had built—to create one inconceivable machine! I suspected that whatever happened next, it would not be dull.

Maxwell said, "We're going to begin adjusting our apparatus today. It may interest you, though I fear there will not be anything interesting to actually see. We will pull some levers and twist some knobs, and then the four units, two on either side of the world, will be connected for the first time via the submarine cable that the governments have only just finished laying on the floor of the Atlantic Ocean, and then we will have to calibrate for a few days."

So Maxwell and Maria led me back to the workshop. Typically, by the way, as it will be pertinent later on, by then Hans had got into the habit of removing himself each morning and I'd not see him again till the late afternoon. He didn't volunteer what he'd been up to, and if I asked, he declined to answer.

----

forming an immense astronomical interferometer array pointed toward the constellation Aquila, two on the west coast of Africa and two on the west coast of South America.—T.K.M.

There was much more equipment in the room than the last time I'd been there. New shiny instruments had been neatly stacked on new racks that had been mounted onto the walls and new sturdy islands and tables had appeared mounded with still more equipment. I was led to the back of the room and we entered a dark alcove I'd not noted before, which was the case, I realized, because it had been screened off. Here there were two tables that seemed to be covered with toy buildings. But when lanterns had been ignited, what I saw reminded me of the table with the movable puzzle pieces by which Maxwell had explained the positioning of the continents. These tables were on either side of the room. The one on the right side of the room, closest to me, held not toys, but a model. It was obviously a representation of the very laboratory where we'd been honored guests all those weeks. It was a tiny reproduction of the main points of the facility, or town—the temple, the buildings, the trains and tracks, the aqueduct and power stations, and the two huge bowls that we'd only just seen completed. After I had oriented myself to the model, Maxwell led me across the room to another table with a similar model.

"This is the laboratory in Ecuador. As you see, its general makeup is similar to ours. We simply call it 'over yonder' usually."

And it was so. A small town with its own array of tracks—with two perfectly equivalent bowls!

"Now step back, Quatermain, and view the set up from that raised platform."

I did so and took in the sight before me. It certainly was impressive. I knew that the space between them represented both the Atlantic ocean and the whole breadth of the South American continent.

I said, "And with this you will listen to the mind of God?"

And then I heard an unfamiliar voice. It said in English with an Italian accent, "Yes, that is our hope."

I looked down toward the voice that had surprised me, and there stood a Roman Catholic priest, which was obvious from his collar. I climbed down from the platform and greeted the man.

Barbicane, who happened to enter just then made the introductions. "Quatermain, this is His Eminence, Alberto Cardinal Cigliutti, Prefect of the Holy Office and Vatican Secretary of State. Under the circumstances, his boss, as you can imagine, has a vested interest in our little experiment, and the Cardinal is here as an observer."

I shook the cardinal's hand and muttered something about an expensive toy, and he responded naturally enough, when I think back on it, "My dear Quatermain, I suppose you are speaking ironically or sarcastically. I can't tell which because my English is not up to such subtleties. Regardless, this attempt to glean something fundamental of the Almighty is one of the greatest works projects since the building of the Suez Canal, which pales by comparison. And it is infinitely more important, as the canal merely makes passage easier between west and east, whereas our goal is to receive the will of the creator of all the universe!"

I said something polite and turned to Barbicane and asked when the show would be on the road. What followed was exactly as Maxwell had predicted. Knobs were turned and levers pulled and orders recorded. To be polite, I hung around for a couple of hours and then retired to the hotel and took a nap.

Ninth Prologue Chapter

They Turn on the Machine

Thus it stood for a few days. Maria, Maxwell, Barbicane, and I would breakfast, then Maria and Maxwell would go straight to the workshop. Though Barbicane inevitably wound up there before long, he would always go elsewhere on inspection tours upon leaving the table.

Then one day I noticed that the hair all over my body had begun to tingle and stand up. Plus there was an unaccountable faint rushing sound in the air like running water that seemed to emanate from everywhere. It was both frightening and distinctly uncomfortable. Soon after I noticed this, I received a message that I was needed in the workshop. Hans, as usual, was nowhere to be found, and I went alone.

Maria met me at the door, clearly very excited. "Allan! All is ready! You're just in time. We need you now to please be a witness. Sh-h-h, James is going to speak." I saw that he and Barbicane and Cigliutti were standing at a chalkboard at the front of the room.

"Everybody!" Maxwell called out. Here, Luna, I should say that the room had somehow managed to squeeze in perhaps one hundred scientists and technicians, most of who were talking and comparing notes.

"Everybody!" They all finally quieted down and Maxwell continued, "The moment has arrived! We've all been working against the clock on an impossible deadline, and we have succeeded beyond our wildest dreams. On both sides of this planet earth we are pointing our telescope toward the constellation Aquila. The power that we harnessed is coursing through all the materials that surround us. Whatever happens next, we will be a better people for it!"

That was all. He stepped over to some equipment and turned a knob. Immediately, everyone in the room began their tasks, including Maria, who had a device over her ears and was listening intently, pad and pencil in hand. The next thing I knew, an array of tubes was flashing and sparks were flying everywhere. There were spinning wheels large and small. Switches were pulled and pushed, and meters and dials were moving like fury. The tingling and buzz that I'd been aware of all day intensified, frighteningly so.

Frankly, I felt more in the way than anything else, but Maria had told me that I was needed, so I remained.

Maxwell was on the raised platform. Cigliutti was next to him. Maxwell began screaming commands. It was controlled pandemonium for perhaps ten minutes.

And then it all stopped, and all was quiet.

Without being told, I knew that something had gone wrong. The room had grown hot and there was an air of disappointment. Maxwell didn't look happy. "All right gentlemen, we will recalibrate and try again in an hour!"

And what I have just described was repeated half a dozen times through the day and the disappointment turned to despondency. But they soldiered on and recalibrated again and again. In time, at nightfall, exhausted, Maxwell announced that they would stop and rest—rather than work—for 30 minutes before continuing.

It was towards the end of this respite that Hans finally appeared at my side. "Hans, where have you been. History is being made . . . I think."

"Well, Baas, if history has to do with spooks, then I have much to tell you. O, Baas! This day I've been haunted by more spooks than—"

But he was cut off, as Maxwell called out. Again, electricity flowed through the whole room, and sparks again flew and containers containing colored liquid began to gurgle and bubble furiously. Hans, despite his endless worldly posing, was clearly in awe of that show of exotic energy.

You could feel the tension increase, and this time the mood in the room swung over to joy.

Slowly, a peculiar steady hissing hum could be heard and soon overwhelmed all the mechanical sounds combined. It was a steady hiss that increased in volume. All the while Hans' eyes opened wider and wider (as mine must have also, truth to tell) and then, suddenly, I felt Hans' body jerk to attention. He seemed absolutely riveted. If it had been a momentary thing, I wouldn't have worried, as such shocks happen all the time—usually a tingling in the spine or a chill—but my concern increased as his eyes grew wider and as he stood thus longer and longer, and then his mouth began to open and close and his lips moved as though he was forming words, mainly without sound—but intermittently he vocalized some clicks that are part of his Hottentot language. I said something to him, but he was able to distinctly communicate "no," by words or change in posture I don't know, but I understood that I ought not interrupt.

Maxwell and the others were clearly riveted as well by the constant hiss that filled the room. I haven't mentioned it yet, but the room was filled with stenographers, listening to every word spoken by every soul in there and recording every one of those words-—Hans and me, too, for all I knew. Indeed, there were machines with pens that recorded all the other sounds, and they were responding wildly to the hum or hiss or whatever it was* I was worried about poor Hans, whose body had snapped to attention and stayed thus for nearly a half hour. But suddenly his body relaxed and folded, and he would have collapsed onto the floor if I hadn't caught him and quietly carried him out of the room.

---

* Editor's note: Though Maxwell and his colleagues could not have imagined its existence, there is little doubt that their magnificent observatory, or earth-spanning telescope, stumbled upon the key (without recognizing it, of course) that has since proven the existence of the Big Bang and the expansion of the universe. They had accidentally isolated the Cosmic Background Radiation (CBR), which formed mere millennia after the Big Bang and which had been extrapolated from Einstein's general theory of relativity and predicted by George Gamow, Ralph Alpher, and Robert Herman in the 1940s. However, the CBR was not officially "discovered," albeit again accidentally, until the 1960s, this time by Robert Wilson and Arno Penzias of Bell Labs in New Jersey, winning them the Nobel Prize in Physics.—T.K.M.

HANS' STORY

CHAPTER ONE

Hans Steals the Diamond

Once we were outside and Hans was steady on his feet, I said, "What on earth happened to you in there? It looked like you were hit by lightening!" A simple enough observation and question, I suppose, and here is the gist of his response.

"Baas! Baas! You will not believe! I've seen and heard your Predikant father, and while I did in fact see him, the conversation was all on his side and thus I mainly heard him."

Now, Luna, Hans was always making the most ridiculous pronouncements, especially having to do with things he could know nothing about—statements rife with superstition.

"What is it, Hans? What do you mean? I'll admit that you seem more pale under that yellow skin of yours!"

"O, Baas, you don't know the half of it."

"What do you mean that you saw my father, the Predikant, and that he spoke to you?"

"Baas, I am easily bored by all the chatter that I don't understand and it hurts my head and that is why I always go off somewhere in the mornings. Well, Baas, as you know, they have here a sort of general store and the folk who tend the store are much like you, Baas, and are very neat and take the garbage out to bins during the day. Well, this morning I chanced to be in the area when I noticed that the door had not been fully closed the last time the garbage went out. Out of curiosity, I peered through the slight space between the door and its jamb, and lo! what do I see but a case full of square-face. Your Predikant father will scold me, I'm sure when I reach the Place of Fires, but I could not help myself nor could I control my hand as it squeezed between the door and its jamb of its own accord and grabbed two bottles. I told my hand and arm that they had sinned but that didn't stop them from uncorking the bottles."

"Hans, you silly fool, stop the speech. You are trying to tell me that you stole a couple of bottles of gin and got drunk."

"Yes, that is it exactly, Baas."

My thought was to shrug off this admission, as it was hardly the first time Hans had transgressed the rules of life as laid down by my father.

"Yes, Baas, but this time it was far more than that. First of all, as I was getting drunk, I felt very guilty—far more guilty than I have ever felt before while stealing square-face and getting drunk and sinning before the spirit of your Predikant father who I served so faithfully since you were a boy, Baas!

"One other thing, Baas, as I slept this morning, I dreamed of that pretty but evil diamond that I found in the temple pool. Do you remember that diamond, Baas? Do you remember who found that diamond and nearly drowned for the sake of that pretty stone? Thus, while you still slept, O, Macumazana!, I took the stone that you always keep wrapped with paper and string from your pocket where you always keep it so that it won't get lost, and I substituted an ordinary stone also in paper and string."

"O, no, Hans, don't tell me you lost it!"

"O, no, yourself, Baas. No, I didn't lose it. But, of course, my guilt was doubled now because I had two thefts on my conscience and was drunk besides and knew full well that your Predikant father was looking up at me from the Place of Fires and that he frowned very sadly as he did so. As all this is going through my mind, I wandered over to the temple because the falling water and rising spray and thunderous roar always seem to relax my mind, and because of my great guilt, I very much needed to calm my head down."

Now I knew precisely what Hans was saying because I have myself felt a special tranquility when I have been at the temple, and, as such, I was sometimes drawn to it myself unaccountably.

He continued: "As soon as I got there, Baas, everything changed. The sun that had been hot and bright went behind a cloud and all became dark and cold. I shivered and my knees felt weak and I sat down on the marble floor with my back to the well and pulled my knees up to my chest and huddled up to myself."

Luna, Hans then paused in his story and looked inquisitively up to the skies, probably toward the Heaven that my father taught him about, and also toward the ground, where many Africans—including Hans' Hottentot forebears, of course, believe their afterlife will be played out—in the "Place of Fires" . . . . But, I'm sorry, Luna, you already know this. Also, I fear I'm repeating myself."

[Luna: That's quite all right, Allan. I wish I could forget most of what I had never asked to learn.]

As I was saying, Hans paused and then he said, "Now here it becomes confusing, Baas. I probably fell to sleep, but I cannot say for sure. Well I remember the sudden cold and my shivering, and I looked over toward the forest edge and I saw something sparkle. At first I thought it looked like a cloud of embers. Then I realized that it was a cloud of embers, and I thought I saw someone step out of the burning cloud. Then I was afraid because I realized that people don't step out of embers and then I knew that it was a spook. I was still cold and didn't want to see the spook, and so I closed my eyes. I think they were closed for a long time, but, of course, after a time I had to open them. I saw that the cloud of embers was still there and that the figure that had been emerging from it had not moved from where I first saw it, but now that I'd opened my eyes, it began to walk toward me, neither slow nor fast and I knew right away who it was, Baas. It was your Reverend Predikant father."

"You were drunk, Hans."

"Perhaps you are right, Baas. So in that case I saw your father while I was drunk. But he was a spook, I'm sure, just the same, Baas. Now, you know how much I hate spooks, even if they disguise themselves as your Predikant father. So I shut my eyes once more and covered my face with my hands, and put my head between my knees, and rolled over on my side and faced toward the well wall.

"Well," Hans continued, "eventually I opened my eyes and looked to see your father still walking toward me, but by then I'd learned that pretending it didn't exist did no good, so I decided to watch and wait. That it was your father, or perhaps a spook who did a good job of seeming to be your father, I had no doubt. In time, he stopped right in front of me and patiently waited for me to pay attention. Finally, I was able to say something."

"What did you say to him?"

"I said to your Predikant father, 'Whoa, Baas! Why are you here? What do you want of me?' And he said, 'Hans, my old friend, do not be scared. I need you to do one or two things for me.'

"'Ask me anything, O, father of Macumazana,' I said, "'and you know I will try,' and he said right back, 'The first thing I need you to do is remember. It is important to remember everything that you will see and hear and feel this day and convey it to my son.'"

"What did he mean, 'the first thing'?"

"I will get to that soon, Baas. There is much more to tell you."

"Hans, why on earth would my father choose to make himself manifest to an old drunken Hottentot like you, rather than to his own son, if anything you say is true?"

"I don't know, Baas, except you know I loved him and he loved me and charged me to take care of you for as long as I lived, a charge I have happily and faithfully fulfilled to this day, and I hope many more, because I care for you as I cared for him, and as you care for me—though you would never say so to me—though mayhap some day when I am no longer here, you will tell anyone who will listen."

"Is there more, Hans?"

"Yes, Baas. Even as I looked, the embers washed over him and in a minute he was covered with them and, in another minute, both he and the embers began to fade, and then they were all gone, and it was as though none of it had ever happened, and I was left wondering if I had dreamed the whole thing . . . . Except that I was still cold and shivered, and I had not moved from my huddled position, and so I knew that it had happened, and right now I am this very moment doing just as your Predikant father required of me: I am remembering and telling you about all that happened at the temple well."

He was nearly panting due to the struggle of telling me all this. I asked, "And all the while, you were clutching the diamond?"

"O, yes, Baas. Never for a second did my fingers loosen from around that pretty stone."

"That pretty stone, as you call it, Hans, will make us both more wealthy than it is possible to imagine."

"Yes, Baas, of course it will. But you should know some other things." Here he gulped and looked all around as though startled. Recall that after Hans' legs had given out from under him, I had led him outside and behind the laboratory building.

"I closed my eyes again, Baas, for a long time, and then opened them half expecting your Predikant father to be standing there again, but, of course, he, or rather, his spook, was gone. Then there was silence for a time. It seemed a long time, and then another voice, a new voice laughed loudly, or rather, an old voice as we both know it well. It said, 'Hans, you yellow dog, attend me!' It said again, 'Hans, attend me!' And then I understood that this new voice was the Great One." That is to say, Luna, the wizard Zikali, also known as "the Opener of Roads."

"'What is it that you want, you old devil?' I cried, knowing perfectly well that he was even then squatting in his hut, as he hates to travel in the flesh because he finds it so much more convenient to let his spirit fly. The voice said, 'I am here with you, as real as if you were standing next to my hut.'

"'So what? You say this, but why should I believe you, as the Baas always tells me that you are nothing but an old cheat? I'm probably hearing things due to my having been thinking a lot about square-face and also drinking it.'

"'Stop yammering, little yellow man, and attend me!'

"This seemed a simple enough thing to do and the wisest course of action, so I did not argue. As you know, when dealing with the Great One, one's first response is to run the other direction because he is so ugly, also so powerful, also for fear he might 'sniff' you out."

"What do you fear being sniffed out about, Hans?"

"Baas, you know that I have my follies as does every man, though some men (and women too) have more follies and therefore are more fools than others and therefore may be prone to seizures of guilt, and I cannot deny that I have done many things in my dirty and slothful life that I'm not proud of. In any case, I determined to merely do as Zikali asked, or rather ordered!

"'Listen to me, you fool!' he droned on. 'When next you see Macumazana, be sure that you pay attention and listen to everything that you hear all around both of you. Listen to the very air itself! Listen and be surprised! Listen and become wise. Be most careful and listen with your ears and listen with you heart! And then when all is done, tell Macumazana all that you heard and all that you saw.' He seemed more than usually mean and angry, Baas.

"Then, Baas, it must have been that I sleepwalked. I soon realized that I was no longer at the temple anymore, but that I had somehow got into one of those long tunnels that connect the big bowls with the laboratory buildings. And then I heard the voice of your Predikant father again, Baas. I could not see him, but it was his voice all the same."

"What did my father say this time to you, Hans?"

"He said, 'Something more, Hans: Hide the stone! Now, Hans, hide the stone in the tunnel. It's important! Trust me, Hans!' Of course, I did not trust my senses, but no sooner than I heard him say this I heard someone enter the tunnel from the opposite end, and so I quickly found a box on the wall and shoved the diamond into it to hide."

314

"God in heaven! Do you mean our diamond is stashed in a box in plain sight of the technicians who fill that service corridor night and day and who are even now trying to repair the machine?"

"That's about the size of it!"

Luna, I was so angry at Hans I could have wrung his skinny neck right there. I wanted to go to the tunnel right then and there, but Hans took my arm and held me back.

"But wait, Baas, I, that is we, are not nearly done. There is more! So much more. And I have promised the spooks that I would tell you all!"

He stopped and seemed to gather his thoughts for a minute, and I waited.

"So then I escaped unseen," he continued, "and waited for the corridor to clear out so I could retrieve the stone, which I had hid for no better reason than the command of a spook who sounded like your Reverend Predikant father. I hid for a while but the tunnel was always full of men, thus I came looking for you."

"And when you found me, you promptly passed out!"

"Not at first, Baas. Much happened before I became so weak and would have hit the floor if you had not caught me. Remember, Baas, that just as I walked into the room, all the

Baases with the beards and their servants and, too, the star lady of whom we are both so fond, were growing happy even as I came in, or they seemed relieved like a great boulder had flown right off their shoulders. Remember that I had just joined you and that we were standing there in that big room with the lightning that jumped off the walls like fleas. And as we watched it all, there came a sound—a sort of hissing sound from out of the lightning—that began quietly and soon filled the room, and it seemed that it was this sound that made all the Baases so happy. You saw! After standing shocked for a minute, with their eyes bugging out, they all got busy again, even more so than they usually are, and as they did things the sound changed, quieter, then louder, then almost shrieking, then a whisper."

Luna, frankly I was amazed that Hans had noticed so much—far more than I, who was mainly irritated by the whole proceedings. Nevertheless, it was just as he described, now that he called it to my attention.

"Yes, Hans, all those things happened. What is so important that you must tell me now, even before we go fetch the diamond?"

"Baas, just this! As that hissing sound began I began to hear a faint voice, a small voice, like a small cat caught behind a cupboard door on the other side of the house. It seemed far distant and so low, but it was accompanied by a quiet drawn-out drumming sound. I could hear the voice, the drumming, and the hissing all at once."

"I tell you, you were drunk, Hans."

"No, or rather yes! But not like this have I ever been drunk, Baas. The distant voice said, or rather whispered because it was so low and almost drowned out by the other sounds, the most strange thing. It said it was the holy trumpet announcing, heralding, the most divine voice yet to come and I was drunk because it, the trumpet, had made me get drunk, and that it wanted me to be drunk, the better to hear with. And no sooner did I understand this, than the voice just disappeared altogether like when you think you might be hearing something in the distance, but then the wind changes direction and it is gone and you are left not knowing if you heard anything at all."

"What did the voice you might have heard want you to hear, Hans?" I couldn't believe that I was asking such an inane question! But when no reply was forthcoming, I asked, "And everything you've said about this strange voice was something you heard—through your ears—and nothing that you saw?"

I don't know what made me ask a question with such a self-evident answer, but Hans responded, "Good question, Baas. I don't know. It almost felt as though I was hearing it through my skin. And then, as I said, it was gone."

"Where is all this leading, Hans?" I asked, my temper growing short.

"Only this, Baas! Ha! All those silly fools with all their machines and whale-boats and brains were trying to hear some sort of message from the Great Baas in the sky. They told us so! Well, they succeeded, but they did not recognize it and will never do so! Yet I, Hans, poor yellow dog drunken Hans, heard the Great Baas' voice and it spoke to him."

"What on earth are you talking about, Hans?"

"Only this, after the small voice that said I was supposed to be drunk came and went, I could hear the hissing more clearly, and I paid attention. At first it was low, but then it became louder and terrible like a room full of snakes, and then the hissing changed and became the flapping of giant wings—just like great wings—and then I thought I could hear words coming from somewhere, but I couldn't make out where they were coming from, but finally I understood that the voice was the hissing sound! I was amazed and at first forgot that I was supposed to remember everything that happened. You will not believe me, Baas, but I swear on your Reverend father's grave that it is true. The hissing sound that filled the room, mixed with popping and crackling sounds, was speaking to me in my own Hottentot click language! O, how I wished then that I could claim to be more drunk than I was. I became scared—very, very frightened, as scared as I have ever been—and then the fear died and I began to feel like I do sometimes when we have reached the top of a tall hill and there is a great green valley below us, or a raging ocean blown around by a storm. What I felt, Baas, was this: It was like a great claw was scraping and tearing at my soul, the very soul your Reverend Predikant father was always telling us about, but I was not so much afraid of it or even hurt by it as I was full of curiosity about what it was and I ached in other ways, not with pain and hurt as you would expect great talons to do, but I ached with yearning to know more. But of course it wasn't really a claw, I just said it felt like one."

"Hans, this story is indeed different from your normal run of excuses for getting drunk, but I am losing interest. If you have a reason for this story, you had better tell me now."

"Just this, Baas. As I said, the hissing spoke to me in my own click language. The voice came through clearly and spoke at length and gave me a message, and it repeated the message several times so I would remember it forever, and once I had memorized it, the language of my fathers faded and changed and again became mere scratching and gibberish."

"Well, Hans, are you going to take all day? Give me the message if you really have a message to give me."

SS—

After I met Hans 30 years ago, I was fascinated by his clicking language and did a monograph on it—never printed of course and I lost track of it years ago. It was a paper much like the one I always planned to write about the Chaldean roots of the Cornish language. In any case, my conclusion was that Khoi (the name of Hans' language) was a strong candidate for the first human language! Imagine that! [Editor's note: M's notion is borne out by several linguists and anthropologists, including John Reader: "[I]t is generally agreed that the roots of the mother tongue...must have been set in Africa perhaps among the ancestors of the Khoisan" (in *Africa: A Biography of the Continent*, p. 110. New York, Alfred A. Knopf 1998).]—*M*

HANS' STORY
CHAPTER TWO

The Message Vouchsafed to Hans

And this is what Hans told me those many years ago:

"'O, Hans the good!'

"Yes, Baas, that is what the voice said to this old yellow monkey, as the Great One usually enjoys calling me.

"'Hans the mischievous. Hans the child. Hans the wise. I wish you to be the vessel of my message to all the people.'

"Here, Baas, despite being haunted by spooks for half the day, I was more surprised to be spoken to by the lightning, or rather by the clicks buried in the lightning, and I responded, 'Great Baas, as you must be or you wouldn't be speaking to me thus. Why are you playing with my head? Leave me alone.'"

"Hans," I said, "I was watching you and I did see your lips move, but it was some time later that you spoke out loud."

"I don't know what to tell you, Baas. I'm only saying what I know, and what I was told I was supposed to repeat back to you."

Chastened, I said, "What else did this voice say to you?"

"Only this, Baas: 'Hans, your fathers and their fathers and their fathers, and also all the mothers, all the way back to the dawn of time, have watched the stars and the sun and the moon move across the sky. Also, your people and all peoples have noted that sometimes the moon will precisely cover the sun, and the light and warmth will vanish! Can anything be more frightening? I ask.

"'Listen, Hans the faithful! Perhaps fear of hunger or of cold or of enemies or of pain or of death can be as frightening. But these are all things that are part of life and are expected, thus assumed, and though they may be feared, they are not strange. For does not every man [i.e., person] fully expect his lot to be touched by these fearsome things at some point during his journey?

"'However, the greatest joy in a [person's] life, indeed, in a whole people's life, is warmth and light from the sun. Thus the fear that comes from the sun vanishing and the world growing dark is the most fearsome thing of all for there is no way of knowing when such a terrible thing will happen. It is not like the sun setting and rising.

"'Or at least this was so up until the various peoples discovered by their industry *my secret pattern*. Man [i.e., humans or humankind] has become fully [human] because he sought to know when in the future the circle of the moon would cover the circle of the sun and plunge the earth into darkness. Behold! In time, each people built tools and discovered the pattern in the randomness. They learned when the fearsome thing would occur, and they became less afraid. They found the secret that I had buried deep within the complexities *I'd created just to goad [humans] to seek it.*

"'I tell you that [humankind's] seeking to predict when the moon will cover the sun is what has made [humans human]. This is the key that directed and honed problem-solving far beyond that needed for mere survival. From this has sprung all that makes [humans human].

"'Thus peoples built grand temples and pyramids and statues and standing stones to observe the sun and moon and sky, and, sometimes, they enslaved whole peoples to build their observatories. Hans, this took many thousands of years, during which time people have done much for both good and ill. *But remember that it all began due to fear of losing the sun during the day—a fear I instilled by making certain that the moon exactly covers the sun. I created a problem that [humankind] needed to solve and thereby progress!*

"'Surely nowadays many people have studied that age-old problem and have for centuries grown to understand thoroughly the remote—I say again—*remote* probability of any such equality in size of the sun and moon, so small a probability that the fact of this equivalence is on the surface preposterous. Yet, too often people just shrug and call it coincidence. *Too few reach the next logical conclusion. If such a thing is preposterous, and yet exists nonetheless as a fact of life, what could it mean? Perhaps it means that someone wished it all to happen in just that manner. But who could wish up suns and moons and propel [human] advancement?*

"'Who indeed? [Humans] now have clear reason to know me. I am right there in the maths and calculations that they treasure so much, but they can also be stubborn, can take things terribly for granted and rationalize. Still, Hans, people will someday understand that *something is happening, has always been happening, that defies reason . . . yet has a cause and that cause is me—for I am that I am!*

"'But first there must come a drawn-out time when the blind will lead and these words I am saying will verily be *the light in the darkness*. Old Hans, share my words. Remember all that I've said and share it with your Baas, Allan, O Hans the child, Hans the wise!

"'For you are my messenger.'"*

SS—

Did you notice that it's Christmas? Happy Christmas! In any case, having just read the interesting new paper by a certain A. Einstein and now Quatermain's memoir with Hans' mentioning eclipses brings to mind certain matters that had once piqued my interest concurrent with my interest in the Cornish and Chaldean languages, both

---

* Editor's note: While some readers might take exception to the idea that a message in the Khoi embryonic language could be embedded 13.7 billion years ago in the Cosmic Background Radiation with the intention of it being heard by one small Hottentot who just happened to be in the right place at the right time, be advised that, while definitely awesome, this scenario is

preoccupations of which came to a head during the
excursion W and I took onto the Cornish moors,
but ultimately came to naught as the distractions at
that time were piling one onto another. The region
where we were staying was one of those Celtic
lands that are dotted with stone monuments and

---

not unique. Futurist and science-fiction writer (and creator of the geosynchronous communications satellite that is at the heart of current world culture) Arthur C. Clarke died on March 19, 2008. Virtually at the same time Clarke died, there appeared in Earth's skies for 30 seconds the light from an exploding stellar source labeled GRB 080319B that just happened to be the most powerful blast ever observed in the universe from earth and which exploded 7.5 billion years ago (3 billion years before earth formed). This seeming coincidence becomes something quite different when you factor in Clarke's 1954 award-winning short story "The Star," the main plot point of which was that the light from a distant supernova (that vaporized an entire noble civilization) traveled 3,000 years and finally reached earth just in time to shine brightly over Bethlehem.—T.K.M.

rings that had in centuries or millennia past sprung up all over that charming land. I was then just beginning to see a glimmer of purpose in the erections that dealt with eclipses, a purpose that stimulated me to venture down avenues of which I'd heretofore paid little attention. In connection with the longitude and latitude of these constructions, I couldn't help but notice that on or near December 21 and June 21 certain of the stones lined up in thought-provoking ways. This led me later to peruse all manner of almanacs and volumes in the British Library, and certain facts took shape that directly pertained to the stones. For one thing, eclipses of the sun occur roughly every 18 months in some part of our world. Naturally these experiences affect humans of all walks of life, often by exciting some of the more primitive emotions such as fear and awe. This reaction is partly a consequence of a remarkable coincidence. The diameter of the moon happens to be 1/400 of the diameter of the sun. But the moon's proximity to the earth is 1/400 of the earth's distance to the sun. The result of this, during a solar eclipse, is that the disc of the moon perfectly covers the disc of the sun—causing any number of atmospheric effects: strange glowings in the resultant darkness, cold, wind, and so on. What must stone-age man have thought of this extraordinary intrusion? Furthermore, I concluded then (an opinion that hasn't changed) that Stonehenge and its brethren were built and conceived as instruments with the primary purpose of predicting the occurrence of eclipses. The builders of these ancient observatories most certainly made all their calculations under the assumption that both the sun and moon revolved around the earth as even I would have assumed had not W set me straight on the matter! This is only a natural conclusion because, for all major purposes, the sun and moon do appear to behave in just that fashion. Now it happens that one of those obvious facts of life that most people entirely take for granted, never thinking of, is the equivalent sizes of the sun and moon! Nevertheless, this illusion of apparent equivalence of size owes nothing to physical or universal laws; there is no simple definable, materialistic explanation for the relative placements of the sun and moon—no discernable cause. It is merely a coincidence! Yet, it is just this coincidence that causes such an awesome fearsome eerie spectacle that stone-age man was inspired to engineer and build their vast calculators.

Considering the incalculable import that the equivalent solar-lunar magnitudes have had on our Western culture and civilization, it would be ludicrous to deny that this exceptional coincidence has meaning! One need only to look at the ratio of measurements to become aware of the remarkable relationship that, presumably blind chance has provided:

Sun's Diameter		*Moon's Diameter*
Sun's Distance From Earth	:	*Moon's Distance From Earth*
865,400 Miles		**2,160 Miles**
92,956,500 Miles	:	*239,000 Miles*
.0090	:	*.0090*

In other words, a pretty damn peculiar one to one ratio! Hans' mysterious voice seemed to know what it was talking about? I wonder!

—M

First Afterword Chapter

Wrapping Up

While at the time, Luna, I honestly feared for Hans, years later when I happened to think upon the odd words of his soliloquy, a memory came with a shock, an electric shock, an eerie shock that shook me to my soul—because just such an eclipse as Hans described in principle saved me and Sir Henry and John Good from serious trouble during our adventure to King Solomon's Mines. We had got in trouble with the Kukuanas in that region and would have certainly been slaughtered had not Good remembered a notation he'd glimpsed in the almanac that he always carried with him. That almanac identified that the following day at one o'clock there would commence a total eclipse of the sun. Well, we there and then claimed to be great wizards with mighty powers and declared that we would extinguish the sun to prove it. We succeeded in creating doubt, sufficient to postpone our executions, and sure enough, the solar eclipse happened right on schedule, with all the resultant reactions in the native mind that Hans had listed out. *[Editor's note: At the "37th thousand printing" of* King Solomon's Mines, *someone—an editor? a publisher?—changed all references and descriptions in the book of this solar eclipse to that of a lunar eclipse! To what avail is anyone's guess.]* But I won't go into any further detail now as that adventure was the first that I wrote up—even before I retired to come here—and my agent thinks it will likely be publishable before long. Thus, Luna, you may soon be able to read all about that adventure in all its boring detail.

Well, getting back to what I was saying, no sooner had Hans divested himself of all this nonsense, than he scampered off as he was wont to do. Naturally, I hurried to the service corridor he spoke of and loitered for ages waiting for the place to clear out so I could fetch the diamond that Hans said my father had told him to hide there. I could just see into the tunnel from where I stood and I spotted the box mounted on the wall perhaps 50 feet from the entrance. Before long, the corridor didn't clear out so much as there was a chance moment when perhaps a dozen stressed, sweating, coughing individuals had gone their separate ways, and for a brief time the spot I needed was accessible! I ran in and made a beeline to the box, opened it, and, to my delight, found the paper-wrapped stone, pulled it out and thrust it into my pocket, and only then did I feel in a position to breath again, ever since

Hans began to tell me his ghost story, as I suppose you would call it.*

***

Well, there you are, Luna. There isn't much more to tell. Hans and I had stumbled onto a most strange enterprise, become reacquainted with an old friend, had been detained against our wills, spent time with some notable scientists and engineers, and observed with our own eyes the expenditure of uncounted millions to build enormous pieces of equipment the like of which I can never adequately describe let alone understand in terms of purpose.

All I can say for sure is that Hans believed to the day that he died that he had touched something divine, or rather that something had touched him, and he felt satisfied that he had conveyed to me that which he had been ordered

---

* Editor's note: Here Quatermain makes an aside that is intrusive to his story, but is interesting nonetheless, so I'm culling it out and here making it a footnote: "Speaking of ghost stories, Luna, now that I've settled into the Grange and I'm noticing the so-called civilized genteel society around me, I find that the ghost story is all the rage. All the popular magazines make a point of publishing

to memorize and convey back to me, but what of it? What would I do with such irredeemable nonsense? Except forget it—as I have in fact done until now, and in fact, it makes my heart sore to remember Hans at such a low ebb. It was likely some sort of trick perpetrated by Zikali just to prove a point—of what I can't imagine—though in later days, he denied any direct involvement. Of course, he knew all about everything that Hans claimed to have experienced, as he is prone to do with anything that is remotely mysterious. Thus I sit before

---

ghost stories, especially in their Christmas numbers. I'm saying this because I simply cannot get over the huge gap that exists between your average Londoner and my African acquaintances for whom ghosts, spirits, witches and witchcraft are assumed to exist and taken for granted. Here, ghosts are treated abstractly (spiritualist societies excepted, of course), but virtually my whole life has been lived amongst peoples whose daily existence revolves around the supernatural. For them, the spirit world is utterly real and alive and is as much a part of their lives as servants and hansom cabs in Piccadilly are for us. Thus you see that the point of a ghost story would be completely lost on most of my African friends and acquaintances! But, of course, you know this already!"—T.K.M.

you today wondering what Hans' experiences or hallucinations all meant, if anything?

I'm close to the end. Poor Maxwell and Barbicane and Cardinal Cigliutti tried over and again to receive some sort of signal from the star in the constellation Aquila, and never heard or measured anything of consequence more than that continuous hiss that I've described. Hans and I remained there for a week further to keep Maria company, but in the end, it was clear that their expensive toy was a failure and that nothing could come of fine-tuning their instruments any further. Heartbroken that all their immense effort, manpower, and expense to hear some whisper from God about the divinity of His son was for naught, they rallied and began to make plans to destroy it all.

Barbicane suggested to me that Hans and I should leave quickly and be well on our way at the end of 24 hours because they had no choice but to erase the laboratory from existence. He did not elaborate, but I could tell he was deadly serious. One wonders what the fate of it all would have been if the experiment had been a success. Certainly I'll never know.

I sought out Maria, and we said farewell, which was of course sad, but I was glad to be on my way finally, and she was clearly happy to be returning to her former life as a professor of astronomy in America. She told me that she and Maxwell and the rest would be boarding a British naval vessel and be leaving before dawn. She told me that they were left with immense amounts of data of an unknown sort, and that she would remain in touch with Maxwell, and perhaps they would be able to extract something of scientific value from the whole experience.

Second Afterword Chapter

Allan Throws the Diamond Away

The next morning, from the top of the same hill from which we first saw the town, as we thought of it then, but which we came to know as an unprecedentedly prodigious laboratory, we spied a ghost town. In the distance out over the ocean was a great naval ship in full sail and moving rapidly toward the horizon.

Then in an instant, the whole facility exploded. With heaven knows how much dynamite—I suppose it must have been dynamite, which was new and controversial then—they destroyed everything they had labored so hard to build. Even the temple that had captured our hearts from the start vanished, as well the incredible aqueduct that fed into it, and presumably all the dams and reservoirs, too, high up in the mountains. It all jumped into the air in fire and smoke that rose it seemed without let-up. Hans and I watched for a time, having very mixed emotions. When the smoke cleared, we saw that some structures had escaped the brunt of the blast, and we could still make out clearly the two bowls on either side of the make-shift town. Of course, I suppose all that silver leaf with which they had covered the bowls must have been stripped away and carted off. In the years since then I've heard rumors of huge pits and ruined buildings being swallowed by the jungle in that region, thus I conclude they never did finish the clean-up and erasure of their occupation. With regard to the two submersible boats, of which Hans and I saw only one, the Nova, we never set eyes on it again, and I simply have no idea what became of them. I would think that they'd be too valuable to scuttle outright, but, as I said, I just don't know. Likewise, I never learned or heard anything more about an equivalent base of operations in Ecuador, not that I was ever in a position to banter with those who would know about anything of the sort in South America!

As we turned to leave and descend the hill, Hans said, "Baas, somewhere in this very strange tale there must be a lesson similar to the sort of thing that your Predikant father used to drum into the heads of all the poor workers and students, of which sometimes I was counted."

"If so, Hans, I'm at a loss to see it. The whole affair seems to have been a detour with little enough value."

"Well, then, if you, Baas, the wise Macumazana, can find no meaning in any of this, then I say curse it all!"

And thereupon, he vented his anger and frustration by cursing just about everything.

"Curse this hill and that great fish. Curse the natives that told you of the white witch doctors. Curse the white witch doctors and all their machines. Curse the temple and the river that ran to it and the mountains from which it was born and curse the rain that fell on the mountains and made the river. Curse that hen's egg of a stone that the river brought down for me to find. Curse me for finding it. Curse its pretty shininess that tempted me so. Curse Zikali for knowing full well what would befall us as he always knows such things. And curse you, Baas, for getting us into this mess to begin with."

By now Hans was breathless and his eyes were red and bulging and I decided it was time for me to step in and calm my servant down. But he wasn't quite done, after all.

"And curse the noise from the sky in which I heard voices, and curse the voices, and curse me for hearing the voices!"

***

Then our life regained some of its normalcy. I decided that I had seen more of west Africa than I cared to and decided not to go back north to catch a ship back to Durban. We hired some porters, reequipped ourselves with oxen and wagons and trekked southeast to see what trading situations I could set up and also to hire myself out as the hunter that was my chief occupation then.

Some months later, Hans and I found ourselves on the outskirts of Zululand, and over a fire we chatted about the sundry challenges we had overcome that day because, as you know Luna, any day in the rough country of Africa is tantamount to a test of endurance. While we sat thus, in time I became absorbed by the flickering wood fire and simply stared into it, when Hans voiced the very subject that was really on my mind.

"How will you spend the money you will fetch from the great stone that I found, Baas?"

Well, I began by mentioning a certain mansion that had come onto the market in Pretoria after its then owner—an officer in the Army had perished in battle—I know not how. Having no wife or other heirs to speak of, his executors had put the property up for sale a year before, and so far as I knew there had been no takers, as apparently the asking price was exorbitant by any standards. So I fantasized in my response to Hans that I intended to march into the responsible agent's office and state that I wished to purchase the house at its current price, and oh, by the way, here is cash on the barrelhead, and a gratuity besides!

"And then, you Hans," I said, "can be head servant and the whole world will be at our beck and call!"

Of course, Hans saw through my weakness and my dreams of avarice.

"Baas, forgive me if your humble servant disagrees with you, but I don't understand why you are happy by such a future. I think you are better off giving the pretty stone back to the earth gods, for they will doubtlessly be very unhappy when they discover that their plaything is missing, and they will track us down and cause us much grief. May your Predikant father forgive me for speaking of such forbidden gods, but still I think we will not hear the end of their anger and our lives will be less than worthless in time—even in the big house that you dream of! Friends you never knew you had will hound you. Offspring that I never knew I had will likewise cause me no end of trouble. And what is the use of being head servant when all the servants will be forever plotting against me and sneaking their filthy hands into my pockets, as you, too, will find out—but the hands you will fight off will be the bigger hands of bigger men, even men with six and eight hands, like insects, and moving so fast that you will never know that they emptied your pockets until it is too late—and then we will regret that we ever carried that cursed stone away from the place where we found it!"

Hans was clearly in one of his lecturing moods, which he slipped into whenever he thought he was wiser than either my father or me, so I just let him have his tirade, after which I figured I would give him a drop of gin or not depending on my mood. I forget what I did then.

**

A few days later we were crossing the Mambuzo River. The sun was straight overhead. I remember that it was a crisp beautiful day and that I didn't mind one bit that I was soaked up to my chest due to the necessity of crossing the river. And, then, on impulse, I reached into my jacket pocket where I had kept the diamond all along and pulled it out. I unwrapped the soaked paper that was covering it and discreetly held it up to the sun and squinted as the sun's rays penetrated its magical substance. But I knew then that the sun's rays were harsh and were never intended for men to stare into for long. Then I clenched the diamond in the fist of my hand, swung my arm around a few times to limber up and hurled the stone into the deepest part of the river as far from me as I could.

Hans, who notices everything, looked at me with eyes as big as saucepans and his jaw dropped.

"Baas . . . Baas . . . ."

"Quiet fool," I countered, "can't you see that I decided that your wisdom won the day."*

Picture this, Luna. We were both standing in the middle of the river. The water was up to his chin, as he was so much shorter than me (imagine me talking of comparative heights!). Behind us were two wagons and on the shore in front of us, our other two wagons had already been secured.

---

* Editor's note: Again, from the sketchy details that Quatermain provides Luna, I suspect that he had had in his possession the Jonker Diamond that would be found again 60 years later in the Elandsfontein region of South Africa, near the area where he threw away the stone into the river. If so, then Hans' predictions about the destiny of the finder of the stone held true, because Johannes Jacobus Jonker, the 62-year-old who found the diamond on his claim, did not enjoy his wealth and soon lost it.—T.K.M.

A dozen porters were all around us, half drowned as we all were, but they were ignorant of the little drama that was being played out between Hans and myself.

"But, Baas, you threw away your big house and the servants that I would boss around!"

"Yes, I did, Hans." I glared at him and we thenceforth did not talk about it again. And, Luna, until tonight I have never spoken a word of this whole matter, and that is pretty much the end of the story."

[Luna: Allan, what a remarkable tale. I don't know what to think! The vastness of the project! The cavalier manner in which it was destroyed. My mind cannot contain it all; not to mention the cavalier way you tossed away your diamond—your Star of Wonder!]

And don't suppose, Luna, that my mind has ever been able to grasp any part of it either, despite Hans and I being in the middle of it all. Still, here I sit a wealthy man as the result of finding untold riches in diamonds. It seems I was fated to experience all these trappings . . . and much of the downside, as well, just as poor dear old Hans predicted, for good or ill I don't know yet!

[Luna: Here I reminded Allan that ironically the very reason we were sitting in my room at that moment was because of the necessity of my getting away from those dreadful, grasping Atterby-Smith cousins of Lord Ragnall (exactly as Hans described!) who are plotting and scheming downstairs even as I write, and who truly believe they and not his wife ought to have inherited his wealth! Yet, this journal must end somewhere, so here are the last words I will record from this evening.]

Luna, I sorely miss Hans! O, dear, I hope, as I so often pray mantra-like to myself, I hope I do find the light of his love burning like a beacon in the darkness as he promised I should do, and that it may guide and warm my shivering new-born soul before I dare the adventure of the Infinite. O, Luna, I've been so lost without him!

Epilogue

Since this narrative says virtually nothing about the "over yonder" facility other than it was along the coast of Ecuador, I spent four months combing newspaper archives on both sides of the Atlantic. I believe I was successful in that I found the following 1915 newspaper feature item, which speaks volumes without my having to say another word!

In the Footsteps of Alexander Von Humboldt
Continuing Coverage of the Third Challenger
Expedition to South America

TITANIC METEORITE CRATERS SPOTTED

Challenger Says "They're Recent"

By E.D. Malone
Special to the
London Daily Gazette

ECUADOR, October 24 —— This morning as we ventured north along the west coast of South America, the dense jungle which had been our constant companion for some days unexpectedly cleared and we, who had just topped a low peak, viewed below us two enormous craters, the remnants of an interplanetary collision, according to Professor Challenger, who declared that no force on earth could have been responsible—

Select Bibliography and
Suggested Further Reading

This book is a love letter to subjects I adore and have been interested in my whole life. But it didn't come easily. It took 11 years of trying desperately to pull words and sentences out of my head* I liken it to pulling taffy through a keyhole on a cold day! I can see myself at the dining room table for hours on end for years struggling to put words into Quatermain's mouth. I assembled countless thick folders and piles and binders and boxes of outlines and notes and tentative text, most hung together with lots of Scotch tape and staples. Yet, it is hard to believe, it is finally done! Is it any good? Frankly, I don't know. My goal was to offer to a few readers a good time and food for thought. Only you can say if I succeeded. Still, I'm very clear that countless genre writers of similar material can write prolific rings around me faster and better. I can only claim to have done my utmost best.

While a lifetime of reading and viewing for both pleasure and research is behind every page of this novel,

---

Crucible of Life took 15 years. Preceding it, the slim *Roof of the World* took four years.

348

specifically for *Dawn of Time*, I've read or viewed at the very least, hundreds of books, magazine and newspaper articles, videos, websites, and other media on the pertinent topics— certainly most available studies—and it would be impossible to list the mountains of material that influenced me before and while this story was being crafted. However, some works either have special meaning for me or could be particularly useful further reading for interested readers. Thus, I studied my shelves to cull out some representative works to share and quickly learned that there is just too much! Therefore, frustratingly, I list here a mere sampling with the understanding that nobody responsible for any part of these listed works has anything whatsoever to do with the unlikely extrapolations and fantasies that I present in this novel:

The Manhattan Project
Groves, General Leslie M. *Now It Can Be Told: The Story of the Manhattan Project*. New York: Harper 1962 (Boston: A Decapo Reprint).

Jaffe, Roland. *Fat Man and Little Boy*. Paramount Pictures 1989 (film).

Kunetks. James W. *City of Fire: Los Alamos and the Atomic Age*, 1943-1945. Albuquerque: University of New Mexico 1979.

Los Alamos: Beginning of an Era 1943-1945. Los Alamos, New Mexico: Los Alamos Scientific Laboratory. (reissued by Los Alamos Historical Society; 2nd edition, February 1, 2008).

Rhodes, Richard. *The Making of the A-Bomb*. New York: Simon & Schuster 1986.

Rhodes, Richard. *Dark Sun: The Making of the Hydrogen Bomb*. New York: Simon & Schuster 1995.

Taurog, Norman. *The Beginning or the End*. MGM 1947 (film).

The Hetch Hetchy Project

The Hetch Hetchy Water and Power System: Origin, Development and Future. San Francisco Public Utilities Commission 2005.

Leonard, James H. *San Francisco Water and Power*. San Francisco: Hetch Hetchy Water and Power System c. 1980.

Miller, Thomas K, "Here's to You. Down the Hetch: Through Granite by Gravity" in *Phoenix*. San Francisco: San Francisco State University, December 3, 1981.

Righter, Robert W. *The Battle Over the Hetch Hetchy: America's Most Controversial Dam and the Birth of Modern Environmentalism*. New York: Oxford University Press 2005.

Wurm, Ted. *Yosemite's Hetch Hetchy Railroad: San Francisco's Water and Power Project*. Fishcamp, California: Stauffer 2000.

Maria Mitchell

Albers, Henry (ed.). *Maria Mitchell: A Life in Journals and Letters*. Clinton Corners, New York: College Avenue Press 2001.

Gormley, Beatrice. *Maria Mitchell: The Soul of an Astronomer*. Grand Rapids: William B. Eerdsmans 1995.

Mitchell, Maria and Kendall, Phebe. *Mitchell. Maria Mitchell: Life, Letters and Journals*. Boston: Lee and Shepard 1896 (A Kessinger Reprint)

Stonehenge and Megaliths

Alexander, Caroline. "If the Stones Could Speak: Searching for the Meaning of Stonehenge" in *The National Geographic Magazine* Vol. 213. Washington, D.C.: The National Geographic Society, June 2008.

Hawkins, Gerald S. *Stonehenge Decoded.* New York: Dell Publishing 1965.

Hoyle, Fred. *From Stonehenge to Modern Cosmology.* San Francisco: W.H. Freeman 1972.

Wernick, Robert (Bernard Wailes, consultant) and the Editors of Time-Life Books. *The Emergence of Man: The Monument Builders.* New York: Time-Life Books 1973.

Victorian Africa

Burton, Richard. *Wanderings in West Africa* (two volumes bound as one). New York: Dover 1991 (first published 1863).

Moorehead, Alan. *The Blue Nile.* New York: HarperCollins 1980.

Patterson, John Henry. *The Man-Eaters of Tsavo.* Stilwell, Kansas: Digireads.com 2005 (first published 1907).

The Khoisan People and Language

Reader, John. Africa: A Biography of the Continent. New York: Alfred A. Knopf 1998.

Wade, Nicholas. *Before the Dawn: Recovering the Lost History of Our Ancestors.* New York: The Penguin Press 2006.

Isambard Kingdom Brunel

Brindle, Steven. *Brunel: The Man Who Changed the World.* London: Phoenix 2005.

Rolt, L.T.C. *Isambard Kingdom Brunel.* London: Penguin 1989.

The Star of Bethlehem
Alexander F. Morrison Planetarium. *The Christmas Star* (Booklet No. 6). San Francisco: California Academy of Sciences 1959.

Brown, Raymond. *The Birth of the Messiah: A Commentary on the Infancy Narratives in Matthew and Luke.* Garden City, New York: Doubleday 1977.

Clarke, Arthur C. "The Star of the Magi" in *The Challenge of the Spaceship*. New York: Ballantine 1961.

Hughes, David. *The Star of Bethlehem: An Astronomer's Confirmation.* New York: Pocket Books 1979.

Kidger, Mark. *The Star of Bethlehem: An Astronomer's View.* Princeton: Princeton University Press 1999.

Maier, Paul L. *First Christmas: The True and Unfamiliar Story*. New York: Harper & Row 1971.

Williams, John. *Observations on Comets, From B.C. 611 to A.D. 1640*. A Nabu Public Domain Reprint 2010.

Robert E. Howard and E. Hoffmann Price
De Camp, L. Sprague; De Camp, Catherine Crook; and Griffin, Jane Wittington. *Dark Valley Destiny: The Life of Robert E. Howard, the Creator of Conan*. New York: Blue Jay Books 1983.

Howard, Doctor Isaac M. *The Collected Letters of Doctor Isaac M. Howard.* Plano, Texas: The Robert E Howard Foundation Press 2011.

Price, E. Hoffmann. *Book of the Dead: Friends of Yesteryear: Fictioneers & Others*. Saul City: Arkham House 2001.

Planetariums
Norton. O. Richard. *The Planetarium and Atmospherium: An Indoor Universe.* Healdsburg, California: Naturegraph Publishers 1968.

James Clerk Maxwell

Balchin, John. *Science: 100 Scientists Who Changed the World*. New York: Enchanted Lion Books 2003.

Hart, Michael H. *The 100: A Ranking of the Most Influential Persons in History*. New York: Citadel: 2001.

Mahon, Basil. *The Man Who Changed Everything: The Life of James Clerk Maxwell*. Chichester, UK: John Wiley & Sons 2004.

Maxwell, James Clerk. *A Treatise on Electricity & Magnetism* (two volumes). New York: Dover 1954 (first published 1873).

Pope Pius IX

Ambrosini, Maria Luisa with Willis, Mary. *The Secret Archives of the Vatican*. New York: Little Brown 1969.

Pius IX. "Ineffabilis Deus" in *Mother of Christ, Mother of Church: Documents on the Blessed Virgin Mary*. Boston: Pauline Books and Media 2001.

Julia, Daughter of Augustus, and Ancient Rome

Casson, Lionel. *The Ancient Mariners: Seafarers and Sea Fighters of the Mediterranean in Ancient Times*. Minerva Press 1959.

Coolidge, Olivia. *Roman People*. Boston: Houghton Mifflin 1959.

Fast, Howard. *Spartacus*. New York: Howard Fast 1951 (a 1960 Bantam Book).

Kubrick, Stanley. *Spartacus*. Universal-International 1960 (film).

Stobart, J.C. *The Grandeur That Was Rome* (5th ed.). New York: Praeger 1971.

Big Bang, CBR, and Interferometry

Gamow, George. *The Creation of the Universe.* Mineola, New York: Dover 2004 (First Published 1952).

Hey, J.S. *The Radio Universe.* New York: Pergamon Press 1971.

Singh, Simon. *Big Bang: The Most Important Scientific Discovery of All Time and Why You Need to Know About It.* London: Fourth Estate 2004.

Tyson, Neil Degrass and Goldsmith, *Donald. Origins: Fourteen Billion Years of Cosmic Evolution.* New York: W.W. Norton 2004.

Solar Eclipses

Menzel, Donald H. and Pasachoff, Jay M. "Solar Eclipse, Nature's Super Spectacular" in *National Geographic Magazine* Vol. 138. Washington, D.C.: The National Geographic Society August 1970.

Monsman, Gerald. Annotation to *King Solomon's Mines* by H. Rider Haggard. Buffalo, New York: Broadview Press 2002.

Steel, Duncan. Eclipse: *The Celestial Phenomenon That Changed the Course of History.* Washington D.C.: The Joseph Henry Press 2001.

Beekeeping

Bodmer, Rudolph J. (ed.). "The Story in a Honey Bee" in *The Book of Wonders.* New York: Presbrey Syndicate 1915.

Grout, Roy A. (ed.). *The Hive and the Honey Bee.* Hamilton: Dadant 1949.

Hambleton, James I. "Man's Winged Ally, The Busy Honey Bee" in *The National Geographic Magazine* Vol. LXVII, Number Four. Washington, D.C.: The National Geographic Society April 1935.

Maeterlinck, Maurice. *The Life of the Bee*. New York: Mentor 1954 (originally published 1901).

Murayama, Hashime. "In Field and Hive" in *The National Geographic Magazine* Vol LXVII, Number Four. Washington, D.C.: The National Geographic Society April 1935.

Continental Drift

Dobson, Jerome E. "Through the Macroscope: Geography's View of the World" in *ArcNews*. Redlands, California: Esri Winter 2011/2012.

Sullivan, Walter. *Continents in Motion*. McGraw-Hill. 1974.

The Maya

Highwater, Jamake. *Journey to the Sky: A Novel About the True Adventures of Two Men in Search of the Lost Maya Kingdom*. New York: Crowell 1978.

Mysteries of the Maya: The Rise, Glory and Collapse of an Ancient Civilization. The National Geographic Magazine. Washington, D.C.: The National Geographic Society April 2005 (among NGS's countless fine Maya pieces over the years).

Stephens, John L. *Incidents of Travel in Yucatan* (two volumes). New York: Dover 1963 (first published 1843).

Von Hagan, Victor Wolfgang. *Maya Explorer: John Lloyd Stephens and the Lost Cities of Central America and Yucatan*. San Francisco: Chronicle Books 1990.

Immense Engineering Enterprises

Ambrose, Stephen E. *Nothing Like It in the World: The Men Who Built the Transcontinental Railroad 1863-1869*. New York: Simon & Schuster 2000.

Broggie, Michael. *Walt Disney's Railroad Story: The Small-Scale Fascination That Led to a Full-Scale Kingdom.* Pasadena: Pentrex 1997.

Burleson, Clyde W. *The Jennifer Project.* New York: Prentice-Hall 1977.

Clarke, Arthur C. *Voice Across the Sea.* London: William Luscombe 1958.

McCullough, David. *The Path Between the Seas: The Creation of the Panama Canal 1870-1914.* New York: Simon & Schuster 1977.

Nineteenth-Century Explorations of Ecuador and Colombia

Sachs, Aaron. *The Humboldt Current: Nineteenth-Century Exploration and the Roots of American Environmentalism.* New York: Penguin 2007

Sanz de Santamaria, Pablo Navas. *The Journey of Frederick Edwin Church Through Colombia and Ecuador April-October 1853.* Bogata, Columbia: Villegas Asociados, Universidad de los Andes, Thomas Greg & Sons 2008.

Von Humboldt, Alexander and Bonpland, Aime. *Personal Narrative of Travels to the Equinoctial Regions of America During the Years 1799-1804* (three volumes) London: George Bell 1908.

Wulf, Andrea. *The Invention of Nature: Alexander von Humboldt's New World.* New York: Knopf 2016.

The Jonker Diamond

TheLazareDiamond. The Cutting of the Jonker Diamond. (YouTube video based on 1936 Movietone News footage) 2010.

Tourneur, Jacques. *A Miniature: The Story of "The Jonker Diamond".* MGM 1936 (short film).

Useful Reference Fiction Found in Many Editions:
Clarke, Arthur C. "The Star"
Doyle, Arthur Conan. *The Lost World* and "The Devil's Foot"
Heard, H.F. *A Taste for Honey*
Verne, Jules. *From the Earth to the Moon* and *20,000 Leagues Under the Sea*

Appendix

The Gospels of Issa, Gaspar, Mariam, and Hans
(Combined)

> There are few persons, even amongst the calmest thinkers, who have not occasionally been startled into a vague yet thrilling half-credence in the supernatural, by coincidences of so seemingly marvellous a character that, as mere coincidences, the intellect has been unable to receive them. [S]uch sentiments are seldom thoroughly stifled unless by reference to the doctrine of chance, or, as it is technically termed, the Calculus of Probabilities.
> —Edgar Allan Poe in
> "The Mystery of Marie Rogêt"

Insofar as four heretofore unknown gospels have happened by pure chance to arrive years apart at my front door—*The Gospel of Issa* as part of Leo Vincey's *Roof of the World* journal, *The Gospels of Gaspar and Mariam* within the Allan Quatermain memoir *Crucible of Life*, and the *Gospel of Hans* through a second Quatermain memoir *Dawn of Time*—it would be immensely hypocritical of me not to state forthrightly that such a coincidence has given me great pause. Of course, being no Biblical or Christian scholar, I am certainly in no position to determine the veracity of these texts; furthermore, one must bear in mind that all any of us has to go on are the rough-and-ready translation (from

358

Aramaic) of Horace Holly (filtered through the sensibilities of Leo Vincey), the two sets of passages presented to Allan Quatermain by Richard Holmes a decade apart (in regards to the latter, my repeated inquiries to the British Museum have elicited no response), and the two sets of pronouncements made in the presence of Quatermain, which he decades later recalled and verbalized extemporaneously as aspects of long anecdotes shared with friends. Nevertheless, I am now taking the liberty of merging the tracts as they seem to me to have points in common; it does not hurt that they, as well, express approximations of my own long-held core convictions.

***

The Gospel of Issa

1. Is it God or is it I who guides this brush? God fills me as milk warm from the goat fills a cup to overflowing.

2. Long ago I ceased to be merely the man who is the son of my parents. I was young when God showed Himself to me:

3. That was the time I ceased to be the son of my parents. I became then an instrument of the Lord. I, Issa, son of Joseph, the carpenter of Nazareth, ceased to be.

4. My whole will from that time forward focused on the fact of God's gracing me with the indisputable awareness of His presence.

5. Why me? What did I ever do to deserve the acquaintance of God? My time and my life have been for these last eighteen years fully a matter of trying to understand what was and is happening to me.

6. I am filled with God. But tell me, if you empty a fig of its meat and fill its skin with mandarin orange pulp, are you left with an orange?

7. Then I am no more God than the fig is an orange. But as that fig, transformed, knows more of oranges than a natural fig, so I know more of God than a natural man.

8. They will say, I think, that I am the son of God. Others will say I am a fraud!

9. I know that the Lord has chosen me for some other than ordinary purpose. I can see glimpses of it, but the details elude me.

10. These things are fact, not to be ignored by me or anyone.

11. I know clearly how the prophets must have felt; what they must have known. As God spoke to Abraham and Moses and Isaiah, so He speaks to me.

12. I truly know that I am to do my Lord's bidding; I am to be the instrument of His will.

13. My Lord wants me to wander through the East and absorb everything I see and hear.

14. So be it. Such is what we have done for nearly eighteen years. Here I am with my brother Didymus Judas Thomas in the land of the Bon, the mightiest mountain country that my Father has created.

15. We have traveled far, about as far from home as is imaginable.

16. I have learned much: the tenets of Hinduism, Buddhism, Confucianism, yoga. These are all fonts from which I have drunk mightily.

17. What is it now that I am supposed to do? Is it time to return? Home has beckoned for months now.

18. Is there anything else to learn in this high land of false magic and superstition? Will I know what to do when the time comes?

19. Now, however, I write this account as You have asked, or, rather, ordered, for my Father does not ask.

20. I am here, Lord; but I don't know why. I have learned much, but I don't know why. We have traveled far, and I don't know why.

21. Everything is so different than that which I was taught as a child in Nazareth.

22. Is it that I am loath to admit to myself what your purpose is for me?

23. In our wanderings, I have noted a common theme. A tenet that explains so much—that answers so many of your children's unanswered questions.

24. Whether in China or India or here in the loftiest mountains, so long as I am in the East, I hear of death and rebirth, and of the soul using the body much as I would ride in a vehicle:

25. How after death, the soul must be born again. Though in a new vehicle, or vessel, according to the merit that the soul exhibited in its previous existences.

26. It is a meritorious approach to existence certainly. Much as a school boy moves from one level of learning to another higher level, so, too, a death marks the potential for a move, for the coming to a crossroads;

27. But as some children need to repeat an entire season of lessons due to slothfulness or poor behavior or inattentiveness, so, too, a soul must sometimes repeat a wasted life in order to attain the merit to move on.

28. Attainment of merit is simple, surely. To do onto others as you would have them do onto you.

29. If a man or a woman follows this tenet for a lifetime, he or she will achieve merit and be closer to God for having done so: In this life and in the next.

30. To be One with the Father, that is the purpose of existence: base man must rise above his baseness to sit at the right hand of the Father.

31. Yet it is slow. God's time is not man's time, nor woman's. A human lifetime is but the single beat of a fly's wing in God's measure.

32. The miracle is that God notices, and more than this, that God cares.

33. But God does care. If God was not Love Incarnate, perhaps all of human existence could have begun and ended without the Father even knowing.

34. But God does know and God does love.

35. Patience is the foundation.

36. An hour, a day, a month, a year, seven years, a single lifetime is not enough.

37. I have had arguments, or, rather, discussions with my brother Thomas.

38. It is self-apparent, I will say to him, that the punishment for the curser is that the soul will forget its previous life and will be cast down into a body that will spend its time continually troubled in its heart;

39. That the punishment for the arrogant and over-bearing man is that the soul will forget from whence it came and will be cast down into a lame and deformed body so that all despise it persistently.

40. Then Thomas will ask, "And the man who hath committed no sin, but done good persistently, but hath not found the mysteries, what will happen to him?"

41. And I reply, "He will seek the light and will find it."

42. Surely, then, my destiny is to teach of these matters and others, such as the righteousness of humility and of seeking and others of which I have learned during our long sojourn.

43. But to whom? Surely, the people of our fathers, the people of Abraham will make naught of such matters.

44. Oh, my brother and I have seen so much in these last years.

45. By caravan, we followed the silk road to Bactra and from thence to Kabul and Palitara. I have seen the holy cities of Juggernaut, Rajagrina, Benares, and Kopilavastu.

46. We have journeyed through many nations and supped with many peoples.

47. I am filled to overflowing with the wisdom of the ages.

48. You told me that I am Your tool. Well, use me! I have much knowledge and have acquired marvelous techniques. What is it all for? I am tired.

49. (Could it be that it was I who recently wrote here of patience?)

50. I know now that I am to teach. Well, then, let me teach! How much more must I learn? I have seen your many faces!

51. Eloi, Eloi! I am lonely. Despite the companionship of my brother, Thomas, I am tired of being a stranger in a strange land.

52. I have learned without doubt that You are Love, but I do not love. I have teachers but no friends.

53. I am feeling sorry for myself, for I am lonely and too wise.

54. I know God as well as I know Joseph, the husband of my mother, Mariam.

55. In the beginning, when I was very young, He would speak to me, and I would respond.

56. He spoke to me and it was clear enough. Not in words would He speak, but in signs and symbols and, sometimes, in dreams, too, He made His wants known. Learning the language of the signs was the challenge.

57. What is school if not a challenge for the student?

58. As a child who does good is rewarded, and is punished for having done bad, so, too, God shows pleasure when a sign is read correctly and displeasure when a sign is misread.

59. Usually some coincidence that inspired wonder would be my reward for right interpretation; a sense of foreboding being the clue that there was misreading.

60. I needed always to plumb my feelings and try to understand what God was trying to say. In time, I built a whole vocabulary.

61. But now I am lost in the mountain country of the Bon people.

***

62. My brother, Issa, is dead. I, Didymus Judas Thomas, who has been my brother's companion for nearly eighteen years as we traveled through the strange lands of the East, am now alone. I am afraid. God has deserted us.

63. Issa was attacked in a dark alley by robbers and was clubbed to death. The morticians here, who feed their dead to the birds, have him in their care now.

64. I cannot bear to stay in this foreign land one day longer. I am leaving for home, Judea.

65. I have much to carry; I leave behind much; my burdens are heavy.

The Gospel of Gaspar

66. Thus Gaspar says:

67. These are the words of Gaspar the Ethiopian.

68. I am dismayed. A significant portion of my life has been given to the study of one man, and more and more frequently I hear reports concerning him that are blatantly false or twisted far beyond the simple truths.

69. Why is this? Can there be so many whose self-interest outweighs the simple truth?

70. In all things, Jesus the Nazarene said, 'Treat others as you would have them treat you. Do good and give as you

can without expecting a thing in return. Your reward will be great, and God will call you his children. Show mercy even as your Father shows mercy. Do not judge, for how can you judge? What right do you have to judge when you have no understanding why a person is the way that person is? Remember, the standard you use will be the standard used toward you.'

71. The one God is real, a spirit that is at the core of everything and everyone. God is always observing how you treat and judge others and how your actions and words, or inaction for that matter, affect others. This spirit doles out according to your actions. Hurt and you will be hurt, love and you will be loved, cause someone to cry in suffering and you will be made to cry with your own suffering. This circle of doing followed by God's response may be experienced immediately or may be held off for a future lifetime, according to the will of God for his own reasons.

72. Jesus explained the way of the world in a simple manner, with parables that even children can understand. He was proud of his ability in this respect. He told his followers and all those who would listen, "Blessed are the eyes that see the things that you see, for I tell you that many prophets and kings have desired to see those things that you see and have

not seen them, and to hear those things that you hear and have not heard them."

73. And yet I, Gaspar, mourn, as none of this do I hear from the caravans. Instead I hear about magical wine and multiplying loaves and fishes. Where is the word of Jesus the Naserene, who told us not to worry about our lives, what we will eat, about our bodies, or what we will wear, for isn't life more than food, and the body more than flesh? Did he not remind us of the way lilies grow, that they do not work or spin, but that even Solomon, in all his splendor, was not as glorious?

***

74. And Gaspar said:

75. Where is the word that tells us how to listen to God, that tells us that God speaks in a special language. When you see clouds in the west, you know that rain will come. You know that wind blowing from the south is always followed by blistering heat. You know the ways of your home and its land and you can read the sky. So why can't you understand the signs that God brings you?

76. God's language doesn't use simple words like fig or tree or wall or camel. Instead, he uses symbols. For instance, if he shows you a circle, you know from common sense that a circle has no beginning or middle or end. It is whole unto itself; therefore, if God shows you a circle, you know that he is gracing you with wholeness and completion.

77. In the same way, a home or house is where you live your life, where you are aware, and where it is that you know all that you know. So if God shows you a house, you know he is showing you your very awareness, or if he shows you an underground vault or perhaps the depths of the sea, you know these places are lightless and the realm of dark and he has graced you with a warning that you need to beware of that which you cannot see, of that which is below your awareness.

78. God communicates to you in two ways. One is obvious and the other is less so. Both are common but only one is spoken of, though even then rarely understood. Through all time, people have spoken about God talking to people in dreams. But what is not said is that, even in dreams, God does not talk in an ordinary way using the dreamer's ordinary language. Dreams are full of symbols that mean

something personal from God to the dreamer; it is the dreamer's duty to discover what is being said.

79. The other less obvious way that God communicates, the way that people seldom speak of, is his placing symbols in our paths during our waking hours. Most such symbols are ordinary and self-evident. So you ask, how is a person to recognize that this or that ordinary thing is a message from God?

80. It is not difficult at all. God causes us to notice such symbols by having them occur in the same space or time as other symbols so that two or more ordinary things coming together is not ordinary at all. When this happens, we feel a jolt of wonder or awe or even love. We all have these experiences, but I tell you, as sure as I am talking to you, that God is thus trying to get your attention, to speak to you. If in your heart you feel such a crossing of paths is wonderful, then I promise God is talking to you.

81. Therefore, fortunate are you to see what you see, for these are the visions of the prophets, and many are the kings who wish to see what you see, or hear what you hear. But they never do, for they seek too hard and are not pure of heart.

82. In this way, there can be nothing that is covered up or nothing that is secret between you and God. The secrets of your mind are held up to God, and God whispers back, or sometimes shouts, as the occasion deserves.

83. But again, it is your duty to understand God's words to you, of what he is saying especially to you! Whether it's easy or hard, God rewards the trying.

84. Now think! There are many people in your towns, in your nations, in the whole world. Think of all the people of all the many ages who lived in all those nations. Now ask yourself this: why would God trouble to speak so to you, who is but one person among so many? Why would he send you a sign, or speak to you in your dreams? Why would he trouble himself with you?

85. He does so because you are holy as all his children are holy. But few listen. But few heed. Few trust. Few love God as he loves them. Instead they choose to be blind. They choose to be deaf. They choose to be mute. God speaks all the time, but he is ignored by so many. His signs and dreams are ignored. His messages are ignored.

86. Where is the voice of Jesus that explains how the world works and how it should be observed? Where does it say that God approaches and needs to be approached with a

serious heart fully open, that this is how God and man come together and that life ceases to be a mystery?

87. Happy are those who show mercy, for, in this life or the next, God will be merciful.

88. Happy are those who have open hearts, for, in this life or the next, they will see the face of God.

89. Great are the keepers of the peace, for, in this life or the next, they will be called the children of God.

90. But where is the voice of Jesus, the voice who held all these wondrous truths? Where are these truths? I do not hear of them from the caravans.

The Gospel of Mariam

91. I am Mariam…. I have brought you here to Sinai from your far off homes to share with you, and through you to the rest of the world, knowledge of the holiest place on earth! I say again, the holiest place on earth!

92. Long have men sought treasures such as the cup from which they believed Christ drank, which is what I caused you to believe was the object of your quest; or the Ark of the Covenant; or for the true mountain called Sinai; or fragments from my son's tree; and so much more.

93. Well, I, of all people, know well what is holy and what is not and what is more holy or less holy, for I am the mother of God, and you have come to this remote spot at my bidding though you knew it not. You, each of you, came now rather than before or later because the time is soon coming when the people of this world must learn the truth of their own existence.

94. They say that God created man in His own image. There is truth to that, not in the material sense, for the material aspect of God can be better thought of as the entire world on which we stand, and, by extension, perhaps the Universe without as well. No, man is created in God's image in the sense of "mind" and spirit. Of all the creatures on earth, man is the only one that can seek God consciously, or who can arrive at God's door through attainment of merit, for God created man to join with and become God—and the destiny of each man, woman, and child is to attain God, whether he knows it or not, wants it or not, needs it or not. And though some men may not consciously strive for this, in time they will arrive there in any case.

95. Of all of God's creatures on earth, man is the holiest by virtue that only man becomes God, as a child becomes an adult at childhood's end.

96. Have you never gone back to the spot of your birth and wondered at the fact that it was there in that precise midwife's home or there in that very room or there in that exact glade that you came into existence, where you were born into this world? Now I bid you think. At such moments, are you not full of wonder for your very existence, for the miracle of your life?

97. I have brought you here to make it clear that mankind likewise has a place where it came into existence, where it was born, and it is time that all of mankind learn of that place so that all may feel that self-same wonder.

98. The Holy Scriptures tell of the creation of the world and a place that is called Eden....

99. The Holy Scriptures tell of the creation of the world...and they tell of God creating man in the land of Eden and that the act of creation took mere moments. These statements are of course true, but who is to determine what is a moment in the eyes of God, who measures time in billions of years? Indeed, God created man in a moment, a mere few million years, and he did this feat in a place that you can call Eden for want of a better name. I have brought you here to identify that real place to you and thus to all men.

100. Before I discuss the realm that is the real Eden of the real world, you need to know more of myself.... I will explain somewhat. As all the world knows well, Jesus asked his beloved disciple to care for his mother. That person is myself.

101. There came a time when the Angel of the Lord came to me. It was Gabriel, the same who had revealed himself to me at so many other crossroads in my life. He made me see in my mind a place on the far side of the Red Sea....

102. He said, "Verily, the spot that I am showing you is holy, more so than Ur was where the Lord spoke to Abraham or the Mountain of Sinai where the Lord spoke to Moses. Though these are surely holy places, the spot I show you is holier still, for it is the holiest spot on earth. And verily, you who are the Mother of God, you are bid to attend this veritable womb of mankind, for are you not the holiest person of the world? Thus is it not right that you should live by and in and protect the holiest place? Are you not also the mother of man? Then it is fitting that you reside by and in and protect the womb of man. Verily, I say to you, the spot I show you is the most holy in the eyes and mind of God."

103. The place the angel showed me was a vast valley that ran the whole length of Africa from north to south, a tremendous valley with many lakes. The angel bade John and I to come to this very spot that is under our feet now—indeed, verily even where you stand before me—which is the northernmost gateway both into and out of the great valley.

104. Let me say a wonderful truth. Remember, thee, how the Lord through the burning bush told Moses that he stood on holy ground? Well I say to you that the ground on which you stand is holier still....

105. That spot, which is under your feet, continues south, making up the great valley of eastern Africa, the bowl out of which sprang man, the crucible where the embryonic spirit, or God-in-the-making called mankind, was forged.... Humans came into being, not all at once, but in stages over time, for that is the way that God performs his miracles, building from the blocks that are available, the stuff of life.

106. My purpose is to share the truth of man's origin with those most able to divine it and appreciate its meaning. After all, we are all the children of God, and God wants his children to grow beyond the quaint stories they tell amongst themselves and to hearken to things as they really are.

107. Listen to me now!

108. If God is as real as, for instance, me, and is by definition divine, and if through the use of the tool called Time, he crafted people in his own image, then it would follow that people are also divine and that the spot where He did his crafting must be holy ground—the holiest of ground.

109. I have drawn you here from afar to tell you my wishes.... First, that all mankind turn away from sin, chiefly your disregard for God and, too, the lust for war. Second, that a chapel be built on the spot of my appearance in my honor. Well, now I ask something similar of you. I ask that all the terrain from where you stand to the southern-most reach of the great valley—the vast bowl that is birthplace of the human race—be designated holy ground and be set aside so all people can come and contemplate their existence, to perceive with their own eyes the spot where God's greatest miracle occurred, and this will make them more mindful of one another and of God, as well.

110. Rest assured that in the fullness of time all these things are possible and will be fulfilled! For you are my tool and, therefore, blessed by God!

The Gospel of Hans

111. O, Hans the good! Hans the mischievous. Hans the child. Hans the wise. I wish you to be the vessel of my message to all the people.

112. Hans, your fathers and their fathers and their fathers, and also all the mothers, all the way back to the dawn of time, have watched the stars and the sun and the moon move across the sky. Also, your people and all peoples have noted that sometimes the moon will precisely cover the sun, and the light and warmth will vanish! Can anything be more frightening? I ask.

113. Listen, Hans the faithful! Perhaps fear of hunger or of cold or of enemies or of pain or of death can be as frightening. But these are all things that are part of life and are expected, thus assumed, and though they may be feared, they are not strange. For does not every man [i.e., person] fully expect his lot to be touched by these fearsome things at some point during his journey?

114. However, the greatest joy in a [person's] life, indeed, in a whole people's life, is warmth and light from the sun. Thus the fear that comes from the sun vanishing and the world growing dark is the most fearsome thing of all for there

is no way of knowing when such a terrible thing will happen. It is not like the sun setting and rising.

115. Or at least this was so up until the various peoples discovered by their industry my secret pattern. Man [i.e., humans or humankind] has become fully [human] because he sought to know when in the future the circle of the moon would cover the circle of the sun and plunge the earth into darkness. Behold! In time, each people built tools and discovered the pattern in the randomness. They learned when the fearsome thing would occur, and they became less afraid. They found the secret that I had buried deep within the complexities I'd created just to goad [humans] to seek it.

116. "'I tell you that [humankind's] seeking to predict when the moon will cover the sun is what has made [humans human]. This is the key that honed problem solving far beyond that needed for mere survival. From this has sprung all that makes [humans human].

117. Thus peoples built grand temples and pyramids and statues and standing stones to observe the sun and moon and sky, and, sometimes, they enslaved whole peoples to build their observatories. Hans, this took many thousands of years, during which time people have done much for both good and ill. But remember that it all began due to fear of

losing the sun during the day—a fear I instilled by making certain that the moon exactly covers the sun. I created a problem that [humankind] needed to solve and thereby progress!

118. Surely nowadays many people have studied that age-old problem and have for centuries grown to understand thoroughly the remote—I say again—remote probability of any such equality in size of the sun and moon, so small a probability that the fact of this equivalence is on the surface preposterous. Yet, too often people just shrug and call it coincidence. Too few reach the next logical conclusion. If such a thing is preposterous, and yet exists nonetheless as a fact of life, what could it mean? Perhaps it means that someone wished it all to happen in just that manner. But who could wish up suns and moons and propel [human] advancement?

119. Who indeed? [Humans] now have clear reason to know me. I am right there in the maths and calculations that they treasure so much, but they can also be stubborn, can take things terribly for granted and rationalize. Still, Hans, people will someday understand that something is happening, has always been happening, that defies reason . . . yet has a cause and that cause is me—for I am that I am!

120. But first there must come a drawn-out time when the blind will lead and these words I am saying will verily be the light in the darkness. Old Hans, share my words. Remember all that I've said and share it with your Baas, Allan, O Hans the child, Hans the wise!

121. For you are my messenger.

Afterword to the Holmes Behind the Veil Series Trilogy

This trilogy of novels is by definition a work of fiction. Furthermore, it is a pastiche of several H. Rider Haggard stories and of various and sundry tales of the Great Detective. Moreover:

(1) The books that comprise this series are not commonplace Great Detective mysteries. Rather, they provide Holmes with four distinct problems at three different periods—youth, middle-age, and two while in retirement. Yet, the narrative seldom does more than allude to the detective, offering scenes that imply his destiny crossing paths with Horace Holly, Leo Vincey, and Allan Quatermain. Thus, he is Behind the Veil, never seen quite clearly.

(2) This trilogy is structured like a child's nesting toy—rather like a set of Russian nesting dolls—insofar as the reader is invited to explore multiple layers within layers, of framing devices within framing devices, books within books, and narratives within narratives.

(4)　　Further, the series can be viewed as a kind of light-hearted homage of the once common practice of casting works of fiction in the form of fact for the sake of verisimilitude. Countless authors have indulged in that conceit over the centuries—from Horace Walpole and Johannes Wilhelm Meinhold through Wilkie Collins, Arthur Conan Doyle, Arthur Machen, H. Rider Haggard, Edgar Rice Burroughs, and A. Merritt to, more recently, Ian Cameron, Michael Crichton, Nicholas Meyer, Lin Carter, and Umberto Eco.

(5)　　The series should also be seen as this author's paean to the progeny of the above literary art form, the pastiche, which often comes equipped with literary conventions such as framing devices, pseudo-prefaces, footnotes, and so forth. My goal has been to take this pastiche convention to a whole new level. None of the apparently ancillary material passages in these books should be skipped over or derided; it is not optional.

(6)　　At the same time, this series trilogy is built on a framework of allusions. For example, the various title pages are parodies of, and allusions to, turn-of-the-century publishing conventions, while the dedications are allusions to H. Rider Haggard's preferred style of trumpeting his allegiance or loyalty or friendship while in his more serious moods, and there are endless allusions to all manner of genre tropes. Of course, this is nothing new, being at heart the same sort of structural foundation employed by, for example, George Lucas in *Star Wars* and Sergio Leone and Quentin Tarantino in their various films.

(7)	Finally, if I may: these three books exist because in the long run I believe, or I am aware, that there is in reality an attentive, deliberate consciousness "behind the veil" and that the key to knowing, or relating to, that consciousness is G.K. Chesterton's remark:

"There is in life an element of elfin coincidence which people reckoning on the prosaic may perpetually miss."

Writing these books was my way of sharing that belief.

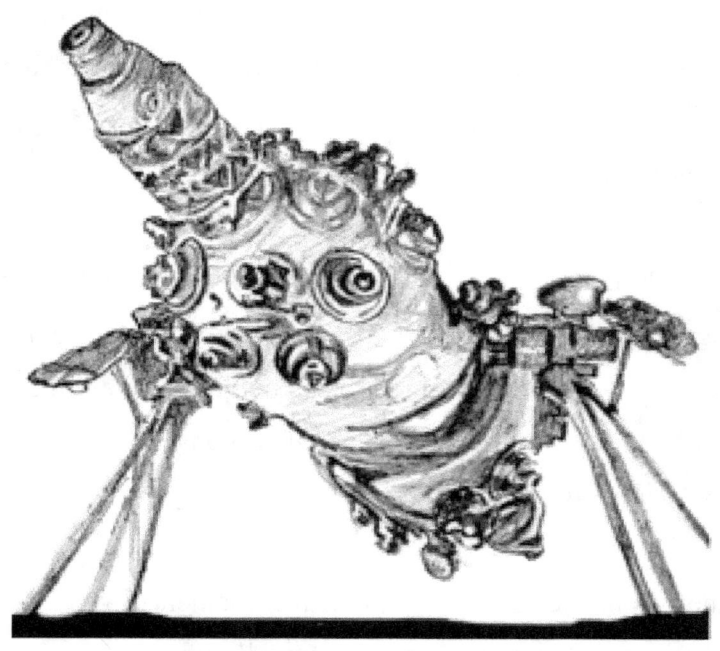

The star projector of the Morrison Planetarium circa 1960.

About the Author

Thomas Kent Miller (often known as Thos. Kent Miller) is author of *Mars in the Movies: A History* (2016) from McFarland publishers, and the three Holmes/Haggard pastiches that comprise this "Holmes Behind the Veil" series.

Visit my Sherlock Holmes memoir-style blog: https://sherlockholmesmeetsallanquatermain.blogspot.com— the story of the writing of one novel. I also maintain a colorful interactive *Mars in the Movies: A History* blog: http://marsinthemoviesahistory.blogspot.com.

I am a member of The Friends of Arthur Machen and The Rider Haggard Society. I have written for *The Weird Tales Collector*, *The Ghosts & Scholars M. R. James Newsletter*, *Faunus: The Journal of the Friends of Arthur Machen*, *The Haggard Journal*, *Wormwood*, Borgo Press, Wildside Press, HarperCollins San Francisco, and Hippocampus Press.

My interests include science-fiction movies, Victorian and Edwardian ghost stories, 19th-century Hudson River School landscape paintings, and home theater. I live in southern California, and I can be contacted at: thomaskentmiller@gmail.com.

Also from MX Publishing

MX Publishing is the world's largest specialist Sherlock Holmes publisher, with over a hundred titles and fifty authors creating the latest in Sherlock Holmes fiction and non-fiction.

From traditional short stories and novels to travel guides and quiz books, MX Publishing cater for all Holmes fans.

The collection includes leading titles such as *Benedict Cumberbatch In Transition* and *The Norwood Author* which won the 2011 Howlett Award (Sherlock Holmes Book of the Year).

MX Publishing also has one of the largest communities of Holmes fans on Facebook with regular contributions from dozens of authors.

www.mxpublishing.com

Also from MX Publishing

"Phil Growick's, 'The Secret Journal of Dr Watson', is an adventure which takes place in the latter part of Holmes and Watson's lives. They are entrusted by HM Government (although not officially) and the King no less to undertake a rescue mission to save the Romanovs, Russia's Royal family from a grisly end at the hand of the Bolsheviks. There is a wealth of detail in the story but not so much as would detract us from the enjoyment of the story. Espionage, counter-espionage, the ace of spies himself, double-agents, double-crossers...all these flit across the pages in a realistic and exciting way. All the characters are extremely well-drawn and Mr Growick, most importantly, does not falter with a very good ear for Holmesian dialogue indeed. Highly recommended. A five-star effort."
The Baker Street Society

Also from MX Publishing

The Missing Authors Series

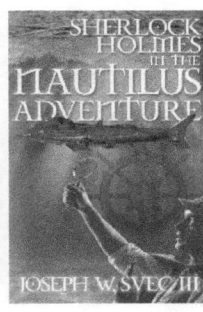

Sherlock Holmes and The Adventure of The Grinning Cat
Sherlock Holmes and The Nautilus Adventure
Sherlock Holmes and The Round Table Adventure

"Joseph Svec, III is brilliant in entwining two endearing and enduring classics of literature, blending the factual with the fantastical; the playful with the pensive; and the mischievous with the mysterious. We shall, all of us young and old, benefit with a cup of tea, a tranquil afternoon, and a copy of Sherlock Holmes, The Adventure of the Grinning Cat."
Amador County Holmes Hounds Sherlockian Society

www.mxpublishing.com

Also from MX Publishing

The American Literati Series

 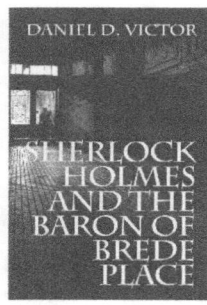 

The Final Page of Baker Street
The Baron of Brede Place
Seventeen Minutes To Baker Street

"The really amazing thing about this book is the author's ability to call up the 'essence' of both the Baker Street 'digs' of Holmes and Watson as well as that of the 'mean streets' of Marlowe's Los Angeles. Although none of the action takes place in either place, Holmes and Watson share a sense of camaraderie and self-confidence in facing threats and problems that also pervades many of the later tales in the Canon. Following their conversations and banter is a return to Edwardian England and its certainties and hope for the future. This is definitely the world before The Great War."
Philip K Jones

www.mxpublishing.com

Also from MX Publishing

The Detective and The Woman Series

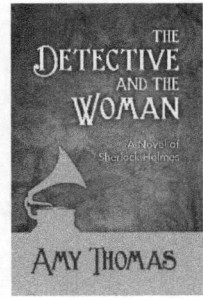  

The Detective and The Woman
The Detective, The Woman and The Winking Tree
The Detective, The Woman and The Silent Hive

"The book is entertaining, puzzling and a lot of fun. I believe the author has hit on the only type of long-term relationship possible for Sherlock Holmes and Irene Adler. The details of the narrative only add force to the romantic defects we expect in both of them and their growth and development are truly marvelous to watch. This is not a love story. Instead, it is a coming-of-age tale starring two of our favorite characters."
Philip K Jones

www.mxpublishing.com

Also from MX Publishing

When the papal apartments are burgled in 1901, Sherlock Holmes is summoned to Rome by Pope Leo XII. After learning from the pontiff that several priceless cameos that could prove compromising to the church, and perhaps determine the future of the newly unified Italy, have been stolen, Holmes is asked to recover them. In a parallel story, Michelangelo, the toast of Rome in 1501 after the unveiling of his Pieta, is commissioned by Pope Alexander VI, the last of the Borgia pontiffs, with creating the cameos that will bedevil Holmes and the papacy four centuries later. For fans of Conan Doyle's immortal detective, the game is always afoot. However, the great detective has never encountered an adversary quite like the one
with whom he crosses swords in "The Vatican Cameos.."

"An extravagantly imagined and beautifully written Holmes story"
(Lee Child, NY Times Bestselling author, Jack Reacher series)

Also from MX Publishing

Our bestselling books are our short story collections;

'Lost Stories of Sherlock Holmes' , 'The Outstanding Mysteries of Sherlock Holmes', The Papers of Sherlock Holmes Volume 1 and 2, 'Untold Adventures of Sherlock Holmes' (and the sequel 'Studies in Legacy) and 'Sherlock Holmes in Pursuit', 'The Cotswold Werewolf and Other Stories of Sherlock Holmes' – and many more......

www.mxpublishing.com

Also from MX Publishing

The Sherlock Holmes and Enoch Hale Series

The Amateur Executioner
The Poisoned Penman
The Egyptian Curse

"The Amateur Executioner: Enoch Hale Meets Sherlock Holmes", the first collaboration between Dan Andriacco and Kieran McMullen, concerns the possibility of a Fenian attack in London. Hale, a native Bostonian, is a reporter for London's Central News Syndicate - where, in 1920, Horace Harker is still a familiar figure, though far from revered. "The Amateur Executioner" takes us into an ambiguous and murky world where right and wrong aren't always distinguishable. I look forward to reading more about Enoch Hale."
Sherlock Holmes Society of London

www.mxpublishing.com

396

Also from MX Publishing

Sherlock Holmes novellas in verse

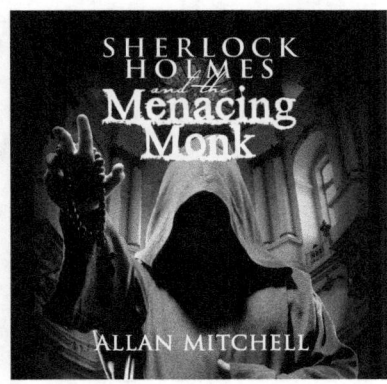

Sherlock Holmes and The Menacing Moors
Sherlock Holmes and The Menacing Metropolis
Sherlock Holmes and The Menacing Melbournian
Sherlock Holmes and The Menacing Monk

"The story is really good and the Herculean effort it must have been to write it all in verse—well, my hat is off to you, Mr. Allan Mitchell! I wouldn't dream of seeing such work get less than five plus stars from me..." **The Raven**